"If you're looking for nonstop action and heart-pounding excitement, then *Angel Falls* is just the read you've been looking to find. Connie Mann deftly weaves danger and suspense into a story that left me sitting on the edge of my seat, flipping the pages."
—Debbie Macomber, #1 NYT Bestselling Author

"Dark, intense, and breathlessly paced, Connie Mann's edgy novel, *Angel Falls*, is exciting, romantic suspense that kept me guessing. With tight writing and fast-paced action, Connie does a fantastic job of grabbing the reader from the first page and never turning loose until the last. *Angel Falls* is not your usual Christian suspense. Filled with intrigue, murder, and sensuality, and set in Brazil's steamy underbelly, Connie's debut is riveting.
—Linda Goodnight, author of *A Prairie Collection, A Snowglobe Christmas,* and *Rancher's Refuge*

"*Angel Falls* is a powerful read from the beginning with a hero and heroine who emotionally grip you and won't let go. The chemistry between Regina and Brooks along with the suspense keeps you riveted to the story."
—Margaret Daley, author of The Men of the Texas Rangers series

"Contemporary and edgy, *Angel Falls* grabs you on the very first page and doesn't let you go until the very last word. With characters so real and sympathetic, readers will empathize with their dilemmas and root for them to overcome every obstacle. With a tightly weaved plot, loaded with twists and turns that only add to the suspense, *Angel Falls* is a highly recommended, exciting, riveting read."
—Diane Burke, author of *Silent Witness, Bounty Hunter Guardian*, and *Double Identity*

"*Angel Falls* is a stark tale of damaged characters and ruthless action set in Porto Alegre, Brazil. But as in our own lives, the most rewarding things come through struggle. As author Connie Mann builds her gripping story, she also grabs the hearts of readers. Their reward is nothing less than a beautiful expanse of forgiveness and redemption."
—Kay Strom, author of Grace in Africa trilogy and Blessings in India trilogy

"Thanks to the excellent research, *Angel Falls* catches the exotic flavor of the Brazilian countryside and the real life dangers of the big cities. The author brings together two damaged souls, thrust together to save the life of a child, who find love and redemption while trying to survive the murderous attempts of an unseen foe. As the tension rises, we see Regina and Brooks learn the healing power of love and the renewal of their faith in God and humanity. The description of Iguaçu Falls makes the reader ready to pack a bag to see them in person."
—Martha Powers, author of *Conspiracy of Silence* and *Death Angel*

"Connie Mann takes her readers on the heart-stopping journey of a woman who puts her life on the line for an orphaned baby boy and her heart in the hands of the man who came to save them. It was a remarkable story I won't soon forget."
—Sharon Sala, author of *'Til Death*, book 3 of the Rebel Ridge trilogy

"*Angel Falls* is a well-written debut romance/thriller with many twists and turns. I enjoyed the wonderful visit through Brazil. Highly recommended."
—Linda Hall, author of *Black Ice*

ANGEL FALLS

Connie Mann

Abingdon Press fiction
a novel approach to faith

Nashville, Tennessee

Angel Falls

ISBN-13: 978-1-4267-5686-3

Published by Abingdon Press, P.O. Box 801, Nashville, TN 37202

www.abingdonpress.com

Library of Congress Cataloging-in-Publication Data has been requested.

Printed in the United States of America

1 2 3 4 5 6 7 8 9 10 / 18 17 16 15 14 13

For Harry,
who shows me daily what it means to love
and be loved.
I love you.
Today. Tomorrow. Always.

Acknowledgments

Angel Falls is hugely special to me and I couldn't be more grateful to those who helped make it a reality:

Ramona Richards, editor extraordinaire, who championed this story for so many years. Without you, it would still be waiting for a home. Thank you from the bottom of my heart.

Leslie Santamaria, dear friend and amazing critique partner, you probably know this story better than I do by now. Where would I be without your constant encouragement, eagle eye, and friendship? I hope I never have to find out.

Tammy Johnson, aka Lucy, who keeps this Ethel laughing, believing, and moving forward. Thank you for always being there.

Diane Burke, Ruth Owen, and the members of VCRW, FHL, and CFRWA. Thanks for cheering me on through the hard years and doing the Happy Dance with me now.

Major thanks to the wonderful folks at Abingdon for taking a chance on this project!

My heartfelt appreciation to my parents for sharing their love of Brazil, and to the combined Blaskowski-Neumann clan.

To Frank LaRoche, United States Army (retired), thank you for your service to our country and your insight into the mind of a Ranger.

Doris Neumann, you straightened out my mangled Portuguese and always encourage me.

Joyce Stevens, your counselor's knowledge of rape victims helped immeasurably.

Any mistakes are mine alone.

Last, but never least, my deepest gratitude and love to Harry, Ben, and Michele, the greatest joys of my life. You never gave up on me and wouldn't let me give up, either. Love you.

1

Porto Alegre, Southern Brazil, Present Day

REGINA DA SILVA TIED THE LACES ON HER CRACKED LEATHER BOOTS AND yanked the hand-knitted wool stockings Olga made her last Christmas up past her knees. Outside, an icy wind fought to get in through the wooden shutters guarding House of Angels orphanage. She straightened the layers of skirts swirling around her ankles, knowing she'd give away all but one before the night ended.

She didn't want to go out tonight, and that made her feel small and selfish. And guilty. So she hefted the wicker basket filled with meat pastries and opened the door—before she changed her mind. On nights like tonight, she didn't know which she hated most—the cold or the memories.

"You are still going out tonight, Regina?" Irene demanded quietly, her voice heavy with accusation. And disappointment.

"Just this one night, Regina, stay home. We'll talk. Laugh, maybe even shed a few tears. *Minha amiga*, even Jesus took time off for his friends."

Regina swallowed hard and glanced over her shoulder at the sagging sofa, where Irene sat with her feet curled under her, cuddling her three-month-old son. The pleading tone almost demolished the fence guarding Regina's mouth.

A gust of wind snatched the door from her grasp and slammed it against the wall, the crash a call to arms. "If I don't go, who will?" Regina asked. She didn't add, "*since you don't go anymore,*" but it echoed in the room nonetheless. Regina tried to keep the hurt out of her voice. She still couldn't believe Irene and little Eduardo were moving to the United States in the morning and leaving her behind. She was thrilled for Irene. She was furious, too, and mad at herself for feeling that way. But she couldn't find words for any of it. So she simply pointed to the basket and said, "Olga has the meat pastries ready and Jorge packed extra blankets." Regina pulled on a pair of handmade mittens, carefully pulling together the hole in one thumb.

Irene sent her a piercing, sad-eyed look. "You can't save them all, you know."

At the familiar argument, Regina met her gaze, eyes hot, and repeated what she always said in response. "Maybe not. But I can save some."

Irene sighed. "I'll pick you up in the morning, then. Be safe, my friend."

Regina kissed her friend on both cheeks, did the same for Eduardo, and then headed out before she caved in to Irene's pleading. The wind hacked through the slums, and Regina hunched farther into her threadbare coat, determined to ignore everything but the task at hand. Especially the memories.

She shifted her grasp on the heavy basket and kept her eyes fixed on the barrel of burning trash ahead. Automatically avoiding open sewers and billowing newspapers, she followed the dancing flames like a ship to a lighthouse. Odd that both lights warned of danger, yet promised safety.

Regina tightened her scarf and snorted. Here on the streets, safety was an illusion, a wish unfulfilled. How many nights had she and Irene spent just like these street children, huddled around a barrel, protecting their right to be there by clutching a switchblade in a shaking fist? They would probably be dead if not for Noah Anderson, who had done exactly what Regina would do tonight. What she and Irene had done together for years.

But everything had changed. Irene planned to take Eduardo to Florida and leave Regina to run the orphanage alone. Her throat tightened, so she stepped up her pace, shoving self-pity roughly away. She had a job to do tonight. The children were cold and hungry and she could help—at least a little. *Keep them safe, God, please.*

Regina knew the exact moment the children caught the scent of meat pastry, for suddenly a swarm of children surrounded her, shouting, "*Senhorita Anjo, um pastel, um pastel.*"

Regina smiled warmly, though she still couldn't get used to being called Miss Angel, even after four years as codirector of House of Angels.

The crowd surged, pressing close, but Regina's willowy height worked to her advantage. "Hello, children. Fernando, Stephan, back up and let the little ones closer." Regina gently pulled the smaller children toward her, trying not to think about just how young they really were. Could Christiane be more than five? Already her beautiful brown eyes held dull acceptance, the understanding that life would never get any better than this—that hopes and dreams were for other, richer children.

Suddenly, the skin on the back of Regina's neck prickled, and she stopped dead on the cracked sidewalk. Someone was watching her. Again. She hugged one of the children as she scanned the street, but saw nothing out of place, no one who didn't belong. Yet there was someone there, someone with evil in mind. Every street child knew what that meant. If you were smart, you ran and hid.

Even fifteen years later, Regina's flight instincts screamed just that. But she wouldn't. Couldn't. The children needed her. She fingered her switchblade and looked back, relieved to see old Jorge in the beat-up orphanage van, lumbering slowly up the cobbled street behind her. The groundskeeper had packed an extra box of blankets, in case the thermometer dropped sharply tonight. And he carried his own knife—just in case. Jorge clambered down from the van and opened the back doors.

"Go get a blanket, children. Fernando, where is the one I gave you yesterday?"

The instant the words left her mouth, Regina wanted to call them back. The twelve-year-old hung his head in shame and shrugged, telling her without words that someone had taken it from him and he hadn't been able to stop him. "Go get another. It is all right," she said gently, trying to spare his pride.

"Thank you, Senhorita Angel," he said, but instead of heading toward the line forming behind the van, he disappeared into the shadows.

Regina tried to call him back, but snapped her attention to the basket when one of the newer boys tried to make off with two pastries. "One," she said firmly, holding his thin wrist until he let go.

Within moments, the meat pastries were gone, the blankets dispersed, and she'd sent at least ten children to the van for a ride to the orphanage. If she could have fit more pallets into the dining hall, Regina would have scooped up more children. And still, the crowd grew bigger than it had been before.

"Senhorita Angel," a voice shouted.

Turning around, Regina saw Fernando running toward her. Panting, he skidded to a stop. "You must come, now. Please."

Regina didn't hesitate. Before she reached the van, Jorge had started the engine and handed her medical bag through the window. He motioned her forward and prepared to follow.

"Let's go," she said, and smiled when Fernando grabbed her bag before galloping off. She couldn't be sure if this was his attempt at gallantry, or a way to make sure she kept up with his punishing pace. As she ran down narrow alleys and grim little streets, Regina prepared to put the nurse's training she'd received in the United States to instant use. She prayed it would be enough. Too often, though, what little she could offer came years too late.

Outside Rio de Janeiro, Brazil

Smoke hung like a heavy blanket in the back alley bar, a place years away from the rich, touristy sections of Rio de Janeiro. The heavy pall obscured individual features, but couldn't disguise that the clientele was poor, rough, and ready for a fight. Chickens pecked at the trash littering the dirt floor, while sweaty locals sat at rickety tables, laughing, arguing, and sucking down alcohol. It helped kill time before the fighting started.

Nathaniel Brooks Anderson had been in enough such places over the years to know the drill. One wrong word and you became the opening ceremony. The knife sheath tucked between his shoulder blades was as necessary as a pair of water-tight boots if he wanted to survive in a place like this.

He leaned closer to the bartender and tried again. "Out of town where?" He kept his voice low, but spit each word from between clenched teeth.

Palms up, the swarthy barkeep shrugged helplessly. "He no say, Senhor. He just leave."

"When?" Stronger men had quailed under that look.

The man looked away and hitched his pants over his sagging belly. "Don't know. A month, maybe more." Another shrug.

Brooks reached across the bar and pulled the man forward by his grimy T-shirt, ignoring the stench of rotting teeth. "Think, my friend. Think hard."

The poor sot's eyes bulged. "I cannot say, Senhor. Please. I don't know."

With a snap of his wrist, Brooks released him, the half-healed muscles in his arm screaming a protest. Besides, this guy knew squat. "So who would know?" he barked.

More shrugging. More apologies. More freaking nothing.

Brooks stormed out the door, the look on his face clearing a path before him. For two weeks now, he'd been getting the same story. After all these years working this part of the world, he couldn't find a single one of his contacts and no one knew where they were or how to get in touch with them. The implications gnawed a hole in his gut. He needed answers, fast. But his chances of finding them lessened with every passing minute.

"He told them to say that."

Brooks turned to see the dark-haired young waitress leaning up against the outside wall of the bar, smoking a cigarette.

"Who told them?"

"The man you're looking for." She stepped closer, her lush figure barely concealed by a white peasant blouse and colorful skirt. She shivered and wrapped her hands around her bare arms.

"Why?" Brooks kept his eyes trained on her face, ignoring the way the dim light spilled from the door and highlighted her curves. No distractions. He needed answers.

Dark curls bobbed as she stepped closer. "What's the information worth to you?" she asked, running a trembling finger over his beard-stubbled chin.

Brooks grasped her wrist, his hold firm but painless. "No games."

Frightened dark eyes clashed with his. "You need information. I need money." She looked away. "And maybe we both need a little comfort on a cold night."

She couldn't be more than eighteen years old and was obviously scared to death. But of what? Brooks carefully scanned the alley behind him. Too many places to hide for his comfort. More than one unwary tourist had been gutted like a fish after trusting the wrong person.

But he couldn't ignore his first lead since he had arrived back in Brazil a few weeks ago. Uncle Sam didn't know—or wouldn't say—what went so desperately wrong on Brooks's last mission, so if he wanted answers, he'd have to get them himself. This girl's motives weren't his concern.

Now his dark eyes catalogued the street ahead in one sharp glance. He'd bet his knife the guy who'd just appeared in the next doorway had sent her. Brooks took her arm in a casual grip. "Friend of yours?" he whispered, turning her in the opposite direction.

Her eyes widened before she looked away. She'd be a wash at poker. "My brother," she admitted quietly.

"Am I supposed to end up dead or just beaten and robbed?" he asked mildly, steering her deftly around a corner.

Her eyes were like saucers in her thin face. "Please, Senhor. We need money."

Brooks looked over his shoulder and then led her down another narrow alley. "You'll get it. After I get what I want."

The ground at their feet suddenly exploded and the girl nearly jumped out of her skin. That idiot almost shot his own sister. Brooks tightened his grip on the girl and picked up the pace. Desperate people were always the most dangerous.

Regina and Fernando were both breathing hard when the boy stopped beside a dumpster, crouched down, and crawled behind it. Regina's vision wavered momentarily as a feeling of déjà vu almost knocked her off her feet. She might have fallen backward through a hole in time. The endless night, the bitter cold, the stench. Even the alley looked eerily familiar. Her stomach pitched and rolled, and she had to force air into her lungs.

"Come Senhorita, please," Fernando said, tugging her sleeve.

Focus on the present, she reminded herself sternly as she crawled between the dumpster and the rotting fence. She flipped on her heavy-duty flashlight and shone it around the small space. At first, all she saw were several of the orphanage blankets. But then she saw a small face, a young girl, barely in her teens, curled on her side. The girl let out a soft moan, cradling her middle, tears streaming down her battered face. When the flashlight beam landed on her torn clothes and the bloodstained blankets, bile surged into Regina's throat.

Dear God no, not another one. Regina clamped her back teeth against the fury and pain screaming for release. That made three girls just this week. Prostitution, even rape, were common in the slums, but not this kind of battering. Someone was prowling the *favelas* and using these girls to vent a frightening rage.

She wanted to wrap this child in her arms and whisper comforting words, but she didn't have time. Emotions would be dealt with later. Right now her medical skills were critical.

Seeing the terror in Fernando's eyes, Regina sent him a reassuring smile, quickly traded her woolen mittens for surgical gloves, and went to work. "Hold the light, just so," she instructed the boy. "What's her name?"

"Leticia," Fernando said, and then added in a whisper, "She's my sister."

Bending over her patient, Regina summoned her most confident smile while she silently begged God to give her wisdom and help her save this child. "Hello, Leticia. I'm Regina, and I'm going to help you."

"Senhorita Angel," the girl whispered, blood trickling from her split lip.

Regina winked, though she wanted to cry. "At your service." She ran her hands quickly over the young girl, assessing the damage. This girl needed stitches and she needed them now.

"Fernando, go get water from the van!" Her voice snapped with authority, moving him from where he stood rooted in horror. This would give him something to do, a way to help.

Regina pulled out her supplies, fighting the urge to grab the girl and run while she still could, just as she had on the street earlier. But Leticia's desperate brown eyes kept her firmly in place, blocking out everything but the next step she needed to take, the next instruction she needed to give.

With Jorge stationed out by the van to give what protection he could and Fernando holding the flashlight, Regina murmured encouragement. "Stay with me, Leticia. That's it. It's going to be okay."

Blood. Dear God. Too much blood. Help me, Father. Regina mopped and probed and kept up a stream of encouraging words, but Leticia's strength ebbed, and she drifted in and out of consciousness. Working against the clock, Regina stitched delicate tissues and bandaged deep wounds. If only she could convince Dr. Perez to come out here with her more often. But thankfully, he'd stop by House of Angels in the morning before he went to his office.

A long time later, when the bleeding finally slowed and Leticia started to come around, Regina released a slow, triumphant sigh. The streets would not claim another victim.

She whistled for Jorge and the old man came running. Together, the three of them bundled Leticia into the back of the van for the short ride to the orphanage.

Fernando immediately clambered in beside his sister and Regina followed, signaling Jorge with a quick rap on the ceiling. Regina glanced at the sleeping children huddled inside the van, then leaned forward and took Fernando's thin hand between her own, desperate to ease the guilt she saw in his face. "You did the right thing. This isn't your fault."

He wouldn't say anything, so Regina raised his chin so he'd have to meet her eyes. "You were very brave tonight. And a big help. Leticia is going to be okay."

Again the shrug and the averted eyes. Regina sighed at his response, but she understood too well. If you expected nothing, you weren't disappointed.

A few minutes later, the three of them were carrying Leticia through the orphanage's back door on a makeshift stretcher when Irene's battered Toyota screeched to a halt behind the van. Regina couldn't help an automatic smile at the hundreds of bumper stickers plastered over every square inch of the old heap. She figured they were the only things holding the ancient rust bucket together.

Irene leaped from the car and helped maneuver the stretcher into the infirmary. "I've been looking all over for you, my friend. Let's go."

Torn, Regina looked from Irene to Leticia's bruised face. Jorge met her gaze. "You go. Olga and I will take good care of the little one. Irene's plane will not wait."

Regina nodded and turned toward the door, but Irene stopped her with a hand on her shoulder. "Ah, that might not be the fashion statement you want to make."

Regina looked down, noticing the blood on her clothes and hands. "Right." After a quick scrub of her hands, a change of clothes, and a silent prayer for Leticia, Regina climbed into Irene's car, carefully gathering Eduardo onto her lap.

"I hear our newest little angel is going to be okay, thanks to you," Irene said, launching the car into traffic without a single look over her shoulder.

At the sound of a horn, Regina braced her feet against the rusted floorboards and wished again for a car seat for Eduardo. But Irene wanted no part of that American obsession. At least not until she got to the United States. Regina tightened her seat belt and her grip on the boy. "It was touch and go for a while, but I think she'll be okay, thank God." And Regina would be back at the orphanage soon, just to make sure. Rubbing her neck to loosen tight muscles, she looked at her watch, then at her friend.

"You're early."

In another hour, the sun would break across the horizon, though traffic was picking up rapidly.

Irene grinned impishly. "I figured we'd have time for breakfast on the way to the airport."

Regina tried to smile, but it fell flat. She'd been dreading this moment. "I hate good-byes."

"Me, too. But it won't really be good-bye. We'll stay in touch, just like always." Irene cut across three lanes of traffic and roared into the parking lot behind a little café. "No sad stuff."

They kept up the steady banter of old friends, carefully avoiding anything that might lead to tears. But halfway through breakfast, Irene, a smile on her face and a bite of roll halfway to her mouth, suddenly looked past Regina and froze, her face turning white. Head averted, she reached for her napkin.

"What's the matter?" Regina asked, swiveling around to see what had caused such a reaction.

"Nothing. Keep eating."

But Regina noticed Irene's trembling hands. Alarmed, she gave the café another careful once over, seeing nothing but the usual assortment of diners, none paying them the slightest bit of attention.

She leaned down so she could see Irene's face. "Tell me what's going on."

"Nothing. Look, I'm just a little jumpy, with the move and everything."

Regina didn't buy it. The silence lengthened unnaturally, but she simply waited.

Finally, Irene burst out, "I want your promise, Regina, your *solemn oath*, that if something ever happens to me, you'll take care of Eduardo. Make sure he has a good home with loving parents."

A chill slithered down Regina's spine, raising gooseflesh on her arms. "Of course. That goes without saying. But why are you asking me this now?"

Irene fiddled with Eduardo's bib and Regina's anxiety inched up another notch. "Irene. What's wrong?"

Irene's head snapped up then, her look fierce. "There's nothing wrong, okay. This is about being a mother. About covering all the bases, just in case."

Regina judged the truth in her friend's eyes and then slowly nodded. "You have my promise, but what about Eduardo's father? Shouldn't you be having this conversation with him?"

"No."

Regina waited, but Irene kept silent on the subject, as always. Regina scanned the café again. Was one of these men Eduardo's father? "Irene—"

"And one more thing—" Irene interrupted, a bit desperately. She met Regina's gaze squarely. "Don't ever fall for a spineless, cheating piece of trash like I did."

Oh, but you got a precious baby out of the deal, Regina's heart cried, *a family of your own*. She knew Irene wasn't proud of having a baby outside of marriage, but they'd both been completely awed that Irene had been able to conceive at all, given the childhood they'd had. Before Regina could put her conflicting thoughts into words, Eduardo let out an unhappy yowl.

His volume steadily increased after they got back into the car. "Got any more ideas on how to calm him down?" Regina shouted above the baby's indignant screams.

"He's dry, you said?" Irene shouted back. She pounded on the horn, gesturing wildly at the driver ahead of them.

"Yes. And he's not hungry, so I don't know what to do." Regina jiggled Eduardo against her shoulder but that only seemed to make him more annoyed.

Irene suddenly swerved sharply to the right and Regina gripped the dashboard to keep from dropping him. "Maybe some juice would help," Irene said. "He likes that."

Regina stopped her friend before she could hop out of the car. "Let me go. Maybe a change of scenery will help." She hoisted Eduardo onto her shoulder and ran across the street to the tiny *mercado*.

She quickly scanned the aisles, then beelined toward the cold drink coolers along the back wall. People stared at the screeching child, but she barely noticed. She snapped a bottle off the shelf, unscrewed the lid and replaced it with a nipple she'd stashed in her pocket. Two seconds after she shoved it between the boy's lips, blessed quiet permeated the store. Regina let out a sigh of relief and headed for the checkout.

"Cute little boy," the elderly clerk replied.

"*Sim*," Regina agreed. "But you should have heard him a few minutes—"

A deafening roar drowned out the rest of her words. The building shook as though a great hand had plucked it off the ground and then tossed it back down. Cans tumbled from shelves, people screamed. Regina lost her footing and went down on her back, Eduardo clutched against her chest. Too stunned to move, she lay still for several seconds. Or maybe minutes, she had no idea.

"Are you okay, Senhorita?" the old man asked, crouched beside her, covering his nose with his sleeve against the boiling dust.

Regina blinked the grit from her eyes and tried to focus. "What happened?"

"I don't know," he said, helping her to her feet.

As soon as she stood up, Regina ran her hands over the baby, who looked back at her with wide, unblinking eyes. He didn't seem to be any the worse for wear, though the shattered juice bottle mingled with the rest of the debris on the floor. But he wasn't screeching, which Regina took as a good sign.

She turned in a slow circle, trying to get her bearings. The store looked like the aftermath of the tornado she'd witnessed during her high school years in Orlando. One glance out the shop's missing front window and she stumbled toward the door. "Irene!" she screamed.

Once outside she stopped, stunned. It looked like the whole street was on fire. Black smoke belched into the air and heat from a wall of flames seared her skin. Her heart thundered in her chest. Where was Irene?

"Irene!" she called again, shielding her face with her arm, trying to see beyond the crush. People milled about, crying, shouting, pointing at something across the street.

The thick smoke shifted for just a moment. "Dear God, no! Irene!"

The flames came from Irene's little car. Roaring tongues of fire engulfed it completely, shooting out the windows, arcing twenty feet in the air.

Regina tightened her grip on Eduardo and tried to get closer, her only thought to help her friend. She hadn't taken two steps when strong arms grabbed her from behind, holding her back.

"Let me go!" She tried to break their hold, but couldn't.

"Go back. There's nothing you can do!" a voice shouted in her ear.

Regina increased her struggles. "I have to help her. Irene!"

Another pair of hands forcibly turned her away from the sight. "You can't help. She's in God's hands now."

Regina's eyes widened in shock, not comprehending. Then she looked back at the car and reality hit her full force. She sagged as understanding sucked all the strength from her legs. If not for those supporting her, she would have crumpled to the ground. "Noooo!"

Her teeth began to chatter, and everything took on an odd sheen of unreality. The baby clutched in her arms became the only real thing in her world.

"I'm okay," she finally managed, and the men slowly let her go. She heard sirens in the distance, but the shouts and chaos all around her seemed strangely muted.

Dimly, as though the sound came from far away, she realized Eduardo had started shrieking at the top of his lungs. Automatically, she shifted his position and began crooning to him. She had to think, but her brain jumbled images and impressions; every coherent thought slithered just out of reach.

Stunned, in shock, she stood in the middle of the crowd, an isolated figure in the sea of turmoil. She looked into Eduardo's sweet, angry face, and her thoughts suddenly focused with razor sharpness: Eduardo. She had to look out for Eduardo.

She raised her head to look around and froze as a shiver passed over her skin. Someone was watching her. Just like last night. Was it the same person?

Instinctively, Regina pulled her coat around Eduardo, hiding him from view. Irene would accuse her of an overactive imagination, but Regina knew better. Until three days ago, it had been years since she'd been the object of covert scrutiny, but it was a chilling sensation you never forgot. Maybe a street child watched her, too scared to approach, but Regina wasn't taking any chances.

Casually, she scanned the milling crowd, looking for any telltale sign—a quickly averted face, a too-interested look—but nobody seemed to be paying her the slightest bit of attention. Which didn't mean a thing. She'd come a long way from the scrawny street child she'd been, but only a fool ignored her instincts when they were screaming to be heard. And they were shrieking at top volume. She had to get away—now.

Head down, she melted into the crowd and made her way quickly, carefully, back to the one safe place in her world: the House of Angels.

The man watched the flames and smiled. He'd gotten some beautiful shots of the explosion. As soon as he got home, he'd send the photos winging their way through cyberspace, thanks to his new computer and the helpful sales clerks' demonstrations on both e-mail and the digital camera. In case anyone didn't want to take him seriously, these pictures should convince them he meant exactly what he said. Though he did wish he could see his nemesis's face when he opened his e-mail. Since that wasn't possible, he would content himself with the fact that the man would know. And would tremble in fear.

When Regina suddenly scanned the crowd as though she sensed his presence, he slid the camera into the pocket of his cashmere coat and fought the urge to go to her. He carefully tucked his hands inside his coat. He wanted to reassure her, tell her he meant her no harm. Actually, he wanted to hold her close, but he knew she wouldn't allow it. At least not yet. He knew of her aversion to men, her well-deserved fear of being violated. He would help her through it, until she welcomed his touch.

When she wiped at her tears, a spurt of irritation shot through him, but he fought it back. She didn't understand. She had no reason for tears. Irene got what she deserved. The guilty had to die. But the time to explain had not yet come. The street children called her Senhorita Angel, and now she had her own guardian angel: him.

As she turned away, a sudden noise stopped him in his tracks. He looked back and anger surged through his veins. She had the child wrapped in her coat! The baby hadn't been in the car.

Breathing heavily, he followed her, his mind working furiously. They couldn't start their life together until he'd completed his revenge.

He would have to rearrange his plans, change the order he'd decided upon. He didn't like it, but for Regina and their future, he would.

He nodded and headed for home. The time had come for the guilty to pay.

The child was the next bill due.

2

"But why did she have to go to heaven now, Tia Regina?" Elena asked, her sweet voice thick with tears.

Regina settled the six-year-old on her lap and brushed a hand over Elena's dark hair, wincing at the pain in her raw palms. For the second time in an hour, she tried to answer the unanswerable question. *God, help me explain what I don't understand myself.* "I don't know, angel. I know sometimes things happen that don't make sense to us."

"Like when my parents died in the bus crash?"

Regina's heart ached. So many of the children had known far too much anguish for their meager years. "Yes, angel. Like that. Sometimes we don't understand, but we must believe that God knows what's best."

Elena's eyes filled. "How can it be best that someone hurt Tia Irene? On purpose."

Oh, dear Lord. Regina took Elena's chin in her hand. "Where did you hear that?"

Elena ducked her head between Regina's neck and shoulder, her words muffled. "Me and Christiane wanted to know what the policeman said. We listened outside the window. He said a bomb went off." She sat up and looked at Regina with frightened eyes. "Is someone going to hurt us, too?"

Anger coiled hot and furious in Regina's heart. Whoever set the explosion had also stolen the first bit of security most of these children had ever known. She looked directly into the girl's dark eyes. "You listen to me, Elena, and you listen close. No one, and I mean no one, is going to hurt any of our angels. Jorge, Olga, and I will make sure of it."

Dark eyes studied her intently. "Promise?"

"I promise," Regina said, meaning every word.

"My heart hurts," Elena whispered.

"I know, angel. Mine, too."

Small arms wound around her neck, hampering her breathing. "I love you, Tia Regina."

"I love you, too, Elena."

"Your hair smells like smoke."

Regina smiled. "Yes, I know. Now, off to bed with you. I'll be in soon to hear your prayers—especially the one about eavesdropping on conversations." She set the child on her feet and gave her bottom an encouraging swat to shoo her on her way.

By the time all thirty children were safely tucked into their bunks, faces scrubbed, prayers said, hugs and kisses given and received, Regina was falling-down tired. She could barely put one foot in front of the other.

Satisfied that Eduardo slept—at least for now—Regina headed for the shower, desperate to clear her thoughts. She needed to think. To feel clean. To wash away the pain. She grabbed a brush and soap and started scrubbing every inch of her skin, trying to remove the dirt. And the horror. First, little Leticia had been severely beaten and horribly raped. Now Irene was dead. Murdered. Dear God.

Regina stood under the hot spray and shook like a leaf in a windstorm, even as she scrubbed and scrubbed, trying to comprehend, to make sense of it all. Why would someone want Irene dead?

Two minutes later, she'd used up all the hot water and an icy spray pelted her bruised flesh, but Regina didn't notice. She braced her hands on the tiled wall and let the sound of the water drown out her sobs. A pain unlike anything she'd ever felt tore at her insides. Arms wrapped around her middle, her legs gave out and she slid down the wall to the cold tile floor. *Oh, Irene.*

The sound of someone pounding on the bathroom door finally penetrated her consciousness. "Regina, is everything all right?" the housekeeper called.

Regina tried to respond, but no sound came out. She hauled herself up by the towel bar and managed to shut the water off after three tries. Struggling into her ratty bathrobe, she eased the door open a crack. "I'm okay," she croaked.

Worry darkened Olga's lined face. "I'll fix you something to soothe your throat, child."

A short while later, Regina sat in the old rocker in Irene's room, a sleeping Eduardo cradled in her arms. Her eyes kept drifting shut, and she worried she'd let the poor thing roll right out of her arms onto the cold floor.

When the phone rang, Regina's eyes snapped open, and she tightened her grip on Eduardo. "No more children tonight, God, please," she muttered, though as soon as the thought formed, she rejected it. If a child needed her, she would find the strength to do what needed to be done. "*Casa de Anjos,*" she greeted hoarsely.

Silence answered her.

"Hello? Who's there?" She kept her voice casual, non-threatening. Street children often called for help and then changed their minds. "It's all right. Tell me who you are."

"I saw you crying on television tonight," a raspy voice said.

Chills raced down her spine. The voice wasn't human. It was disembodied, mechanical. Regina held the phone slightly away from her ear, as though the evil could reach through the telephone line. "Who is this?" she asked again, only this time she couldn't help the edge that crept into her voice.

"Irene didn't deserve your tears."

Her heart hammered against her ribs and her hands shook. "Please tell me who you are."

"The guilty must pay," the voice said again, and Regina heard the click as the caller hung up.

She slowly replaced the receiver and buried her face against Eduardo's sweet-smelling neck, trying to combat the memory of that dark, evil voice and its terrifying implications. Had she just spoken to Irene's killer?

Olga elbowed her way into the room. "I'm sorry I didn't get the phone, but my hands were full." She set the tray down and then turned, eyes widening. "What is it? Who called? Another orphan?"

Regina tried to steady her breathing. "I don't know."

"Then who?" Olga marched over and scooped Eduardo out of Regina's arms, in full mother-hen mode. "Why do you look so frightened?"

Regina didn't want to scare the older woman any more than necessary, so she asked a question instead. "How much of what the police said earlier did you hear?"

Olga looked away and shuffled her feet.

"It's all right. It's important that you and Jorge know what's going on." The elderly couple bore as much responsibility for the orphanage as she and Irene.

"I know the policeman said Irene was murdered, but that idiot is *loco* if he thinks you had anything to do with it." She raised her eyes heavenward briefly. "I don't understand God at times like this, but I know something is very wrong. First

Irene, and now you sit here—pale as a ghost—after a midnight phone call."

Regina took a deep fortifying breath. "I intend to find out what happened to Irene."

Olga gasped and muttered a quick prayer. "That is dangerous, Regina. Let the police handle it."

"And do what? Sit here and do nothing in the meantime? I can't do that. And I don't trust the police."

"Not do nothing. Take care of the other children. Take care of Eduardo. That is what Irene would want."

Regina's eyes filled and she had to swallow hard before she spoke. "Irene always took care of me. And today, when she really needed me, I wasn't there for her." She swiped her cheeks. "How can I sit by and do nothing to help?"

Seeing the arguments forming on Olga's lips, Regina asked, "Have you had any luck getting in touch with Noah or anyone at the Orlando office?"

"No, and that is very strange."

Regina patted her hand. "Please keep trying."

When the private line rang in his plush downtown Porto Alegre office, Francisco Lopez jumped guiltily and shoved the incriminating photo into his bottom desk drawer. He still couldn't believe Irene had tried to cut him out of her life. How dare she? Didn't she know how much he loved her?

Francisco deliberately calmed himself before he answered. He'd been dreading this call, but had been expecting it. The man operated with the precision of a Swiss watch.

He ran a hand through immaculately coiffed black hair, smoothed his silk tie, and wondered, for the thousandth time, how his life had gotten to this point.

When the phone shrilled again, he picked up the receiver and barked a greeting. Never let anyone, from political opponent to blackmailer, see a single one of your weaknesses.

"What do you want? I've already paid you."

"Yes, you've been very generous. But unfortunately, that was merely a down payment. Especially after today . . ."

"What do you mean 'after today'?" His volume belied the fear dancing in his belly. What did the man know?

"Tsk, tsk," the voice taunted. "Such a temper, especially for a man who wants Brazil to see him as the logical choice for president. Although what you did today in broad daylight seemed rather bold."

Francisco's palms began to sweat. Had the man seen him leaving the café? "What are you talking about?"

"Turn on the television, Colonel. I'll be in touch concerning the cost for my silence."

Francisco fumbled with the television remote, but when he finally understood what the announcers were saying, it slid from nerveless fingers. He dropped his head in his hands as the knowledge pummeled him. His beloved Irene was dead, gone from his life forever. Grief sucked him under, but gradually, his political mind pulled him back up. This had not been a random accident. Bile rose in his throat. The monster blackmailing him had killed her—and somehow, he could make it look like Francisco did it.

He paced his lavishly decorated office, searching for answers, a plan. There had to be a way to stop this man—without revealing his involvement with Irene. If his wife found out, she'd cut off his money, and with it, his chance for the presidency.

But first, he had to find out about the boy. There were too many loose ends. He picked up the phone and dialed a familiar number. "Noah Anderson, please."

Rio de Janeiro

The images began again, and Brooks thrashed his head on the threadbare pillow, his entire body braced in an attempt to stop them. But their pull was as relentless as the sea. His fists gripped the sheet and sweat beaded his forehead as memories sucked him under.

The sounds of the jungle were all around, the air thick. His camouflage clothes clung to his back; his boots slid on the slippery ground. He stopped, signaling the men behind him to hold up. The guard wasn't where he'd been that morning.

He pointed to Jones and Woody. In a crouch, they raced to the spot, silent despite heavy packs and the weapons cradled in competent hands. When they motioned that the guard was dead, icy dread settled in Brooks's gut. Someone had beaten them here. A low cry pierced the air, and he and his men raced through the underbrush, praying they were not altogether too late.

When they spotted the woman and child lying in the small clearing, Brooks whispered, "Cover me, Jax," to his fellow Ranger and best friend. Brooks sprinted through the trees, eyes darting back and forth. Every instinct screamed that they'd been set up, but he could not walk away from the hostages he'd come to save.

He dropped to his knees beside the woman and cursed the neat hole left in her forehead by her assassin. Her body was still warm, and she was fully clothed, so it didn't appear she'd been raped. It wasn't much to tell a husband, but it was something.

Jaw clamped in fury, Brooks turned his attention to the nine-month-old boy. Hope flickered briefly, but vanished when Brooks saw the sucking chest wound, blood pumping out with every heartbeat. He ripped the plastic covering from a first aid dressing and placed it over the wound, knowing it wouldn't help. Big blue eyes gazed solemnly at him, darkened by confusion and pain. One breath, then another, and the child slipped away.

Brooks squeezed his eyes closed, cursing the tragedy of a mother and child lost to the whims of a drug lord. He gently closed the child's eyes and did the same for his mother.

Then he leapt up, icy determination in his eyes. They'd been set up. Betrayed. He intended to find out how. And why.

When shots erupted, Brooks ran for cover, taking a hit to his right arm just as he reached the tree line. He tied off the wound, then returned his gun to the fight.

Pain slashed with white-hot agony, but he gritted his teeth and kept firing. Whoever had ambushed them wasn't going to win. Not as long as he could still lift his gun.

Several yards to his right, Jones took a hit, hitting the ground with a nearly silent thud. Brooks crawled over to him, but Jones was already dead. Shaking with rage, Brooks fired again and again, but the shots kept coming. He looked down and saw blood dripping onto the ground. Relief that the pain had eased changed suddenly to desperation. He was losing consciousness. The spots before his eyes grew bigger, flooding his field of vision. He couldn't give in. He had to protect his men.

Another muffled groan and Brooks watched, helpless, as Woody went down. He, too, was dead. Cursing, Brooks leaned against a tree and tried to raise his gun. Once. Twice. Then he couldn't even see it anymore, though he focused with everything he had. Slowly, the ground rushed up and swallowed him whole.

In the next instant, Brooks saw himself walking in Arlington Cemetery, between rows of gleaming, condemning headstones.

Each bore the name of one of his men, and like the talking trees in fairy tales, taunted him as he walked past. *Your fault, your fault*, they chanted. He wanted to run, but responsibility held him fast.

Suddenly, two more voices joined the condemning chorus: Beatrice Simms and her little son, Richard. "It's all your fault."

Brooks sank down against a tree, oblivious to the pain shooting down his arm. Because of his failure, four people were dead. He forced the condemning words out. "I don't know what went wrong. I'm sorry, so sorry."

A hand slowly brushed his thigh, penetrating the dream. Brooks grabbed it and rolled over, pinning the owner securely under him, his left arm across her windpipe. He found himself looking into a terrified pair of brown eyes.

He lifted his arm and scanned the room while panic clawed at his gut. Where was he? Familiar shapes clicked into focus and he released a pent-up breath. Night. Hotel. Brazil. Girl.

On a mission, a lapse like this could leave a man dead.

He rolled off the bed and studied the woman over his shoulder. After they evaded her pistol-toting brother, they'd gone to the hotel bar, and he'd ordered drinks. Money changed hands before she told Brooks that his long-time contact, Hector, had forbidden anyone to talk to him. Oh, and the man seemed terrified, but she didn't know why.

End of story. He exhaled sharply and rubbed the back of his neck. So how did they get from the bar to his bed?

Eyes glued to his face, the woman leaped up and scuttled into the bathroom.

He had his back to the room when she cautiously returned. He couldn't meet her eyes. In one night, he'd become just like his father. Take what you want with no thought for the woman or the consequences. He only hoped he'd had enough sense to use protection.

"Nothing happened, Senhor."

He whipped around and she grinned ruefully.

"Except that you pinned me to the bed and scared me to death."

When his cell phone rang, she turned to go.

"What's your name?" he asked.

"Maria."

He forced himself to meet her eyes. "I'm sorry, Maria."

"You said that all night long, too, in your sleep. I hope you figure out what you're sorry for, Senhor."

Before he could respond, his phone rang again. He flipped it open and barked, "I'm off the payroll," before snapping it shut again.

"Will you be all right?" he asked.

Maria pulled the money Brooks had given her out of her blouse. "My brother will be happy you were so generous."

As she prepared to slip out the door, his arm snaked out, blocking her path. "Not that generous."

Her eyes widened. "I don't understand."

"Picking my pocket was a bad idea."

She paled and her eyes darted around the room. Slowly, she reached into her blouse again and came up with the contents of his wallet.

As he opened the door, the phone rang again. "Give your brother my best."

Maria scuttled out the door, and Brooks growled into the phone again.

"Nathaniel, don't hang up! I need to talk to you." Carol Brooks Anderson kept her eyes trained on her husband's still face as she spoke to her son. All around Noah's Orlando hospital room, machines beeped and clicked in a steady, reassuring rhythm that should have calmed her racing heart, but didn't.

"Hello, Mom," Brooks said. "How are you?"

His distant tone grated. "I don't like being hung up on, young man."

"Yes, ma'am."

Carol could almost see his half-smile, so like Noah's. Torn, she clutched the printout from Noah's computer in a damp fist, and hesitated, not sure what to say, where to begin. Had seeing this photo from Brazil caused Noah's heart attack?

"What's up, Mom?" He still sounded distant, impatient.

Carol bit her lip and took the plunge. "I need your help."

"Sorry, I'm unavailable," he said bluntly.

"How's the investigation going?" Carol didn't know all the details, no relative of an Army Ranger ever did, but she knew something had gone wrong on his last mission, knew also that the wife and son of a good friend of theirs had been killed in South America around the same time. Knowing Nathaniel, he wouldn't rest until he put all the pieces together.

"It's going nowhere." Each word sliced the air, sharp as a knife blade.

"I'm sorry. But I need your help anyway." Carol took a deep breath, and then shot the words out, rapid-fire. "Your father has suffered a heart attack. A severe one. They're not sure if he'll recover."

"That has nothing to do with me."

Carol glanced toward the hospital bed. "Oh, Nathaniel, he's your father."

"I can't help you."

"You *have* to. Since Noah can't do this himself, I need you." She paused, glanced again at the horrifying digital photo she'd discovered on the monitor in Noah's office. Irene Perriera's car, blown to bits and a warning that no one Noah loved was safe.

She shuddered. Why would someone kill the director of one of the orphanages? Irene—and Regina—were like daughters to her and Noah. It made no sense. Regina could take care of herself. But Eduardo . . . "There's a little child, Nathaniel, a baby. I need you to bring him to the States from House of Angels. That's all. It will only take a few days."

"Get one of his minions to do it. I'm busy."

"I can't. There are things you don't understand . . ." her voice broke off abruptly. She couldn't tell him her suspicions about the baby's parentage or that she thought Eduardo was in danger. After Nathaniel quit the Rangers, he'd sworn off the life. But if anyone could keep that baby safe—and make sure Regina and the other children were all right—her son could. When she spoke again, her voice sounded brisk. "This is important, Nathaniel. If you won't do it for Noah, do it for me."

The silence stretched, measured by the machines counting Noah's heartbeats. "Sorry. No can do. Take care, Mom."

Brooks flipped the phone closed and tossed it onto the bed, Carol's I-love-you echoing in his head. His mother never asked for help, so Noah must be hovering at death's door. The sharp flash of pain caught him off guard. Noah didn't deserve his sympathy or his loyalty. Those things had to be earned, and his old man had blown any chance of that straight to hell a long time ago.

But his mother? Different story entirely. She deserved better than this from him. Besides, after two weeks combing every hellhole around, he still had no answers, just suspicions, bruises, and a light wallet. A two- or three-day detour wouldn't make much difference.

Resigned, Brooks picked up the phone and started packing.

Porto Alegre, Brazil

Regina woke to the sounds of a baby crying and wondered why Irene wasn't getting up to nurse Eduardo. All at once yesterday flooded back, bringing razor-sharp pain and fresh tears.

She shoved her feet into her slippers and fumbled for her bathrobe, crooning softly, "Shh, Eduardo. I'm here, angel, it's okay." She scooped him up and padded to the kitchen. To her surprise, Olga already had a bottle in a pan of water on the stove. If only they could stretch the budget to buy a microwave.

"It's almost ready," Olga whispered.

Regina leaned over and kissed her cheek. "Thank you. I'll go change him, and then you go back to bed. No sense both of us being awake."

While Eduardo sucked contentedly, Regina looked around Irene's bedroom. Their budget left nothing for frills, but Irene had left her unique imprint on the room. A brightly colored blanket covered the single bed and a red scarf draped the water-stained lampshade on the bedside table.

A piece of paper peeking out from a half-closed drawer drew Regina's eyes again and again. After she put Eduardo back in his crib, Regina approached the nightstand, hating the idea of rifling Irene's possessions. Even as street kids, the other's backpack stayed strictly off-limits. But things were different now. They had a murderer on the loose and a baby to protect.

Muttering an apology, Regina pulled open the drawer and a handful of photos and papers tumbled to the wooden floor. She scooped them up and spread them out on the bed. Bills, a few café receipts, but no letters or cards. She'd been hoping for at least some clue to the identity of Eduardo's father, a place to start looking for answers.

Disappointed, she shuffled through the meager pile of photographs. The first was old and faded; two parents with eight children, none of them smiling. Regina wondered idly if any of the Perrieras would see the news and attend the funeral. For Irene's sake, she hoped so.

Regina flipped through the pictures, smiling over the ones of newborn Eduardo. There was even one of her holding him. Tears slid over her cheeks, but she brushed them aside. There would be time for tears tomorrow.

She glanced through the rest of the stack, then stopped, stunned, at the last one. Behind Irene, arms protectively curved around the baby filling her womb, stood Noah Anderson.

Surely her eyes were deceiving her. Regina dropped the picture in her lap, drew a deep breath, and looked at it again. No, it was Noah. Tall and solid, with his salt-and-pepper hair, warm smile, and booming laugh, it could be none other than the founder and president of Noah's Ark International. The man responsible for House of Angels. The one who had rescued her and Irene from the streets that long-ago night, taught them about God's love, gave them hope. He was Eduardo's father?

Regina strode to the window, revulsion and betrayal sending chills up her arms. Bitter cold covered the city, and Regina shivered, thinking of the children on the streets. Tomorrow, she'd order more blankets.

Her mind veered back to the photograph, and she shook her head. No. There had to be a rational, innocent explanation. Noah made frequent trips to Brazil. He'd probably laugh out loud when she told him.

Except she wouldn't tell him, not until she knew more. She had to think logically. The cold hard facts were that Irene had a baby with a married man, and now Irene was dead. The photo showed Noah with Irene. Regina loved and respected Noah and Carol, but Irene was the only sister she'd ever known. Eduardo's safety took priority over everything else.

The terrifying voice on the phone had said the guilty must pay. Regina had no idea what that meant, but she'd start by protecting Eduardo and the rest of the children. And she'd find answers.

No matter what.

3

THIRTY SILENT CHILDREN SAT AT LONG TABLES IN THE ORPHANAGE DINING room, shoveling rice and black beans into their mouths. After this morning's funeral, no one felt much like talking or laughing. Regina knew she should lighten the somber mood, lead by example, but her heart raced with panic.

The frightening mechanical voice had called again, right after she and the children returned from the funeral. Only this time, the caller had demanded to know why she hadn't taken the baby to the church with her. She thanked God she'd followed her instincts and left Eduardo home with Olga and Jorge.

But that meant this monster was after the baby. Shaking, Regina had notified the police. They dismissed her as a grieving female with an active imagination. Regina wanted to grab Eduardo and hide in her room with her knife, but the children needed her. So, she sat in her place at the head of one of the tables trying to coax a smile out of shy Claudio when Olga hurried over, her brown eyes huge.

"Regina, a man came to the door and said Senhor Lopez sent him." Olga leaned closer and lowered her voice. "He said he's a guard and he's to start work later tonight. I didn't dare open the door. He said he'd be back later."

Regina forced a smile and gave the twelve-year-old's hair a quick pat. "Claudio, why don't you take the other children into the courtyard to play? Ask Jorge to go with you." The high walls should keep them safe.

After Claudio scampered away, Regina sighed. "I expected him. Senhor Lopez made the offer after the service this morning. Given the situation, I didn't feel we could refuse."

"But an important man like the Colonel? Why would he do that?"

The thought had crossed Regina's mind as well. "I know he and Tio Noah and Tia Carol have been friends for many years. By the way, still no word from the Andersons?"

"None. I've left messages on every contact number we have. I thought surely either Tio Noah or Tia Carol would be at the funeral."

Regina thought the same thing. This was Noah's first orphanage, and he'd always taken such pride in it. Besides, he had arranged Irene's job in Orlando. He should have been here. Unless he had something to do with Irene's death?

Regina shivered. She couldn't think like that. She'd call Orlando again, but first she confirmed the guard's identity with Francisco Lopez and reiterated that the man had to stay out of sight of the children. They'd been terrified enough.

Standing by the phone, swaying from exhaustion, Regina jumped as though someone had goosed her when a knock sounded on the front door. *No more visitors, please.* She wavered, at the end of her strength.

Slowly, she walked toward it, fingering the knife hidden in her skirt. She hated keeping it where the children might see it, but she didn't have a choice. She wouldn't take any chances.

She had her hand on the doorknob when Jorge hissed, "Senhorita, wait."

She looked over her shoulder to see the old man barreling down the hallway brandishing a kitchen knife like a sword. She wanted to tell him to go back to the children, but she read the determination in his eyes. His age was not the issue; his honor demanded he protect the women and children under his care.

Regina smiled and waved him on, quietly showing him the lethal blade now tucked into her own sleeve. She hoped she never had to use it again, but she could if she had to.

Drawing a deep breath, she peered through the peephole, but whoever stood there was so tall she couldn't see more than a leather-jacket-covered chest.

"Who's there?" she demanded in Portuguese.

"Irene Perriera?" a hard male voice demanded.

Regina's palms began to sweat. Whoever this was didn't know Irene was dead. On the plus side, the voice didn't sound like the one from the telephone, either, but she couldn't be sure.

"Who wants to know?"

A distinctly American voice growled in Portuguese, "Carol Anderson sent me."

Regina looked through the tiny glass again. The man had stepped away from the door and this time she caught sight of a pair of cowboy boots. "State your name."

"Are you Miss Perriera?"

Clearly, this was a man used to getting his way. Well, he wasn't getting so much as the tip of those battered boots in the door unless he answered her questions.

"Look, Senhor, you showed up at my door uninvited. Now, unless you are willing to tell me your name, I will bid you good day."

He gave a very male, very put-upon sigh and then said clearly, in English, "My name is Nathaniel Brooks Anderson of Key West, Florida, and I'd appreciate it very much if you'd open the door so we can have a conversation."

Somehow, his irritation—and the fact that he sounded very much like Noah—eased Regina's apprehension slightly. It had been quite a few years since she'd heard this harsh, precise voice, but she knew one thing. It didn't belong to the man on the telephone. That voice had been disguised and belonged to a weak man, a coward. This deep, commanding one belonged to another kind of man entirely.

She opened the door a mere crack and felt Jorge step up behind her, knife at the ready. "What can I do for you, Senhor Anderson?"

They eyed each other over the threshold. She took him in at a glance, from the tips of too-long dark hair tied at his nape to the worn knees of well-washed blue jeans. She pushed her glasses up the bridge of her nose and compared this man to the one she'd met in an Orlando shopping mall years ago. He had crow's feet at the corners of his eyes and he wore his hair longer, but they were unmistakably one and the same.

Just as it had then, a frisson of something close to fear whispered up her spine. Her eyes widened as they skimmed over the well-developed chest and arms wrapped in a black T-shirt and leather jacket. She refused to think about his size and the way those jeans clung to his shape. Everything about him bespoke a hard-edged masculinity, a frightening virility.

"Just Brooks."

"Pardon?" She pulled her eyes back to his face, flushing when she realized he'd given her as thorough a perusal as she had him.

Almost against her will, those dark gray eyes pulled her into their depths. She blinked in shock, and something akin to recognition. He had old eyes. Eyes that—like hers—had seen too much. She shoved the thought roughly away. She didn't want to feel any empathy, any connection to this man. To any man. She didn't really know him, didn't know what he was doing here.

He was Noah's son.

Confusion swamped her. Anyone associated with the Anderson family had always meant safety and shelter to her. But after finding the photo, her whole world had shifted. It felt like someone had shaken up all the puzzle pieces, and none of them fit in the same place as before. She gripped the doorjamb, the knife carefully hidden.

"Not Mister," he said again. "Just plain Brooks."

Regina ignored that and moved on to important matters. "Take your hands out of your pockets."

He raised one dark brow, but pulled both hands out of the battered bomber jacket and held them out for her inspection.

"Why did Senhora Anderson send you here?" she asked.

Annoyance flashed in his eyes. "She didn't tell you I was coming?"

"I'm sure I would have remembered," Regina drawled. She had the satisfaction of seeing puzzlement furrow his brow.

He turned to scan the street in one quick, efficient movement. Regina followed his gaze, but saw nothing except an old car parked some distance away. "Let's take this conversation inside."

Before she had a chance to protest, he'd grabbed her arm, closed the door, and propelled them both down the hall.

"Let me go, Senhor," she demanded, trying to wrench her arm out of his grip. It was like pulling wood out of a vise.

He headed straight for the office and pushed her unceremoniously into one of the desk chairs before releasing her. She rubbed her arm, temper and panic fighting for dominance.

She wouldn't let any man push his way into her orphanage and manhandle her. She didn't care what his last name was. The fact that he knew exactly where the office was ratcheted her fear up another notch.

Regina squared her shoulders and pushed her glasses firmly back into place. She reached for the telephone. "You will state your business immediately or I will call the police."

He leaned back and stretched his long legs all the way under her chair. Fingers laced across his chest, he regarded her as though showing up unannounced at a stranger's home occurred every day. "It's really very simple. You have a baby here by the name of Eduardo Perriera." He paused as though waiting for some reaction from her. "My mother asked me to bring him to the States."

Regina studied his insolent pose and her panic coalesced into indignation. Flames fairly leaped behind her eyes, burning her eyeballs. This man acted as though he'd come to pick up a crate of bananas. Taking Eduardo away from the only home he'd ever known—from her—seemed to be no more than an errand to him. Something to kill time between assignments, or whatever he did for the government. Another thought struck, snuffing out her anger with its terrifying implication. What if there was more to it than this?

"Why should I believe you?" she demanded. She could see Irene's car exploding all over again. Gripping the arms of the chair for support, she briefly closed her eyes to block out the scene. In an instant, her mind replaced that image with another: the photo of Irene and Noah before Eduardo's birth.

When she opened her eyes, she saw a flash of surprise in Brooks's face. He was obviously not used to having his motives questioned, but he *was* used to hiding his emotions. She could read nothing in those fathomless gray eyes. "Why would I lie?" he asked reasonably.

Regina stood up on wobbly legs, to give herself at least a height advantage over him. "I can think of several reasons."

He folded his arms over his chest as though he didn't care one way or the other. "So enlighten me."

Before she could come up with a response, the doorbell rang again.

Brooks watched the orphanage director pull herself up to her full height, as though bracing for an attack. With her unruly dark hair bunched into a loose ponytail at the nape of her neck, black-rimmed glasses sliding down her nose and shapeless, faded dress brushing her ankles, she would fade into the background, become almost invisible walking down a crowded street. She looked like a million other young mothers.

But when he saw that stubborn chin go up again, he realized that what she lacked in looks, she more than made up for in spirit. He imagined she did a fine job keeping a pack of unruly children in line.

The office door swung open and a relatively short, though extremely well-dressed, man strode into the room, expensive leather shoes beating out an elegant rhythm. A short, round woman, who bore a startling resemblance to Mrs. Claus, padded in behind him, grinning from ear to ear. The man reached for the Senhorita standing stiffly in the center of the room and kissed both her cheeks.

If Brooks hadn't been watching, he would have missed the way she inched back a fraction when the man invaded her personal space. Interesting.

"Regina, *meu amor*, I came as soon as I heard," the man exclaimed, and Brooks's eyebrows shot up at the mention of her name. "I am so sorry I missed the funeral, but business kept me in São Paulo."

Brooks sat up straight. Unbelievable. He hadn't bothered to ask the woman's name, just assumed it was Irene Perriera. Too late, he remembered his mother's old saying about assumptions.

"Thank you, Jair," Regina said, gracefully pulling her hands out of his.

Jair, apparently, didn't want to let her go, for he tucked one hand beneath her arm and then noticed Brooks sitting in the chair. "*Bom dia*," he greeted politely.

Brooks responded in kind, but made no move to rise or shake the man's hand.

Regina looked from one man to the other and rushed into introductions. "Senhor Brooks, this is my friend, Senhor Jair da Costa. Jair, this is Senhor Brooks Anderson."

Brooks inclined his head and watched as Regina got more and more flustered.

The gray-haired woman he figured for the housekeeper set a tray on the table and poured coffee. But first, she handed the woman what looked to be a wet washcloth. Turning her back on the elegant Jair, Regina scrubbed her hands as though prepping for surgery. She scoured until he thought she'd draw blood.

When she looked up and found him watching, she froze. In one smooth motion, she tucked the washcloth in the pocket of her skirt and turned toward her guest, presenting Brooks her back and deliberately shutting him out.

An odd fragment of memory clicked into place. Brooks had met Regina in Orlando where she had gone shopping with his mother. She'd been late arriving, busily shoving a packet of baby wipes into the pocket of another shapeless skirt. How had he forgotten? He rubbed his jaw and decided the local liquor had pickled his brain.

Or maybe that was a convenient out.

He'd lost his edge, the focus a Ranger needed to stay alive. He'd screwed up not once, but three times today alone. Even raw recruits understood that success or failure hinged on the details. He'd missed several standing out in plain sight, waving red flags.

Failure rose like bile, choking him. What had he missed that other, deadly day? What obvious sign had he overlooked, what warning had he dismissed that would have changed everything?

"Would you like coffee, Senhor?" the housekeeper asked, startling him.

"Please." Jerking himself back to the present, he looked up and noticed Regina studying him. Expression blank, he returned stare for stare.

When Jair asked what brought him to Brazil, Brooks merely raised a questioning brow at Regina.

"He's here visiting the orphanage on behalf of his family," Regina supplied.

Jair began rattling in Portuguese and Brooks lost the thread of the conversation. If he worked at it, he could keep up with a native speaker, but he didn't figure this Jair character had anything worthwhile to say.

Instead, he watched Regina. Behind the glasses, the woman had a lovely face, despite the dark circles under her eyes. Her high cheekbones emphasized her plump, kissable lips. Whoa. Back up. Regina ran an orphanage, ergo she belonged squarely in the untouchable, maternal-woman category, as opposed to the party-girl category. He wondered why it mattered either way when Eduardo's name yanked his mind back to the conversation.

"What will happen to poor Eduardo, with Irene gone?" Jair asked.

"He'll stay here," Regina said firmly, then fiddled with a curl that had escaped the rubber band at her nape. Idly, Brooks wondered if her dark hair was as soft as it looked.

"It is such a tragedy, what happened to her." Jair clucked sympathetically, while the housekeeper nodded her head in agreement.

Brooks snapped to attention. *Wait a minute.* "What happened to Irene?" He demanded in Portuguese. Three startled faces turned his way.

"You do not know?" Jair asked. "Is that not why you are here?"

"What happened?" Brooks asked again.

He gave Regina credit for meeting his look head-on despite the agony shadowing her brown eyes. "Irene died yesterday."

"How?" He forced a bland expression. This wasn't his problem.

"There was an explosion."

"What kind of explosion?" *Stay focused. Gather the facts. Get the kid. Get out. Don't let those brown eyes get to you.*

"Her . . . her car blew up." Regina brushed angrily at an errant tear.

His gut tightened involuntarily. He suspected it would take a lot to make this woman cry. "Was there a collision?"

"No."

Unease tiptoed up his spine. "Who do the police consider as suspects at this point?"

"Why do you assume the police are involved, Senhor?" Jair asked.

"Because unless there's an accident, most cars do not explode."

Regina's eyes flew to his and her chin tilted up defiantly. "They say everyone is a suspect right now."

Ah. And she didn't like being considered an "everyone." His training had questions crowding his tongue—like whether anyone had seen anything, if Regina had been there—but he bit them back. *Stay focused.* "Look, Regina, I'm sorry for your loss, but if you'll just get the boy, I'll be on my way."

Her eyes widened as if he'd just sprouted another head. "I don't think so, Senhor," she hissed.

"What?"

"Eduardo is not going anywhere with you."

"Why not?" *What was going on here?*

"Because I don't know you."

He gritted his teeth. "Lady, you know exactly who I am."

"Well, I don't trust you," she blurted.

"What's that supposed to mean?"

"Never mind." She moved to the door and motioned for him to leave. "Please go. I apologize that you made the trip in vain."

Brooks started to argue with her and then stopped. She didn't want to give him the kid, fine. He'd go back to the airport and catch an earlier flight. His mother would have to find someone else. "Have it your way, then." He sketched Regina a brief salute and walked out the door.

As he approached his rental, he realized the car he'd seen earlier had disappeared.

4

THE SILENCE AFTER BROOKS LEFT PULSED WITH TENSION.

"What an odious man," Jair commented. "Really, Regina, I don't know why you let someone like him in the door."

Regina would have pointed out that she hadn't invited him in, but she didn't have the energy. Between these two men clouding the air with warring testosterone, the grief of Irene's funeral, and that anonymous, blood-chilling phone call, she was numb with exhaustion. Until this moment, she hadn't realized how much effort it required to make polite small talk with this man.

Jair stepped closer, and Regina took her usual half-pace backward.

"You need to get out for a bit, *meu amor*," he crooned. "We'll have dinner. A quiet night out is just what you need."

Regina kept from slapping his hand away by reminding herself that Jair was a very nice man. And a very generous contributor to House of Angels. The fact that she didn't like to be touched—or referred to as his loved one—had nothing to do with him personally. Probably.

She sent a helpless look Olga's way, but the older woman beamed at Jair, delighted to have such a gentleman showing an interest in Regina.

"I'm sorry. Not today." And with that, she left the room.

Her annoyance simmered well into the evening. Had everyone gone crazy? Brooks Anderson wanted her to hand Eduardo over like a discarded package, and Olga wanted her to go out to dinner. No matter how well-intentioned Olga's matchmaking, Regina wouldn't let Eduardo out of her sight. Certainly not for Jair.

As for Brooks Anderson . . . no way was he getting his huge hands on the boy.

She was stomping down the hall after she'd checked on the children when the doorbell rang. *What now?*

As if on cue, Jorge appeared in the hallway, kitchen knife of choice at the ready. Her own knife waited safely in the pocket of her skirt. She looked through the peephole and called, "Who is it?" though if the cowboy boots were any indication, she already knew.

"Brooks," came the growled response.

Something inside Regina shifted at the unmistakably male timbre of his voice, though she refused to acknowledge it. "What do you want, Senhor Brooks?"

"I need to talk to you, Miss da Silva."

Regina sighed. "I believe we said all that needed to be said this morning."

During the silence, Regina pictured him grinding his teeth.

"Please open the door." He said each word quietly, but Regina found herself responding to the command behind them.

She slid the deadbolt back, but left the safety chain on. "How can I help you?"

As he had this morning, he looked over his shoulder before directing the full force of those flinty gray eyes her way. "We need to talk. But not out here."

Slowly, against her better judgment, she released the safety chain and waved him in. While Jorge secured the door, she led the way into the office, where he draped his large frame into the same chair he'd occupied that morning.

Regina perched in the chair behind her desk, adjusting her glasses with hands that badly wanted to shake. Yet despite his size and overwhelming maleness, she wasn't physically afraid of him. Even more surprising, he didn't repulse her like Jair did. In some long-denied corner of her heart, she sensed his threat came from what he could make her feel.

She wrapped her sweater around her shoulders as tremors raced up her spine. Just the idea of feeling something for a man besides revulsion terrified her. Even the way he watched her made her tremble—like a cat before a mouse hole. Confident. Lazy. Determined. "Why are you here, Senhor Brooks?"

He met her gaze head on. "I just learned that Eduardo Perriera needs some medical tests done right away. My mother asked me to bring him to the States. I'm not leaving without him."

Regina's eyes widened. Eduardo was fine. There wasn't a thing wrong with him. Why would Carol lie? Even more alarming, if Regina didn't hand over the boy, what would Brooks do?

She was still scrambling for a reply when his head snapped up. In a blur of motion, he leaped out of the chair, grabbed her arms and shoved her into the hallway before landing on top of her in one smooth motion.

For an instant, all her energy focused on catching her breath. *What in the world?* But as soon as the tiniest bit of air filled her lungs, panic set in, and she struggled to get out from under him, fighting with all her might.

Instead of fighting back, he merely shifted his considerable weight to hold her more firmly under him. "Hold still and be quiet."

His voice slid over her, a mere thread of sound. The "or else" didn't have to be stated for her to know it was there. How many times had she heard those same menacing words growled in her ear?

Memories assaulted her and a small whimper escaped her throat. Immediately, a callused palm closed over her lips. *No. Dear Father, no. Not again.* Regina twisted and bucked and tried to take a chunk out of his hand with her teeth.

He must have read her intent, for his hand loosened just a fraction, and he looked her right in the eye. "Lady, I've had a very long day, and getting shot would just about top it off. I'm not going to repeat myself. Hold still."

The word "shot" had the effect of a slap. Her vision cleared, and she fought to hold the panic at bay, even as his weight pushed her into the hard wooden floor. She had no doubt she would have bruises along her back tomorrow.

In the sudden quiet after her struggles, she heard nothing but their breathing. Hers rapid and shallow, his slow and deep. She heard another noise, a slight pinging. It came three times in rapid succession, and then stopped. She raised questioning eyes to his and was surprised at the anger she saw reflected there.

"Rifle. Muffled."

It took a moment for his meaning to sink in. "You mean someone's shooting at us?" The whispered words were barely out before he clamped his hand over her mouth again and leaned in even closer.

"Lady, if you can't keep quiet, I'm gonna have to find a way to do it for you."

His eyes bored into hers and something shimmered in the air between them. A gossamer thin connection, delicate as a spider's web. With it came an elemental awareness, an acknowledgment of the differences between male and female that neither welcomed. It raced back and forth from one to the other like a desperate spider trapping an unwary fly.

For one terrifying moment, she thought he planned to kiss her. He gazed at her lips and then lowered his head, but at the last second he drew back, his jaw tightening.

Regina breathed a sigh of relief, but as the minutes dragged by her fear returned. Maybe if she held herself completely still, he'd forget about her. Eyes closed, she slowed her breathing until she feared her lungs would burst.

He shifted slightly away. "Quit holding your breath," he growled into her ear. "I'm not going to hurt you."

Regina opened her eyes and found herself neatly trapped in his gaze. Rage stormed in the icy depths, tempered by rock-hard determination.

"Where's the back door?" he mouthed.

She jerked her head in the direction of the hallway.

"Stay quiet and out of sight until I get back."

He waited for her nod before he rolled off her and disappeared from sight.

Regina flipped her switchblade open and followed.

5

BROOKS HEADED DOWN THE DIM HALLWAY IN A CROUCH, SEARCHING FOR the old man he'd seen earlier. He didn't want to take him out by mistake.

He passed a connecting hallway and peered around the corner, relieved to see the man standing guard before a corridor to what he assumed were the children's rooms. Good. Brooks sent him a thumbs up and indicated that he was going outside. Gray hair standing up in tufts and thin body looking like a stiff breeze would take it down, the old guy nevertheless brandished that knife like he knew how to use it, and the steely strength in his faded eyes told Brooks what he needed to know.

With a quick prayer that the feisty director would stay where he'd told her to, Brooks eased the knife from its sheath. He slipped out the back door and flexed his right hand, relieved the knife didn't clatter from his grip.

Time to go hunting.

Eyes tilted down lest reflected moonlight give away his location, Brooks slowly made his way to the front of the building. In the distance came the faint hum of traffic, but here in this side courtyard, all was quiet. A cat yowled, and from somewhere nearby, the stench of garbage wafted on the still night air.

The scrape of a heel on brick had him blending farther into the shadows. Another scrape, a muffled cry, and then the thud of a body hitting the ground.

Had the old man come out here after all? Visions of men being cut down by machine gun fire danced before his eyes. Brooks broke out in a cold sweat and every muscle in his body screamed for him to run and never look back. Only the terror in Regina da Silva's eyes and the thought of those innocent children kept him rooted in place. He wasn't worth much, but right now, he was all that stood between them and a very determined shooter with an expensive silencer.

He wiped sweaty palms on his jeans and waited. He knew how to slow his body down and wait, for however long it took. His work for Uncle Sam required weeks and months of waiting in return for fifteen minutes of pure adrenaline.

The minutes ticked by. Not too far away, he heard a moan. Good, meant the victim was still alive, but if he didn't keep quiet, the shooter would be back to finish the job.

No sooner had the thought registered, than a shadow separated itself from the night. Of medium height and build, the man moved with confidence, secure in his power.

Brooks tightened his grip on the knife and waited for his chance. After several minutes, the man stepped into a circle of moonlight. It glinted off his weapon.

Soundlessly, Brooks pulled back his arm to send the knife flying. But just as he let go, his injured muscles spasmed and threw off his aim. He heard the quiet *oof* as blade entered flesh, but no thud of a body hitting the ground. Instead, he heard a muffled curse and pounding feet.

Even before the sounds registered, Brooks was racing across the yard. He rounded the side of the house in time to see the man scale the iron fence and leap across the street. By the time Brooks cleared the same fence, the man had taken a dive into the parked car and sped away.

Disgusted with himself, Brooks scooped the bloody knife from the cobblestones where the shooter had dropped it and wiped it on a clump of grass before returning it to the sheath in the middle of his back.

He jogged back to the fallen man. As he approached, he heard a gasp. A female gasp.

Sure enough, there was the incredibly stupid Miss da Silva making enough noise to wake the dead while she examined the man lying on the ground.

He crouched down and nudged her aside with his knees. At least she'd had sense enough to put pressure on the wound in the man's shoulder.

"Who is this guy?" he demanded as he reached back for his knife and prepared to slice his shirt into thin strips.

"Back away from him," Regina hissed.

His head came up, and he found himself looking at the business end of a long switchblade. "What are you doing? He needs help."

"I think you've helped him plenty. Now back away. I'm going to call for help."

He stared her down. "I don't think so. The last thing we need right now is the police asking a bunch of questions. I can take care of it here." He returned his attention to his shirt and sliced off a neat section, wadded it up and pressed it to the wound.

When she continued to point that knife at him, his patience snapped. He snatched the knife from her hand and pressed her palm over the makeshift bandage. "You want to do something useful, then hold this. Firm pressure."

He ignored the way she muttered to herself in Portuguese. From the few words he picked up, it wasn't flattering to him or anyone in his lineage.

When she wound down, he fixed her with a determined glare. "You want to tell me why you didn't stay put like I told you to?"

Her chin came up, but she never let up on the pressure bandage. "I don't take orders well, Senhor."

Yeah, well, ain't life grand. Just his luck to be stuck with a stubborn, prickly female. So much for the pleasant fantasy he'd spun on the plane after listening to the piped-in music about the girl from Ipanema.

Jaw tight, Brooks ran his hands over the man's arms and legs, searching for other bullet wounds. Their hands bumped, and he realized she was doing the same thing. "We need to see if the bullet went through. We'll have to lift him far enough to check."

She nodded once, which he took for assent.

"Okay, keep the pressure on and I'll get behind his head so we can see what's going on. Ready?"

A quick look confirmed that the bullet had gone clean through. Good. Gently, he set the man back down. "We need to get him inside."

Without waiting for a reply, he swung the man over his shoulder in a fireman's carry. His patient moaned, but it couldn't be helped. They couldn't stay out here and wait for the shooter to come back.

Miss da Silva marched ahead to open the door and gestured to a bedroom just down the hall. Following a spate of Portuguese, the housekeeper materialized with a pan of water and rolls of bandages. He eased the injured man onto the crisp clean sheets and the older woman immediately shooed him out of the way.

"Senhor Brooks, let Olga tend him. I will take a look at your shoulder."

"Just Brooks. And I'm not sure I want you anywhere near me." He nodded toward the switchblade again clutched in her hand, then pointed at his jacket. "The blood isn't mine. Just point me toward the bathroom."

Stubborn to a fault, she led the way instead. And then followed him all the way in. It was not a very big room.

"Look, lady, I'm fine."

"Stop calling me lady." She tossed the words over her shoulder as she scrubbed her hands at the clean but rusty sink.

He couldn't help a half grin at her audacity. The woman had clearly been scared witless tonight, but she was still spitting like a scalded cat. He did prefer demure, moldable women, but he admired guts in either gender.

"Then stop calling me Senhor."

Behind all that hair he caught a glimpse of those lovely lips reflected in the mirror. For some reason, he wanted to see them smile, rather than muttering or shouting at him. She rewarded him with the briefest of smiles before the fear rushed into her eyes again.

He waited until she turned to dry her hands before he said, "Give me some privacy here while I clean up."

Her chin came up at his tone. He leaned in just a bit, and her eyes went wide and she backed up a step. But when she made no move to leave, he shrugged out of his jacket and pulled his cut-up tee shirt over his head. His head snapped around at her sharp intake of breath.

He reached for the knife sheath, then realized she was staring at his shoulder. He touched a hand to it and it came away bloody.

"You are hurt," she accused.

"Not today," he muttered. "Look, it's an old injury."

"I'll get bandages," she said, then she hotfooted it on out of the small room.

While he had the chance, he checked his forearm; glad to see he hadn't torn anything open again. After however many stitches it had taken to sew him up the first time, he didn't relish a repeat in some dirty foreign excuse for a hospital.

"Let me see."

Before he knew what she had planned, she'd snatched his arm and held it in both her hands. "No new tearing. That's good. Now, let's have a look at that shoulder."

Her matter-of-face tone registered. "Are you a doctor?"

She leaned up on her toes. "Nurse. USA trained." She was tall for a woman, but not tall enough to work on his shoulder comfortably. "Have a seat," she said, indicating the rim of the tub.

She set out her supplies while he shrugged out of his sheath and sat, still and silent. He didn't want to make her any more nervous. And he sensed that underneath her bravado, she was uneasy. He thought about her reaction to that stuffy Jair fellow this morning and decided, maybe, she didn't like men in general.

Either way, he studied her as she bustled about tending him. He'd bet his knife she was hiding some very nice curves under that shapeless blouse. He shifted position on the edge of the tub, uncomfortable with the direction of his thoughts. She was wife-mother material. Clearly off-limits.

She looked down and caught him staring. Immediately, she froze and that pretty mouth puckered up like she'd swallowed a lemon. The muttering started again, too. In record time, she stepped back and announced, "All done, Senhor." She held a T-shirt out to him, careful to keep as much distance as possible between them. "This is one of Jorge's shirts, but I think it will fit."

He nodded, and after adjusting his sheath, pulled the shirt over his head, ever mindful of his newly bandaged shoulder.

"We need to talk. You and I have a few things to get straight, and I'd rather not do it in the bathroom."

Back ramrod straight, she nodded and led the way down the hall.

6

REGINA LED HIM BACK INTO HER OFFICE AND INDICATED THE CHAIR ACROSS from her. "Please, have a seat." Amazed at the steadiness of her voice, she kept her hands in her lap so he wouldn't see them shaking.

Someone had tried to kill the guard.

Her stomach flip-flopped wildly. *Dear God, what do I do now?* Across from her, Senhor Anderson sat in the same chair as before, but his apparent laziness had changed to watchfulness.

He glanced at the black diver's watch on his wrist. "He's been gone for eighteen minutes. That's long enough to get himself patched up and come back to finish the job. We need to be ready."

Regina felt all the blood drain from her face. Somehow, the man coming back had never occurred to her. "The children. We have to protect the children."

He patted the air with his hands when she sprang out of her chair. "Easy. We will. How many are there?"

"Thirty."

"Who else is here?"

"Just Olga and Jorge."

"Who's the man he shot?"

"The guard."

His eyes didn't widen exactly, but he seemed to grow even more alert. "Since when have you had a guard?"

"Since Irene's funeral."

He expelled a frustrated breath. "Look, you obviously have some trouble here. Frankly, I want no part of it. I'm just here to pick up the boy."

Could he really be that unfeeling after the way he'd helped them tonight? "And you don't think Eduardo had anything to do with tonight?" she asked sweetly.

When he narrowed his eyes, she nodded in satisfaction. "I have all the necessary papers. Just sign them, and me and the kid will be on our way. Then you can let the police handle whatever else is going on."

"You're just going to walk away, without a backward glance?" She could barely get the words past the resentment clogging her throat.

"That was the idea, yeah," he muttered, scrubbing his jaw.

"Not on your life," she shot back. How could this man be related to Noah and Carol Anderson—a couple who'd spent a lifetime helping others? Maybe he wasn't, a little voice said. She'd met Nathaniel Anderson a long time ago, and then only briefly. Maybe this man was an imposter.

And maybe there really was a tooth fairy.

No, this was their son. It was his motives she seriously questioned. "There is no way I'm letting Eduardo or *any* child out of here with you. How do I know you aren't working with this lunatic?"

"Are you listening to yourself? Carol sent me, remember? The wife of the guy who rescued you as a kid, if I understood my mother correctly."

She had to think. Fast. "Show me your passport," she demanded. Since that beady-eyed policeman had first come by the orphanage and declared her a suspect in Irene's murder, she'd realized the police weren't going to be any help. The slimy little official would probably arrest her just to get his hands on her. Goosebumps crawled up her arms. They were on their own.

Brooks stood and pulled his passport from his hip pocket, then tossed it on her desk. "Satisfied?" he asked, leaning his knuckles on the desktop. "Time's wasting, lady. Get the kid."

"No."

"Fine. I'll get him myself."

The knife slid out of her sleeve like silk on skin. Instantly, she had the edge pressed against the pulse in his throat.

"Let's get something straight, here, Senhor Anderson. Around here, I call the shots. And I'm telling you in no uncertain terms that Eduardo is not leaving here with you."

With a speed that made her dizzy, Brooks had the knife out of her grasp and her pinned to the desktop, his upper body holding her down.

"Now I don't mind you rubbing your curves on me, lady," he drawled, "but I'd prefer to do it when we're not in danger of getting shot."

He let her up and pocketed her knife. "Never, ever, point a knife unless you plan to use it. Get the kid."

She sputtered at his casual manhandling, but quickly realized that could be dealt with later. Right now they had a lunatic with a gun on the loose. And if she believed this terrifying man, the lunatic would be back.

Her stomach pitched and rolled, and her brain flitted wildly from one option to the next, but in the end, she found only one answer. Eduardo. "Fine. Give me ten minutes to get his stuff together and tell Olga and Jorge what's going on."

"You've got four minutes, so you'd better talk to them while you pack his things."

Regina ran to her room, calling for Olga as she went. She grabbed a worn duffle bag from under the bed, and threw clothes, underwear, and socks into it. She also raided her emergency stash of *reais*, and threw them in with her passport and Eduardo's.

She fired off rapid instructions in Portuguese as she went. "Olga, take the van *and* the truck, go twice if you have to, but take all the children out to your son's farm. I'll contact you there."

She raced into Irene and Eduardo's room, Olga hot on her heels. She scooped up as many diapers and baby clothes as she could find and threw them in on top of her own stuff. Olga dashed to the kitchen and returned with formula and bottles.

Before they had everything near ready, Brooks strode through the doorway and grabbed the bag from her hands. "Time's up. Give me the kid."

Regina scooped the sleeping Eduardo from his crib, gave Olga a quick kiss on the cheek, and turned. "We're ready."

Brooks stopped in mid-stride. "There is no 'we.' "

He glanced down the hall at Jorge, who stood with his knife in one hand and his other wrapped around his wife's substantial middle, then back at her.

Regina jutted her chin in the air. "I'm Eduardo's guardian. Where he goes, I go." When he started to protest, she held up a hand. "Take it or leave it, Senhor. You want Eduardo, you get me, too."

Panic fluttered in her chest, and she fervently hoped he hadn't noticed the quaver in her voice. *What am I doing? Going off alone with a man I don't know?* She looked down at Eduardo and stiffened her spine. For him, she would walk through fire, even with this man.

And at the first opportunity, she planned to get her knife back.

"What about the children?

"Olga and Jorge will take them out of the city to a farm."

"And until we get away? How will you keep them safe?"

She raised an eyebrow. "I thought you didn't care about them."

When he took a menacing step toward her, she quickly outlined her plan. "We should be hearing sirens any minute now. Jorge set fire to the small shed out back. He and Olga will take the children, while we leave with Eduardo."

It took him only a moment to think it through. "What about the guard?"

"They will take him, too. In the bed of the truck."

He nodded once and strode from the room, tossing orders over his shoulder as he went. "Jorge, help me load the guard. You two round up the kids and get them out of here."

Another quick check of his watch. "It's been too long."

7

Regina's heart contracted painfully as she kissed half-asleep children before hoisting them into the aging van or the even more decrepit flatbed truck. Some of the older ones, like Rico and Fernando, saw this as a grand adventure, and their eyes shone with excitement. Others, like three-year-old Luisa, clung and cried, confused by the thickening smoke and noise as neighbors poured out of homes and apartments to gawk. In the distance, sirens screamed, adding to the confusion.

Beside her, Senhor Brooks worked quietly and efficiently, loading the children. If his injured shoulder pained him, he gave no sign. She wondered how he could be so aloof and detached, but then, as she watched, she saw him pat an arm here, tousle a curly head there, whisper something to another disoriented child. So, the big, tough American had a soft spot for children. Somehow, she felt much better about leaving the city with him. There were still questions she needed answered, but there would be time for that. For now, they had to get the children safely away.

Scooping her ankle-length skirt in one hand, Regina raced to the driver's window of the van. Olga had the seat all the way forward so she could reach the pedals and was wedged in close to the steering wheel. On impulse, Regina leaned in and gave the older woman a hug. "Go with God. *Tchau.*"

Olga returned the hug fiercely, then cupped both Regina's cheeks in her work-worn hands. "It will be all right, *minha filha.* Jesus will protect us."

My daughter. Tears threatened, so Regina swallowed them back. Tears could come later. "Yes, He will. Go. You must hurry."

She blew a quick kiss to the children who peered anxiously out the van's dirty windows, then hurried to the truck. "Take care of them, Jorge. I'm counting on you."

The old man seemed taller now, stronger than he had in years. The light of battle gleamed in his dark eyes. "Don't worry, I will protect them with my life."

Regina managed a smile. "Let us pray it does not come to that."

The sirens were getting closer. "Go, Jorge. I will contact you when I can."

He nodded once and the truck lurched off down the street, brakes screaming, gears grinding deafeningly.

Whirling, she ran back into the building to get Eduardo, only to meet Senhor Brooks striding down the hall, the sleeping baby tucked under his arm like an American football.

"Where is his bag?" she asked. She had left it on the bed.

"Already in the car. Let's go."

In seconds, they were across the street and in his rental car. The crowd of gawkers continued to swell, and a collective gasp went up when the shed roof burst into flames. Fire trucks lumbered up the cobbled street.

Regina looked out the car window and back at Brooks. "Why aren't we leaving?" She couldn't stop the note of panic that crept into her voice.

He kept watching. "He's not here yet."

For a moment, she couldn't speak. "You mean you're waiting for him?"

Surely, surely she'd heard wrong.

This time, he deigned to look over at her. The coldness in his eyes chilled her, made her instinctively shrink away. This was a predator, a hunter, and he waited for his prey to make an appearance.

She shifted Eduardo to her other shoulder. "You can't mean to use us as bait?" The words were a mere whisper.

"It's the only way to get those kids away safely."

"What about us?"

The half-smile he sent her chilled her insides. "We're going for a little ride, lady, so hang on to the kid."

As the minutes dragged by, Regina felt the strength born of adrenaline seep out of her. She knew she needed to stay alert, to get Eduardo to safety, but her head felt so heavy. Before she knew it, she'd leaned back against the seat, hugging Eduardo close. At least he slept, she thought drowsily, kissing the top of his head. She didn't think a squalling baby would help matters.

She must have dozed, for the next thing she heard was the engine turning over and Senhor Brooks muttering curses against the shooter.

"That's it, come on. Look this way." His hands were wrapped around the wheel with calm competence as he expertly eased the car out onto the street and slowly chugged up the hill. The smoke thickened as firemen worked to contain the fire. Several police officers tried to keep the crowd from coming too close.

The man beside her said nothing more, simply maneuvered them past the chaos. As he topped the hill, he came within inches of a car parked on the right side of the street. The same car, Regina realized, that she'd seen outside the orphanage several times. Was this the shooter?

Brooks hunched over the steering wheel so he could see out her window and gave the other driver a lazy two-fingered military salute before he gunned the engine and sped away. Glass shattered from somewhere in the rear of the car. "Get down!"

Regina clutched the dashboard with one hand and a now-squirming Eduardo with the other. "Are you crazy?" she shouted. "That's the shooter!"

"You got any better ideas?" he shot back, eyes trained on the rearview mirror.

Brooks careened around a corner, and Eduardo screamed in earnest. Regina braced herself and began crooning softly to him. She risked a glance over the seat and immediately wished she hadn't. She could see the nondescript little Fiat gaining on them.

They whipped around another corner. "Turn left! Turn left! This street is a dead end." His look said he clearly didn't like to be challenged, especially about his driving. Too bad. "I grew up here, remember?"

His jaw tight, he fired words like bullets. "Get us on a main highway so we can lose him."

"Take a right here. At the next intersection, make another right. A few blocks down is the highway on-ramp."

He followed her instructions to the letter, but when he got to a red light, he merely honked his horn and barreled through. This American drove like a Brazilian.

Regardless of the hour, the highway teemed with cars, everyone determined to get to their destination in the next thirty-five seconds. Brooks darted out and around lumbering trucks, rusty buckets of various makes and models, and sleek sports cars that thought they owned the road. He drove just like they did: one hand on the wheel, the other on the horn.

Regina sang softly. Eduardo screamed at the top of his lungs.

"Do something about that squalling, would you?"

She stiffened, but kept singing. "Where's my bag?"

"Trunk." He gunned the engine and passed a flatbed loaded with chickens, ignoring the driver's shouts.

Regina settled Eduardo in the crook of her arm and gave him her index finger to suck on. Tense silence filled the car, blending with the traffic noise and magnifying her panicked heartbeat. This couldn't be happening. *Were they really fleeing a madman with a gun?* This had to be a nightmare, and she'd soon wake in her narrow bed at House of Angels, with Irene in the next room.

Brooks glanced in the rearview mirror and gritted his teeth. "He's still behind us."

It wasn't a dream. Regina took a steadying breath and pointed to the next off-ramp. "Get off there and we'll lose him in the back alleys." When he hesitated, she said, "I know these streets like the back of my hand. Unless he grew up in the *favelas* like I did, he won't know his way around. Only those who've lived in the slums know them."

She thought he planned to ignore her. He kept going straight ahead in the left-hand lane, but at the last second, he whipped across three lanes of traffic and roared up the ramp.

"Left or right?" he demanded.

"Left, then right immediately." Regina looked over her shoulder.

The brown Fiat sped past the ramp.

Her shoulders relaxed a fraction. "He kept going."

"How far to the next exit?"

"Couple of kilometers. Not far."

He sped toward another intersection. "Now what?"

"Right. Then left at the next street."

Abruptly, they crossed into another world. Precariously tilted shacks looked to once-proud buildings for support. The smell of garlic mixed nauseatingly with the stench from open sewers. Blank-eyed men huddled around burning barrels of trash. Children with eyes that had seen too much peered from around corners and darted into dark alleys.

Brooks slowed and his arm shot out in her direction. She instinctively reared back, then forced herself to stay still when he merely locked her door.

He pulled up in front of what had once been a pretty little church, but was now merely a burned out shell. He brushed her knee as he reached into the glove box for a map, and Regina could have sworn he did it deliberately, just to jangle her nerves further. Her heart hammered as she watched him, cautious.

He unfolded the map over his knees, all the while scanning the area with those deceptively casual glances. She'd already learned the man didn't do anything without a reason. And he had an amazing ability to do two things at once. He may be studying a map, but she'd bet her next *cafezinho* he knew the exact location of everyone on this street.

She shifted Eduardo and pointed to the map as inspiration struck. "Go north to Gramado," she said. "It's a tourist town they call the Europe of Brazil." At his raised eyebrow, she added, "Its architecture and atmosphere are supposed to look like a town in the Alps. The place is always crawling with tourists."

"I know it." He refolded the map with impressive speed. "Let's make sure we've lost our friend before we head that way."

He pulled the keys from the ignition, got out of the car and opened the trunk. Seconds later her bag landed in the back seat with a thump and then he was back in the car and steering them on a roundabout route in and around Porto Alegre.

And always, he kept one eye glued to the rearview mirror.

The man stopped at an intersection in one of the worst *favelas* of the city and slammed his right hand on the steering wheel. His left shoulder throbbed in time to his heartbeat, and a red haze burned before his eyes. He angled his chin so he could get a better look at the wound. The blood seeping through the bandage precipitated another round of heartfelt curses.

He had not been expecting Brooks to be at House of Angels, much less armed. His contact had told him the man was burned out—useless. He believed Brooks was too drunk most of the time to be any kind of threat whatsoever. So, he'd been unpleasantly surprised to see him at the orphanage earlier. But his contact said Brooks's mother had talked him into picking up the kid. As a favor to her.

He applied more pressure to the wound, hatred building. He'd underestimated his enemy once. He wouldn't make that mistake again.

He slowly cruised the streets, seeking his quarry. If luck smiled on him, he'd spot them before they left the city. That they would leave, he had no doubt. It was what he would do.

He continued up and down streets, always watchful, confident that a calm and orderly search would eventually bring him the results he wanted.

Half an hour later, his efforts were rewarded. He spotted the taillights of the Toyota disappearing around a corner.

He smiled as he stomped down on the accelerator.

Several streets away, Brooks got that niggling feeling at the back of his neck. The one that meant things were not as they should be. The same one he'd gotten before his last mission exploded in a hail of gunfire. He turned his head to tell Regina to hurry and stopped short. The bossy Miss da Silva knelt on her seat, trying to hold an increasingly fussy Eduardo while she rooted around in a bag the size of a bathtub. With that mane of hair forever hanging in her eyes, he marveled the woman could see past the end of her nose, horn-rimmed spectacles notwithstanding. His eyes narrowed. For all her motherly looks, the woman had surprisingly shapely legs. Who'd have thought it?

Annoyed with his thoughts, his words were sharper than he intended. "Hurry it up. We may get company."

Her head snapped up and thumped against the car's ceiling. The baby quit fussing and began squalling in earnest. Brooks looked in the side mirror again. He thought he'd spotted the Fiat when he made that last turn..

He ducked in a narrow little alley that was dark as sin, cut the engine and waited. Eduardo's screams pierced the stillness. "Shut that kid up. Now."

The woman lunged back in her seat, shoved a bottle between the kid's lips and treated Brooks to a glare that could have melted steel. Whoever said brown eyes were soft and puppy-dog sweet had never been on the Senhorita's bad side.

Eduardo let out one last half-hearted cry and then settled down to serious sucking.

Brooks twisted in his seat and kept his eyes on the mouth of the alley. Mentally, he counted off the seconds. One, two, three. He'd only gotten to thirty-five when the Fiat slowly cruised past. He rubbed a hand across the back of his neck, making the muscles in his forearm and shoulder scream in protest.

He looked down and saw the child suckling happily. Then he looked up at his companion. Regina met his gaze calmly, but he could see fear shining in her eyes.

He saw it, but didn't want to. Didn't want to see this little kid, either. Both of them depending on him to get them to safety. He almost laughed at the irony of it. Of all the possible options, these two had a worthless shell of a man to protect them. They'd be better off climbing out of the car, flagging down the Fiat, and begging the shooter for mercy. Or even calling the local police, futile though that would undoubtedly be. In this part of the world, the wheels of justice turned slowly, if at all, and then only if one applied enough grease to the appropriate palms.

He squeezed his eyes shut, then snapped them open again and started the car. Closing them proved dangerous. Every time he did, he saw another child, another innocent, gunned down. His fault; his failure.

He had to get away. His gut roiled as obligation settled over him like an unbearable stench. He couldn't do it. He would dump these two somewhere safe and catch the next plane to the States. Or he'd call his buddy Jax while he hunted down answers about their last mission.

Brooks wasn't sure what he'd landed in the middle of. He just knew he wasn't man enough for the job.

Five minutes passed, then ten. Eduardo finished the bottle and Regina quietly put him to her shoulder to burp, rubbing his back all the while. She almost began singing, as much for Eduardo's sake as her own, but one look at the granite-hard profile beside her convinced her of the wisdom of silence.

Eduardo eased into sleep, and Regina breathed a prayer of thanks, though her heart continued to hammer against her ribs. Part of her fear stemmed from the man trying to kill them, but her traveling companion inspired a different kind of anxiety. He was too big. Too masculine. Too used to getting his own way.

She pushed her glasses up the bridge of her nose and glanced out the rear window, but saw nothing but darkness.

Maybe they'd finally lost him. She wanted to believe that, but she couldn't, not really, and knew Brooks didn't either.

She caressed Eduardo's cheek and her flagging strength returned. She had a job to do—only one—and she would do it. As soon as they were safely away, Senhor Brooks better be prepared to answer some tough questions.

Her eyes narrowed.

Like why the shooting started mere minutes after he showed up on her doorstep.

8

Brooks checked his watch. It had been forty-five minutes since the last time they saw the Fiat. If their assailant had any experience, he would be combing the streets in a grid pattern. So if they backtracked the way they'd come, and if the man was going the other way . . . Brooks stopped his list of ifs and concentrated on the task at hand. He'd never been on a mission yet where the ifs weren't as long as his arm. You covered the possibilities as best you could and prepared for anything.

Except he hadn't prepared. He had zero supplies and no contingency plans. Hadn't thought he'd need them for a two-day errand for his mother.

He shook his head. *Okay. First things first. Get out of the city. Stash the woman and kid somewhere safe. Then hop the next plane out of the country.*

He backed the car to the mouth of the alley and did a quick scan of the area. "Stay down," he commanded.

Then slowly, so as not to arouse undue interest, he headed back the way they'd come and onto the highway.

Regina popped her head up as soon as they cleared the on-ramp. "You're going the wrong way," she pointed out.

"We're going south."

"Gramado is north."

"You watch the kid. I'll do the driving."

She hitched her chin up and ignored him. Fine. Let her sulk. He had other things to worry about. He would swear the Fiat had been on their tail when they reached the highway.

He changed lanes again, eyes on the rearview mirror. Another car changed lanes. Might be him. Too soon to tell. Brooks sped up and passed two lumbering produce trucks. The other car kept pace. He tightened his hands on the wheel. Their man was still with them.

Beside him, the woman continued to stare out the window and ignore him. Why that rankled him he couldn't say. He only knew he didn't like it. "Who is this guy?" he demanded.

She pretended not to hear him.

"Answer me." His temper began a slow burn.

"I don't know."

He leaped across two lanes and cut off a Mercedes. The driver gestured angrily. "Don't know or won't say?"

"I said I don't know."

He watched their tail mirror his moves. Furious, the Mercedes driver rolled down his window and started shouting. "Then give me your best guess. I like to know why I'm being shot at."

Regina whipped around in her seat. "Is he shooting again?" Eduardo protested her tight grip. She crooned softly.

"He just took out that Mercedes's back tire."

Oncoming headlights highlighted a face gone white. "We have to get away."

"I'm working on it," he grumbled, changing lanes again, this time putting a panel truck between them. "Give me directions. I don't have time to read the map. Just weave us around the city so I can lose him."

He glanced in the side mirror, then back at her. "And while we do that, start talking, lady."

From the corner of his eye, he saw her straighten up like she had been poked with a gun barrel. "Take the next exit and make a left. As for the other, I have no idea who he is. But maybe you do."

He again waited until the last possible second before wrenching them off the highway and back onto the city streets. He deliberately ignored her last statement. "Do you often get people shooting at the orphanage? Seems my mother would have mentioned it."

"Turn right here, go around the traffic circle, and take the second right. It's never happened since I've been there." She paused to look at him. "Not until you showed up."

He'd already come to the same chilling conclusion.

She guided them down a dizzying progression of streets. "Turn left here. About halfway down the block there is an all-night parking garage."

As he slowed down, she scraped back her curly mane and rooted around in the pocket of her baggy sweater for a scrap of fabric to tie it back. She had a nice profile—and a good head on her shoulders. She didn't scream or faint in the face of danger, and she protected her cub as fiercely as any mama bear.

He knew instinctively that Regina's fear wasn't just from their situation. She was afraid of him. Since he'd always been an ornery cuss, her reaction wasn't unusual, but she visibly shook whenever he got too close. Since any girl who grew up in the slums had probably been raped, a prostitute, or both, that would certainly explain her aversion to men.

He refused to think of that brief moment of connection on the floor of the orphanage and his reaction to her nearness. He had no room in his life for a woman like her. Considering her reaction to that Jair fellow, no room in hers for a man either.

He turned into the parking garage and slid between two vans, well beyond the feeble light from a low-wattage bulb. Just to test his theory, he put his arm along the back of the seat. Regina almost shot through the roof.

Definitely afraid of men. He'd hate to use that knowledge against her, but would if it came right down to it. He didn't ask any questions since voices would echo in the garage. He'd get his answers. Later.

Regina leaned over the seat again and fished a clean diaper and container of baby wipes out of the bag. Once she had Eduardo dry and gurgling happily on her lap, she pulled out another wipe and washed her hands and face. She tossed it into a plastic bag with the diaper and grabbed another wipe. This time she raked it over her hands until he figured she'd scrape the skin clean off.

Without thinking, he covered her hands to stop the motion. She jerked and tried to yank her hands free, but he overpowered her easily. "Stop."

When he looked in her face and saw the panic behind those awful glasses, he found he didn't like it a bit. But it might just keep them alive.

He waited until she stopped struggling before he let her go. "Get some sleep. We'll head north in the morning."

Yeah, right, Regina thought. They had some madman with a gun after them, and the frightening hunk beside her wanted her to sleep. She stifled a yawn. It must be after four in the morning. She figured he was waiting for daylight when there were more cars on the road and they could get away easier. Thankfully, he hadn't rented a flashy car. The olive green Toyota faded into the background. Her stomach lurched. Had he planned that, too?

Senhor Brooks had questions. Well, she had her own. And as soon as they lost this lunatic, she would get answers.

Her stomach rumbled, but she put it out of her mind. It wasn't the first time she'd gone without food. The important thing was Eduardo's safety.

She cuddled him close, breathing in that sweet baby smell, her heartbeat finally slowing. "Help me keep him safe, Father," she murmured, her eyes drifting closed.

When something warm and hard closed over her mouth some time later, Regina woke with a lunge, a scream forming in her throat.

"Easy, lady, it's just me," Brooks breathed into her ear.

His deep voice sent a shiver down her back.

"If you promise not to scream, I'll take my hand away."

He took her nod for assent and removed his hand before starting the car. "We need to get out of here."

She saw the open map in his lap and realized that while she'd been sleeping, he'd been plotting their escape.

Brooks snaked down the levels of the car park and finally came to the cashier. "Tell him you missed your friend last night and ask him if he's seen a brown Fiat come this way."

Her back stiffened at his dictatorial tone, but she couldn't fault his idea. She leaned forward and spoke to the attendant, a skinny young man with greasy hair. Hearing his response, she sent the boy a dazzling smile. "*Obrigada.*" Her smile vanished as she turned back to Brooks. "He says he hasn't seen the car."

They nosed out into the street, and she noticed Brooks had donned aviator sunglasses. She swallowed. He had looked forbidding before, but he looked flat-out dangerous now. She knew he'd joined the military some years back, but never had that been more obvious. Could she trust him?

Without hesitation, he threaded them back through several streets they'd traveled last night, and then wove off and on the highway several more times. Though she couldn't tell behind the glasses, she knew he divided his attention between the road ahead and the traffic increasing behind them.

After about an hour, he pulled into a small service station. Before she got her hand on the handle he'd put his arm out to stop her. She jumped and spun to face him, almost colliding with his nose. Seeing her face reflected back at her in his sunglasses unsettled her further. "Let me get out first."

Heart thumping, she gathered up a smiling Eduardo and retrieved a diaper and some formula mix.

He thrust a wad of bills into her hand. "Get whatever supplies you need for the kid. We need to be back on the road within ten minutes."

If her hands hadn't been full of baby and baby supplies, she'd have snapped the general a salute. And if she hadn't needed to use the facilities so badly, she'd have stayed in the car just to defy him. She could hear Irene saying, *choose your battles carefully*. Some things just weren't worth fighting over.

When she and Eduardo came back out with—according to her trusty Timex—three minutes to spare, she found Brooks leaning against the side of the car, arms crossed over his chest, booted feet crossed at the ankles. To anyone else, he would look like he hadn't a care in the world, but she could see the impatience radiating off him in waves.

She followed his gaze and realized that from this vantage point, he had a clear view of all the entrances to the building as well as the service road to the station itself.

Before she could get into the passenger side, he put his hand on her arm. She tried to shake him off, but he held on and all but shoved her into the vehicle.

"Get behind the wheel. If you see the Fiat, hightail it out of here."

She hopped back out so fast Eduardo squeaked a protest. She leaned in close and poked his chest with her finger. "Just a minute here. Where do you think you're going? You're not just leaving us here!"

He towered over her and put his face just inches from hers. "Lady, I can answer nature's call here, or I can do it at the side of the road. Your choice."

She clicked her jaw shut and got back in the car, smoothing her skirt before settling Eduardo on her lap. "Well, be quick about it, then."

He snapped her the same saucy salute she'd have liked to give him before, which only made her angrier. The man was insufferable. He was rude. He was arrogant.

And he made her nervous. She didn't like that one bit.

On pain of death, she'd never admit her relief when he returned moments later and helped her change places. Her equilibrium took another dangerous dive when he leaned over to tuck in her skirt, then brushed a hand over Eduardo's dark curls.

As they headed north, the terrain changed. The smog and smell and traffic of Porto Alegre gave way to rolling hills dotted with cattle and goats. With every kilometer, the tight band wrapped around Regina's heart seemed to loosen a bit and breathing became easier.

Except when she looked over at Brooks. Then her heart did a funny little flip she didn't like at all. It made her feel all jittery inside, as though she'd driven too fast over a dip in the road and the car went airborne.

"Did you get him some more formula?"

When she merely nodded, he dropped a bag on the console between them. "Snacks. Help yourself."

Regina studied him out of the corner of her eye. Orders she'd come to expect from him. But kindness, no. She didn't know what to make of it. "*Obrigada*," she said, and bit into some crackers.

By mid-morning they reached the quaint tourist town of Gramado. Regina squinted, trying to see it through the eyes of a stranger. Narrow winding streets with tidy buildings made to look like Alpine chalets, flower boxes in every window. It had long been one of the most popular places in the state of Rio Grande do Sul, especially in the spring when the azaleas were in bloom. They passed Lago Negro with its paddleboat rentals and footpath that wound around the edge of the lake.

Brooks took them right to the center of town. He parked in front of one of the dozens of small restaurants and, once inside, found them a table in the corner. He waited until the waitress had taken their order for *café com leite* and hard rolls before he crossed his arms on the table and leaned in close.

"Start talking, lady. Now. From the beginning."

Her hackles rose at his tone. Somewhere during the long night she'd realized he couldn't possibly be working with the shooter, but she still thought Brooks was hiding something. She just couldn't figure out what. "Take your sunglasses off," she retorted.

He regarded her silently for several long moments before he slipped the lenses off and tucked one earpiece into the collar of Jorge's well-worn T-shirt. Regina looked into his flat gray eyes and realized his emotions and feelings were just as hidden now as they had been behind the shades.

"After I tell you what happened, I expect answers, too."

She took his grudging nod for assent.

So, where to begin? She cleared her throat and fussed with the buttons on Eduardo's sleeper. "My friend Irene, a . . ." she began.

He reached across the table and tilted her chin up with one long finger so she had no choice but to meet his eyes. A tremor passed through her, but she did her best to ignore it.

"Fair is fair," he said, matter of fact.

Regina fiddled with her glasses. "My friend Irene," she began again.

"Eduardo's mother."

She huffed out a breath. "Would you mind not interrupting?"

"Sorry. Just want to make sure I know all the players," he said, but didn't sound the least bit sorry.

She took a fortifying breath. "Irene and I have been friends since we were children living on the streets. Your father, er, found us as teens and arranged for us to go to the States to school. We finished school and both even went to college. Scholarships. I studied nursing; Irene business. We came back to Brazil four years ago and became the orphanage's codirectors."

When he opened his mouth to speak, she held up a hand like a traffic cop. "Just let me finish, okay?" She hated asking for even that much, but she wasn't sure she could maintain her composure if she didn't get it all said quickly.

He inclined his head and she rushed on ahead of the tears clogging her throat.

"About a year ago, I guess, Irene met a man in a café and told me she'd found the man of her dreams. He was a bit older, but he was kind, warm, established, and would take good care of her. When she found out she was pregnant, she just glowed. She felt guilty about having sex before marriage," she added hastily, not wanting to give the wrong impression, "but after the childhood we'd had, she didn't think she could ever have children." She swallowed hard, fighting back the images of that horrible night when the shooter's bullet had destroyed her own chance to ever bear a child. But this wasn't about her; it was about Irene.

Regina paused when the waitress brought their food, shoving emotion aside and focusing on the bare facts. She broke off a piece of her roll for Eduardo to suck on. "When Irene told the man she was pregnant, he panicked and finally admitted that he had a wife and three daughters—one of whom was almost the same age as Irene!"

She lowered her voice as several patrons turned their way. "Irene was devastated. And furious. She felt so betrayed."

"Who was the father?" Brooks broke in.

"I don't know. She wouldn't tell me. And yes, I did my best to get the information out of her." Regina took a sip of her coffee. "Anyway, I guess she told Noah, because he arranged for her to go to the States to have the baby there. He said he would help with immigration and everything.

"But Eduardo had his own timetable," she said, stroking a gentle hand over his round cheeks, "and arrived two months early. That changed everything. Irene told me she'd broken it off with the father, because she wouldn't live a lie and wouldn't destroy another woman's family, either. She made me promise that if anything ever happened to her, I would make sure Eduardo was raised in a good home."

Her voice trailed off as she reached the hardest part of her tale. "Irene still planned to go to the States. On the way to the airport on Tuesday, Eduardo wouldn't stop fussing, so we stopped at a small *mercado* to buy some juice. There were no parking spaces, so I told Irene I would take Eduardo and run inside while she waited in the car."

She tightened her grip on the boy and lowered her gaze. "I was paying for the juice when a terrible explosion knocked us to the ground. As soon as I got up, I raced outside." She swallowed hard. "Irene's car had blown up."

She squeezed her eyes shut against visions of the searing heat. The impenetrable flames. The terrible helplessness.

"I tried to get to her, but I couldn't save her. So I took Eduardo and ran," she finished in a whisper.

"It wasn't your fault," Brooks said harshly.

She met his eyes then, and this time the shutters were open and she could see the storm raging in them. Rage churned like a living thing, writhing in the icy depths.

"Don't blame yourself," he commanded.

Regina gave a harsh laugh and wiped at tears she hadn't realized were there. "Easy for you to say."

"No. Not easy." His voice turned hard and flat, and Regina sensed that was the most honest thing he'd yet said to her.

In the blink of an eye, the shutters dropped over his eyes again masking all emotion. "So you think the shooter is the one who killed Irene? What did the police say?"

Regina raised her hands in a gesture of confusion. "They first called it murder, but according to the papers, they ruled it an accident. Explosion in the gas tank."

"Had you smelled gas before you left the car?"

She watched him over the rim of her coffee cup. "No. Nothing."

"You think it's the baby's father."

It wasn't a question, but she answered it anyway, searching for a reaction, some clue whether Brooks was involved in this or not. She still wasn't convinced his father, Noah, didn't have something to do with this. "Not the father, but maybe someone who works for him. I got the impression he was somebody important and that he'd been using an assumed name around her."

His look sharpened. "Important, how? Government?"

She studied his hard features, but they gave nothing away. "I don't know. She wouldn't say. If she had . . ." She let the thought trail off.

"Think back. Had she seen him on TV, maybe? Shown some unusual reaction to a face on the news?"

She snorted. "Senhor, we don't own a television set, much less have time to watch one."

Brooks finished his coffee and set the cup back in the saucer. "Okay, do you know someone around here? Some place you can lay low for a while? I'll make a few calls and get the police investigation headed in the right direction. Once they catch the shooter, you and the kid can go back home."

He was dismissing her. And Eduardo. Just like that. Relief that he wasn't involved turned to indignation at his cavalier attitude. "Oh, I see. And what are you going to do while we're in hiding? Get a tan? And how long might that be, anyway? I have an orphanage to run. I can't hide those children for an entire police investigation." Her voice rose. "This isn't the good old US of A where the police are your friends. Truth and justice don't hold a candle to bribery, and I don't have that kind of money. Besides, I thought Eduardo needed tests right away."

He saw the interested glances aimed their way and ground out, "Keep your voice down."

Her expression turned mutinous. "How dare you . . ."

"Look, lady, the way I see it, you have two choices. You can go into hiding with the kid while the police sort this out, or I can take him to the States, and you can go back to your precious orphanage. Either way, I'll make a few calls to the right people to help things along."

"Oh, thanks a lot. And you're going to waltz out of here. Just like that."

His stare unnerved her, unblinking as a cat's. "You got it."

"I don't think so, Senhor Brooks. We—the three of us—are in this together, whether you like it or not."

"I'm just an errand boy, Senhorita da Silva. I came to pick up the kid. If you won't give him to me, fine. I'll just head out and the responsibility for his health and well-being will be on your shoulders."

In her twenty-eight years, Regina had met a slew of selfish, unfeeling men, but this one topped them all. Never had she met someone so cold and heartless. That this could be the same son so adored by Carol Anderson amazed her. Regina wouldn't walk across the road with a cup of water if the insufferable beast were on fire.

But there were two points that had to be made perfectly clear before he walked away. She met his unblinking stare head on and said words she wouldn't have believed a week ago. "Your mother lied to you. There is nothing wrong with Eduardo."

The tiny twitch of his rock-hard jaw offered the only indication that she'd scored a direct hit. The thought brought her no satisfaction. Her next revelation would be even worse.

Regina dug in the voluminous pocket of her sweater and drew out the photograph. She smoothed a few wrinkles out of it before she raised her head so she could gauge his reaction. "Whether you like it or not, Senhor, you are involved."

She set the photograph in front of him and waited.

9

BROOKS STEELED HIMSELF. WHATEVER AND WHOEVER HAD BEEN CAPTURED in that photo, he wasn't going to like it. He could tell that much from the look on Regina's face. Expression blank, he leaned over and picked it up.

His features froze and his jaw clamped tight against a tide of anger he hadn't felt since he'd been a naïve kid. He set the picture down before his hands started to shake. This wasn't real. He'd wake up and find himself safely in his dumpy garage apartment in the Florida Keys.

But it was real. The photo was just like the one he'd received on his eighteenth birthday. He blinked and looked again. There stood his father—whiter hair now than in the other picture—with his arms around a pregnant woman. The only difference between the photos was the woman wrapped in his arms.

Brooks looked up. "Irene?"

"Yes."

"Where did you get this?"

"I found it among Irene's things. After she died, I went through her drawers looking for clues." Disappointment and sadness showed in her eyes. "I never expected that."

He kept his voice neutral. "You think he's the father?"

"I don't want to. But it all points that way, doesn't it?"

Brooks nodded once, then scooped up the photo and the check. "Let's get out of here and find a place to lay low for the day."

He loaded them into the car and found a tidy chalet up the hill and off the main road. He ignored Regina's raised eyebrow when he paid cash and signed them in as Mr. and Mrs. Smythe.

The sloped roof of their attic room forced him to duck just to get inside, but it provided an excellent view of the road and the surrounding area. "Why don't you and the kid get some shut-eye? I have a few calls to make."

She grabbed his sleeve before he could make his escape and heat streaked down his arm at her touch. Her hands were rough, the strong hands of a woman who mothered thirty-odd children and could be tough when she had to be. Why that appealed to him, he couldn't have said.

Her grip tightened. "You'd better not run out on us."

Since he'd considered it, his voice turned gruff. "Lady, if I decide to leave, you'll be the first to know. I'm no coward."

Her chin came up. "No? Then how come all I've heard from you is how this isn't your problem?"

He swallowed the words screaming to be said and took back every nice thing he'd thought about her. The woman had no mercy and went straight for the jugular. "Don't let anyone in and don't go out. I'll be back."

"You'd better be. Because you're not going anywhere without this." She waved his passport at him and then tucked it smugly into that ratty sweater.

If he went after her now, he might break her scrawny little neck. Or kiss her senseless. No matter how tempting, neither was a viable option. It took every ounce of his self-control not to slam the door as he marched out.

Regina plopped down on the bed and let the shakes come. She couldn't believe she'd stood up to him that way. Even more amazing was the fact that he hadn't smacked her for her audacity. He'd been tempted. That much she knew. But he hadn't.

Something inside her eased a fraction. That Senhor Brooks could be lethal, she had absolutely no doubt. She'd seen how he behaved in the car when they were being chased, and how he'd responded when the shooting started. The man was a trained killer. But he wasn't cruel. Selfish, yes. A coward? Possibly. But in a life-and-death situation, he hadn't hesitated.

Her cheeks flamed as she remembered the way he'd tackled her in her office and protected her with his body. He hadn't even tried an "accidental" grope. On some level, the man had a code of honor.

Every once in a while, when he thought she wasn't looking, she saw shadows in his eyes. Pain, deep and dark, lingered there. She couldn't be sure how she knew; only that she did.

And when he'd seen the photograph? The sharp sting of betrayal. She'd felt it herself when she found the picture. Noah had always been her hero, her idol, the one man all others should aspire to be like. He'd introduced her to Christ through his words and actions. To discover Noah's feet of clay and have him tumble from the pedestal she'd kept him on tore at her soul. Her heart filled with sudden empathy. How much more difficult would this be for his own son?

Beside her on the bed, Eduardo yawned and settled more comfortably into sleep. If the photo meant what they thought it did, then Eduardo and Brooks were half-brothers. It was a lot to deal with.

And then she thought of Carol. She'd lied to her son about Eduardo. Why? Did she know the child was Noah's and want

Eduardo in the States to keep the secret from coming out? But that wouldn't make sense. It would be easier if he stayed in Brazil.

Regina yawned, exhaustion pulling at her. Something else nagged at her, some stray thought she should remember, but it hovered just out of reach. With Eduardo dozing, she should get some sleep, too. They were safe—at least for the moment—so she slipped off her shoes and glasses, loosened her hair, and climbed under the covers next to Eduardo.

They had vanished. The man sat on his expensive silk sheets and threw his cell phone across the room. It bounced off the flocked wallpaper in his apartment and landed behind the marble-topped dresser. No one had seen them. He'd driven around all night. Nothing.

Finally, this morning, he'd had an idea. He began calling the *Rodoviaria*, explaining to the highway patrol that he'd somehow gotten separated from his friends from America and desperately needed to find them. They tried to be helpful, but unfortunately, no one had seen them.

He hopped up and winced at the pain in his shoulder. He would think past it. Just like he had in prison. He dropped down and began one-handed push-ups, not stopping until sometime after 200, when his shoulder opened up and blood dripped onto the white tile floor.

He bandaged his shoulder again and picked up the photo of his sister, kissing it gently. "They will pay, *minha irma*. Don't worry, sister, they will pay."

He closed his eyes and blocked all thought. A bit of quiet meditation would help him find the answers he sought. After a time, his eyes popped open, glazed with pain but burning with a fervent light.

There were only so many routes out of the city. He would take each one and personally ask at the *Rodoviaria*. They couldn't have disappeared. Somewhere, someone had seen them.

And he would find them.

The boy had to die.

Regina slept soundly when Brooks let himself into the room. Afternoon shadows lengthened across the bed where she and the boy slept. Brooks lowered himself into an upholstered armchair and watched them, emotions churning in his gut.

The boy was his brother. He was having a hard time accepting that fact. The child slept on his stomach, with his little rump pointing straight up. Looked cute like that. Vulnerable. Brooks's heart pounded as he studied the tiny profile. Eduardo didn't have the gray eyes common to males in the Anderson family. But the nose . . .

He rubbed a weary hand over his face. He'd picked up the phone to call his mother three different times while he was out, but he hadn't. According to her, Noah could die. Dollars to donuts Noah had asked her to get the kid to the States, but hadn't told her about his latest fling. Noah wouldn't have mentioned Brooks's own heritage years ago if he hadn't been forced into it. His mother had suffered enough. Brooks wouldn't add to her pain now. What good would it do? The woman, Irene, was dead, and it looked like Noah might soon be, too.

The thought brought a heaviness he hadn't expected. He'd thought his old man's death would be cause for celebration. Freedom, at the very least. But lately, his thoughts turned more and more to the man who'd sired him.

Like pictures in a digital photo frame, snapshots of his childhood flashed through his mind. Himself as a toddler, hands in his pockets in perfect imitation of Noah's stance. Another shot, of father and teenage son on a camping trip. He'd tried to hide from these long-ago images, to harden his heart, but they snuck in while he slept, mingling in his nightmares with the screams of his men.

Brooks shook the memories away, frustration clawing at his gut. He needed answers about the ambush, knew he'd never sleep through another night until he did, but if he left now, he'd be signing the woman and child's death warrants.

Beatrice and Richard Simms's faces flashed in his mind, and he shook the images away. He couldn't protect Regina and Eduardo any more than he had them. But if he didn't try, they were as good as dead. The feisty orphanage director and her switchblade were no match for a trained lunatic with an expensive gun. He was all they had.

With a harsh laugh at God's sense of humor, he realized he'd need some shut-eye, too, if they were going to keep going tonight. He slid his feet out of his boots and eased down on the bed opposite Regina, the baby between them. Just half an hour, that's all he needed.

The half hour passed, and still sleep wouldn't come, though the bed's other two occupants dozed on. He propped his head on one arm and looked over at Miss da Silva. Regina. In sleep she looked softer, more feminine. Without those awful glasses, you could see her long lashes and elegant little nose. He studied her face, reaching a finger out to touch her, before he realized what he was doing.

His gaze wandered over the ever-present cardigan and loose blouse. He had a hunch Miss da Silva was hiding quite a bit behind all this dowdy armor. Not that he cared, he reminded himself. He had to keep them alive until they figured out who was after them, that's all. If she wanted to downplay her assets, never get married, who was he to argue with her?

Not his problem.

He kept telling himself that until his eyes finally slid shut. The dream came again, but this time the child had Eduardo's face. And the cries for help came from the alarmingly sensual mouth of a certain Brazilian orphanage director.

10

"Wake up, Madam Director. We need to hit the road." The voice was deep and quiet, a disturbingly male growl.

With reflexes developed on the streets, Regina shot to her feet, arms raised protectively to fend off an advance.

"Whoa. Ease up, lady." He crossed his arms over his chest and regarded her curiously.

Disoriented, Regina tried to marshal her senses. Eduardo still slept peacefully on the bed, but he was wearing a different sleeper. Her eyes widened. "You changed him?"

He shifted uncomfortably. "Yeah, well, he was screaming fit to wake the dead, and I didn't see you hopping up to help the kid."

Regina pushed the hair out of her eyes, horrified. "I slept through him crying?" That had never happened before. How could she protect him if she didn't even wake up to tend him when he cried?

As though he could read her mind, Brooks said, "Don't beat yourself up. You needed the rest."

She opened her mouth to argue with him, but changed her mind. "Thank you."

He shrugged as though it was no big deal. "I was awake anyway."

Regina turned back to the bed to scoop up Eduardo, who had apparently awakened with the sound of her voice and now waved pudgy fists in the air. She was crooning to him when she heard a thump and saw Brooks toss her bag onto the bed and dump the contents out in a heap.

"What are you doing?" she demanded, mouth agape while he rifled her things.

He ignored her and began separating all her belongings into what looked like two different piles. "We need to travel light," he said, voice clipped. "You've got way too much stuff."

Regina marched over to the bed and started shoving her things back into the bag, her movements hampered by Eduardo, who squirmed in her grip.

Brooks took her arm in a grip that was firm, but not painful. When she struggled, he carefully tightened it, but not enough to hurt. Again, she had the sense of supreme strength ruthlessly controlled. She had to tip her chin up a bit to do it, but she looked him right in the eye. "Let me go."

"Not until we get a few things straight, lady."

"Stop calling me lady."

There went that eyebrow again, and she could have sworn she saw a glimmer of amusement lurking in the shadows of those gray eyes. "What would you prefer I call you?"

She ignored his attempt at humor. "Just Regina."

"Okay, Just Regina, here's how this is going to work. I give the orders. You follow them, no questions asked."

"Ha! That's what you think," she retorted seconds before his meaning sunk in. "Wait a minute. I thought you were leaving."

He kept sorting and muttered something that sounded a lot like, "So did I," but she couldn't be sure.

She reached out a hand to touch him, then thought better of it. "Look at me," she commanded.

He did, but he sure took his sweet time about it. All the earlier amusement had vanished, replaced by the deadly seriousness she'd glimpsed the previous night. The warrior had returned.

"Are you going to help me?"

"I'm going to help my brother and finish the mission I promised my mother. Eduardo and I are going back to the States." He moved one shoulder in a dismissive gesture. "You're free to do as you like."

His attitude grated against her temper like flint to rock. Flames danced in her eyes. "In case you missed this little fact the first time, Senhor, Eduardo and I are a package deal—at least until he's safely on a plane to Florida. No way are you waltzing out of here with him while there's a crazy man with a gun looking for him." She had just started warming to her topic when he quietly interrupted.

"How do you know he isn't looking for me?"

She stopped. Opened her mouth. Closed it again. "Why would someone be after you?"

His mouth fixed into a grimace. "I'm sure you know I'm military. Ex-military," he corrected quickly. "I've made some enemies."

Oh, she could believe that, all right, though from what she'd seen, she pitied anyone unfortunate enough to get on this man's bad side. But she didn't think that was the case here. "Did I mention the phone calls?"

He straightened. "What phone calls?"

"After Irene died, I started getting calls. Late at night."

Brooks took a step in her direction, but, with an effort of will, she held her ground.

"What did the caller say? And why haven't you mentioned this before?"

"He never really said anything. And it never came up, that's why."

His hands tightened into fists as his sides and Regina eyed them warily. He took another step until she had to tilt her head back to meet his eyes. "Look, lady—"

"Regina."

"Look, Regina," he drawled the word insolently and had her setting her jaw, "if I'm going to risk my neck, I want to know exactly what's going on, so I'll know what I'm up against."

His haughty tone had her throwing caution to the four winds. "Yeah, well, Mr. Military Man, we don't always get what we want, now do we?"

Very calmly, he plucked Eduardo from her arms and settled him in the middle of the bed, then gave him the car keys to gnaw on. When Brooks turned and advanced on her, she retreated from the look in his eyes. Icy cold and turbulent, those eyes started a churning in the pit of her belly.

In two long strides, he had her backed up against the wall. One more step brought his feet on either side of hers, his hips inches away, palms flattened against the wall on either side of her head.

As scare tactics went, it was effective. The urge to struggle, to flee almost overpowered her. But she had learned long ago that men used their size to intimidate and bend females to their will. Even though she knew she was no match for him physically, she was done cowering, begging, or pleading.

She glanced at Eduardo and licked suddenly dry lips. She didn't like this man. He was arrogant and rude. And even though his size intimidated her, she needed his strength on her side. On some instinctive level, she knew if he committed to keeping them safe, he would do it with his very last breath.

Eyes on hers, he deliberately leaned closer, so their bodies brushed. She closed her eyes and focused on Irene and Eduardo. This was a game to him. He was testing her somehow—gauging her reaction. She met his gaze without flinching, her mind made up. If sex was the payment for his protection, she would allow it. Whatever it took to assure Eduardo's safety.

But instead of pawing her, Brooks eased back and tucked her hair behind her ear in an oddly tender gesture, as though she'd answered some important question.

Regina told herself the goose bumps popping out on her skin were from terror, nothing more. *Help me, Father.*

"Relax, Reggie. I just wanted to see how far you'd go for the kid."

Her eyes shot up to his in outrage. "How dare you . . . !"

He ran a finger down her nose, a flicker of amusement flashing briefly. "I dare quite a bit. But we're getting off the subject. You want the kid safe, right?"

She nodded once, stiffly.

He raised her chin and kept it firmly in his hand. "Then here's how this is going to work. I give the orders; you follow them. We'll get rid of this psycho, and then I'll get the kid safely to the States."

"Why?" she managed, trying to see past the shutters guarding his eyes.

"Why what?"

"Why are you doing this?"

His expression hardened. "You worry about taking care of the kid and following orders. Let me worry about my reasons."

Abruptly, he released her and turned back to the bed. Her knees threatened to buckle, so she braced her palms against the wall for support. After several deep breaths, she realized he was still calmly sorting through her possessions as if he had every right.

She stalked over to him just as he efficiently tucked several changes of her serviceable white cotton undies into a side pocket of the bag. The pile he was putting back into the bag was much, much smaller than the one he'd shoved away.

"Stop it. I need all that."

"No, you don't." In went her toothbrush and deodorant. Her sleep shirt got tossed away.

She grabbed it and tried to put it back in the bag. He freed it from her grasp and went back to his task.

Several pairs of socks made the cut, but not her sandals. Half her blouses went in, along with a pair of overalls. Her only dress, two skirts, a paperback—all were tossed into the discard pile with one deft flick of a tanned wrist.

To her surprise, he tucked her Bible into a zippered compartment. But when he reached for the small carved wooden box and prepared to toss it across the bed, she lunged for it with both hands. "No. That goes with me."

He pried her fingers loose. "Too heavy."

Inexplicably, tears filled her eyes and the word came out sounding pathetic, even to her own ears. "Please."

Brooks raised his head and studied her face for several long seconds. Then he opened the lid, and Regina saw him glance at the pitiful little pile of photos inside. He fingered a small lock of hair and studied the imprint of Eduardo's foot, done at the hospital the day he was born.

Silently, Brooks closed the lid and placed the box in the bag. Regina released the breath she wasn't aware she'd been holding.

He pointed one long finger in her face. "But if it comes down to it, we leave it behind. I won't jeopardize this mission for the past."

With quick, efficient movements, her things and Eduardo's were repacked. He bundled the remaining items into his torn T-shirt.

"Grab the kid and let's go." He grabbed the shirt and both bags, satisfied with the weight of hers. "At least you didn't pack a bunch of feminine baubles."

He subjected her to a thorough once-over that stiffened her spine, then turned for the stairs before she could protest.

She snatched up the baby and hurried to keep up with his long stride, one thought reverberating inside her head. He was going to help them. *Thank you, Father.*

11

LADY PROVIDENCE HAD GRANTED HIM SUCCESS TODAY. JUST BEFORE darkness fell, he had found the road they'd taken. He'd had to drive to the *Rodoviaria* substation on every highway out of the city of Porto Alegre, but his patience and logical methods paid off. The officer at the last substation confirmed that he had seen a young couple with a baby matching that description at a nearby *posto de gasolina*. It had taken a fistful of *reais* to bribe that information from the uppity young man, but he had what he needed.

Now he just had to catch up to them. Once the baby was dead and his debt to his sister paid, he could move on to other things. Like Miss da Silva. He grinned widely as he recalled the luscious curves he'd glimpsed between the curtains of the orphanage windows. Amazing what a good pair of binoculars could reveal.

Oh, yes, revenge, and a warm and willing woman, too. And he'd make sure she was willing. She wouldn't shy away from him this time. He knew all about her pitiful little childhood, but he figured she'd learned a few tricks out there on the streets that she wouldn't mind trying on him. People often took a whole different view of things when their lives were on the line.

He checked his map. If he had to guess, they were headed for Vacaria. A fairly small town, but at least it had a decent hotel in the middle of it. It was where he'd go, in their shoes.

He set the map beside him and pressed down harder on the accelerator. His other car would take these hills without a problem. He sighed. This would soon be over. Then he could go back to the life he wanted. The life he deserved.

If possible, this night seemed darker than the one before. The hills were getting steeper, and Brooks saw fewer and fewer power lines. The occasional light flickered from the window of a small farmhouse. Highway BR 116 was fairly well maintained, but it took all his concentration to keep going. Doubts gnawed away at his conscience, getting more persistent with every mile. He was out of shape, too out of shape to do this. He couldn't even go one night without sleep. In top form, he could go several and not have it affect him a bit.

He should have let Regina and the boy take their chances on their own. He looked over at her. That unruly mass of curls shielded her face, but he could tell from her voice that she was smiling down at Eduardo as she moved his arms and legs back and forth. His childish giggle filled the car, and Brooks's guilt increased. He couldn't handle the responsibility.

Unaware of his dark thoughts, Regina turned to him and smiled. It was a tentative smile, with traces of doubt hovering around the edges. Her innocent naiveté reminded him of the child she held in her lap and made him angry. She shouldn't trust her life and Eduardo's to him. He wasn't a good bet.

"Vacaria shouldn't be too much farther," she said. "The San Bernardo Park Hotel is fairly new and has a very nice restaurant."

After miles of self-recrimination, his voice came out harsh. "We'll see. We can't risk making ourselves easy targets."

She cocked her head, puzzled. "We did before."

"Then, we had no choice. We had to protect the other children, give them time to get away. It's always wiser to avoid a confrontation if you can." His logic sounded cowardly, even to him. He wondered if she bought his path-of-least-resistance thinking.

"They teach you that in the military?"

He snapped his head around to look at her, but between the hair and the dark, he couldn't decide if he heard sarcasm or genuine curiosity in her voice. But her insight added fuel to his fire. "You just worry about the kid—"

"Certainly, Senhor Military Man. And his name is Eduardo, not 'the kid.' "

He gritted his teeth. She was the most irritating female he'd ever met. He decided he preferred her scared speechless. "Look, Regina," he said it slowly, so she wouldn't miss his use of her name, "you take care of Eduardo," here he spit each syllable out individually, "and I'll worry about our strategy."

"Fine. As long as you don't do anything *estupido*."

They rode in silence until the lights of Vacaria shone in the distance. He'd had the radio on for a while, but the constant chatter grated on his already-taut nerves. Though it did amuse him to hear American pop music in Portuguese.

He spotted the hotel up ahead. Fairly new, the two-story building boasted stucco walls and a red roof. On top, a neon sign proclaimed *Hotel* in big block letters. He scanned the decaying buildings on either side of the hotel. If they stayed here they might as well hoist a banner announcing their presence.

He kept going.

"What are you doing? You passed it."

"Can't stay there. Too obvious."

She followed the building with her eyes until it disappeared from sight, her disappointment obvious. He heard her stomach rumble and wondered if she'd swallow her pride enough to ask him to stop for food.

She didn't.

He stopped at another service station, filled the tank, and stocked up on more baby supplies and snacks. This time, at least, he found several *pastelles*. The meat-filled pastry wouldn't taste great cold, but it would fill their bellies.

When the meager lights of Vacaria faded into nothing, Regina stifled a sigh. She didn't want to admit how much she'd counted on a decent night's sleep in a real bed. A real meal, with silverware, not snacks from a vending machine. She smiled to herself. How quickly she'd gotten spoiled. As a child, she'd have given just about anything—had, in fact—for the same prepackaged food she disdained now. *Forgive me, Father.*

Beside her, Brooks drove with quiet competence. The man was a mass of contradictions and made her tremble, but on a deeper level, she knew she had nothing to fear from him. At least not in the life-or-death sense.

Throughout the years she spent in the States, and even after she returned to Brazil, the military exploits of Noah Anderson's eldest son were spoken of in awed tones by the women and with exaggerated pride by his parents. No one mentioned the rift between father and son, or questioned how secret missions were found out about. Her traveling companion had a reputation as a man of honor. An Army Ranger.

So why the reluctance to help? Why would he only agree when he discovered Eduardo was his brother? The questions burned the tip of her tongue, but she held them back. He wasn't a man who invited questions or exchanged confidences.

She shifted a sleeping Eduardo to her shoulder and tried to stretch her cramped legs and ease muscles that had been in one position far too long. She marveled at how much heat little Eduardo generated. Cradling him was like holding a portable heater, and though the night was cool, his sweat had left a damp circle on her skirt.

Or was that sweat? A hasty diaper check confirmed her first diagnosis.

Brooks must have heard her sigh, for he slanted a hooded gaze her way before resuming his careful scanning of the countryside.

"Are we going all the way to Passo Fundo tonight?" she asked.

"No."

She waited for more information, but none was forthcoming. Well, wasn't the man just a brimming fount of information. "So where are we staying? We'll pass Lagoa Vermelha, but it's even less impressive than Vacaria."

"I'll let you know."

Regina clamped her jaws together and reminded herself that she had asked, no begged, for this man's help. But would it hurt for him to tell her what was going on?

Several minutes later, he pulled off the road into a heavily forested area. The little car heaved and bucked as he wove through the trees and took them deeper and deeper into the dense undergrowth. Finally, she couldn't see anything but trees. Even the night sky was obscured.

"Where are we?" she asked, exasperated.

"Here," he tossed over his shoulder as he got out of the car and came around to open her door. She could have sworn she saw a spark of humor glinting in his eyes as he helped her and Eduardo out.

She jumped when he put his large hand under her elbow as she exited the car. But as time went by, she had started to worry that her reactions to his touch had less and less to do with fear and more with something else. Something nameless she refused to examine too closely.

Regina stood beside the car and her mouth dropped open in shock when he produced a light blanket from the trunk and handed it to her.

"You might want to wrap the kid up in this. It's chilly out here."

After tucking the blanket around Eduardo, she looked up to see Brooks pull two sleeping bags from the trunk. She wondered what else he'd purchased while she slept.

He turned off the headlights and turned a battery-operated lantern on low. It provided just enough light to see one step in front of her. Mercy, she'd forgotten how dark the woods could be. Irene had railroaded her into one camping trip in her life, and that had been quite enough, thank you very much. Give her a big city any day. Sure, the wildlife walked on two feet there, but it was familiar. She knew how to handle the things that went bump in the night in a big city.

But out here . . . she suppressed a shudder.

Brooks moved several feet away, swept the light over a relatively flat little clearing, and set the lantern down. Dropping to his haunches, he unzipped the first sleeping bag.

A suspicion began to take root in her mind. "What are you doing?"

"Zipping the bags together."

"Oh, no, Senhor. We may be out here in the middle of nowhere, but I'm not sleeping with you."

He didn't bother to turn around. "I didn't ask you to."

"Then what . . . ?"

"We're up pretty high. It's already cool and will get a lot colder before morning. We need to keep the kid warm."

Her face flamed, and she was very glad he couldn't see it. Why did she always jump to conclusions?

Finished, he spread the makeshift bed on the ground, then turned to her. When those long arms reached out, she stiffened, prepared for him to assert his masculinity, even though he'd told her he wouldn't. Instead, he took the sleeping child from her. Before he turned back to the sleeping bags, he leaned in close to her ear.

"If I want a quick roll in the hay, Senhorita, I'll let you know. But you're not my type."

Regina stiffened. "Not your type! And what, pray tell Senhor, is your type?"

He merely raised a brow. His arrogance made her so mad she forgot she didn't want him to want her. She didn't want any man to want her. Still, it was an affront to her gender that he didn't. Men wanted women, unless there was something really wrong with them. It was the women's job to say no. Wasn't it?

Fear rushed back as she remembered that night had fallen and she was in the woods, alone with a man she didn't really know. She hunched farther into her sweater and kept her gaze trained on him, watching for any sudden moves. She didn't want his attention. She wanted to be left alone. If men found her attractive, they took more than she wanted to give. Lots more. She shuddered at the memories.

After settling Eduardo snugly in the middle of the sleeping bags, Brooks straightened and subjected her to a very slow and thorough perusal, from the crown of her head to the tips of her serviceable shoes. "There are two kinds of women in this world. Nice women who become wives and mothers, and pretty little things just out for a good time. I don't plan to marry. Ever." He turned and disappeared into the woods.

When he returned, Regina still didn't know which category she fit into, and he didn't say. Instead, he handed her a penlight, a small packet of tissues and a foil-wrapped moist towelette.

"You might want to keep a sharp eye out for snakes."

She accepted his offering and backed away. She would not show her fear. She wouldn't. So what if snakes terrified her. He must be kidding. They weren't in the rain forest or anything. They were just off a two-lane highway, for heaven's sake.

The thought did little to comfort her, but since her bladder had been protesting loudly for the last fifty kilometers, she marched off into the brush. Hadn't she heard somewhere that if you made lots of noise, snakes and other critters would run away, or slither, or whatever it is they did? She shivered.

The little penlight's minuscule beam forced her to walk with her head down. She pushed her glasses up her nose and immediately tripped over an exposed root. Gracious, the vegetation grew thick out here. Penlight in one hand, she held the other out in front of her and pushed low hanging branches and vines aside. She had gone too far. She couldn't see the lantern's glow anymore, which meant he couldn't see her, either. The thought should have been comforting, but instead she noticed all the chirping and rustling in the underbrush, and her knees began knocking.

Calm down. Stop. Take a deep breath and then head back the way you came.

Regina turned to do just that, but a hand reached down and grabbed hold of her hair, holding it fast. She screamed and struggled, but it wouldn't let go.

"No! Let me go!" Her heart thundered in her chest as she realized the madman had found them. They were going to die. *Eduardo, please God, don't let him hurt Eduardo.*

Brooks suddenly appeared in a crouch, knife blade gleaming in the feeble glow of her penlight. While she continued to struggle, he scanned the area, then calmly stood, knife pointing toward the ground.

"Stop screaming; you'll wake the baby," his voice sounded hoarse, angry.

The baby? The madman had found them, and he was worried about waking the baby? Tears stung her eyes from the pain in her scalp, and she felt just like she had the time friends coaxed her into the fun house at a county fair. Reality had somehow shifted. Nothing was as it should be.

Brooks advanced on her, slowly, deliberately. She thought her heart would thump right out of her chest. He was working with the madman. Nothing else made sense. They were working together and now he'd brought them out here to kill her. And Eduardo. *No, God, no.*

Brooks reached out and grasped her chin. She tried to wrench away, but the grip on her hair wouldn't let her. Fresh tears seeped from her eyes.

"Hold still, while I cut you loose."

Regina wasn't going without a fight. After all they'd been through, she would not stand by like a lamb at the slaughter and wait to feel the knife. She struggled harder, ignoring the increasing pain.

Unperturbed by her struggles, Brooks pressed his body up tight against hers and gripped her head with one hand. With the other, he raised the knife. "If you don't stop fighting me, you're going to have a mighty big bald spot."

The world seemed to shift again. "What are you talking about?" The words were a thread of sound. The terror all but choked her.

"You've got your hair so tangled up in this branch, I'm going to have to cut some of it off just to get you loose." He shifted his grip. "That's it. I've almost got it."

Seconds later the terrible pain ended and had he not already been holding her, she would have toppled into his arms. The madman hadn't found them. They were safe. She'd just gotten tangled in a tree. Without warning, thick sobs broke into free, noisy, embarrassing sobs that wouldn't stop.

He had been sure they'd be there. The San Bernardo Park Hotel was the nicest place for miles around. It would be just the place for a rich American to go. He cruised the parking lot once more just to be sure he hadn't missed their car.

He shifted against the stiffness in his shoulder. They weren't far away. He could almost smell them. He'd find them. And when he did, Noah's son would have one more thing to answer for—this hole in his shoulder.

He pulled over and changed the bandage. The wound had turned red and angry looking. He'd have to keep a close eye on it. He'd seen too many men in prison die of blood poisoning.

The streets of Vacaria were dark and quiet this late at night. He used the same method he had in Porto Alegre to patrol the streets. Up one street and down the other in an ever-widening grid. He'd find them.

And then they would pay.

It was only right. An eye for an eye.

Almost, Teresa. Almost.

Brooks gathered Regina close before they both fell headlong into the underbrush. He couldn't decide if he was more surprised by her sobs or by the way she clung to him. Weeping women made him nervous. Not knowing what to say, he settled for soothing noises like the ones she made whenever the kid squalled, and then patted her back, too, for good measure.

When the sobs slowed to a trickle, he began to relax. He eased her away from him and cupped her face in his hands. Tears sparkled on her cheeks and terror lingered in her eyes, but this was the first time she'd let him touch her without recoiling from the brush of his hands.

"Where are your glasses?" he asked gently, amazed that there was any tenderness left in him at all. But she looked so small and fragile, not at all like the little spitfire he'd been traveling with up till now.

She blinked slowly, like someone waking from a dream, and flicked her tongue over her bottom lip. "I-I don't know. I must have lost them."

"I'll find them. Go on back to camp." He reached for the penlight she'd dropped on the ground, but she clamped a hand on his arm.

"No. Please. I, um . . ." her voice trailed off.

So she wasn't a country mouse. Who would've thought it? He picked up tissues, towelette, and penlight and handed them to her. "Just go behind that bush. I'll stay here, but I'll keep my back turned."

She nodded once, and he could have sworn she blushed, but in the dark he couldn't be sure.

In an amazingly short period of time, they were back in camp, her glasses perched on her nose. She rushed right over to Eduardo, who seemed to have slept right through the hullabaloo.

Satisfied that he was all right, Regina fetched a brush from her bag and then settled on the sleeping bag to brush her hair, carefully keeping her back to him. In the light from the lantern he saw that the section he'd hacked off barely brushed her shoulder, while the rest hung a good five inches longer.

Kneeling beside her, he reached back and drew his knife from its sheath. She eyed him warily and leaned away from him. His temper strained its leash. "How many more times am I going to have to pull your fanny from the fire before you stop worrying I'm going to skin you alive?"

"I'm sorry, Senhor. It's a reflex."

"Yeah, well that doesn't say much for the company you keep, does it?"

"No, Senhor."

"Stop with the Senhor, already. It's Brooks."

"Okay, Senhor Brooks."

He ground his teeth. "Just Brooks."

She cocked her head to one side. "Why not Nathaniel?"

"I won't answer to it."

She wanted to ask more questions, he could tell, but apparently her Brazilian manners overcame her American curiosity.

Before she peppered him with more questions, he settled behind her and grabbed her mass of curls in one hand. "I had to cut off some of your hair to free you. Let me straighten it out."

He took her barely perceptible nod for a yes and carefully pulled his knife through the thick mass he held in his hands. He spread her hair out over her shoulders. It was still pretty ragged at the tips, but it looked a lot better than before.

On impulse, he reached over, picked up the brush from the blanket, and began running it through her hair in slow, smooth strokes, stopping every now and then to untangle a snarl.

Who would have thought such a big man could be so gentle? Regina wondered. For an instant, jealousy reared its ugly head. How many other women had he done this for? The thought formed before she remembered she didn't care. Didn't want him to do anything for her. But right now, it felt too good to be pampered. Had anyone ever treated her so tenderly? Not that she could remember. A sigh escaped and she allowed her shoulders to relax. "You've done this before."

"A time or two. My sister has hair like yours and it was forever in a hopeless tangle. I sometimes helped her out."

"Your mother didn't do it?"

"Sometimes. But Mom was often busy with other things."

She heard the trace of irony behind the words, but thought better of probing. This rare peace was not something she was anxious to end.

The silence lengthened, but it was not the tense silence of before. This was the calm of friends who don't have to fill every moment with sound. It seemed odd to think of him as a friend. Until now, Irene had been her only friend. She really knew very little about him. Wasn't sure, exactly, if she wanted to know more.

The slow stroking continued until her eyelids drooped. When he set the brush down and slipped off her glasses, she wanted to beg him not to stop, but bit her tongue. It wouldn't do to get too dependent. Or to let her guard down too far. He was still a man, after all.

Slowly, gently, those big hands crept up under her hair and began to massage her scalp. The sensation was unlike any she'd ever felt. He applied pressure here and then made small circles there with his fingertips. Unconsciously, she pushed back into his hands.

"Feel good?"

"Umm." She didn't think she'd ever been so relaxed in her life.

Before he gave himself time to consider the stupidity of his actions, Brooks tightened his hold on her head and eased her back into his lap. Her eyes blinked languidly at him, questioning. They were beautiful brown eyes. With those ugly glasses hiding them all the time, he'd never gotten a good look. He ran a finger over each finely sculpted eyebrow, and then traced the curve of her cheekbones.

His gaze steady on hers, he inched closer, drawn to the warmth in her eyes like a hapless moth to a flame. Before the action completely registered, he'd lowered his head and brushed his lips across hers.

They were soft and warm and giving, and for one drawn-out minute, responsive.

Then she bit him. Hard.

He yelped and wiped a hand over his lower lip, furious to see blood there.

She scrambled to her feet and towered over him, her knife pointed right at his heart.

He slowly unfolded his length from the sleeping bag and took a careful step toward her. "I warned you once, Reggie, about pointing a knife unless you're prepared to use it."

"Feel free to call my bluff," she tossed back, and took a step closer.

She was beautiful when she was riled. Her shorter hair swirled like a cloud around her head, and without those butt-ugly specs the woman was traffic-stopping gorgeous. She was also madder than a wet hen.

Eyes directly on hers, he made his move. In two steps, he had the knife out of her grasp, and both her hands behind her back, held tightly in one of his. With the other he drew her up against him.

"Let me go."

"When I'm good and ready."

They stared each other down for several more heartbeats. He couldn't tell if that thundering heart belonged to her or to him. She was furious, but he would swear he'd seen attraction in her eyes moments ago, too. He ran his tongue experimentally over his lip. He still tasted blood, which made him mad all over again.

"It was just a friendly little kiss, lady." And darned if he knew where the impulse had come from. She wasn't his type.

"If I want to be kissed, I'll let you know."

Their gazes locked, clashed, for several long seconds. He hated the wounded rabbit look that was back in her eyes. Her anger he could readily accept, but her fear of him was something else.

"Get some sleep. We'll have to be up and gone early."

He abruptly released her, re-sheathed the knife and, tossing aside his boots and jeans, climbed into the sleeping bag.

12

REGINA REMOVED HER SHOES AND CLIMBED INTO THE SLEEPING BAG, INCHING back until the zipper dug into her spine. She curled her knees up and reached over to pull Eduardo closer, snuggling him into the curve of her body.

"I won't attack you while you're sleeping."

Regina wanted to snap and snarl at him, but she just couldn't summon the energy. Besides, he sounded more weary than annoyed. So was she. Her body craved sleep. She spent her days running after energetic children from dawn to dusk, but she'd never, ever spent a twenty-four-hour period like this one. From phone calls, to being shot at, to fleeing across the country with a complete stranger.

She hoped all was well with Jorge and Olga and the children. She should call them. She knew Brooks had a cell phone. She'd seen it when she'd taken his passport. She reached down into her pocket to reassure herself it was still there.

"Thank you for helping us, Brooks. When I asked God for help, you weren't what I expected," she said ruefully.

Beside her, Brooks stiffened. "I'm here because my mother asked me to be. End of story."

No, there was a lot more. With a sigh, Regina realized she was no closer to understanding her travel companion than she had been when they met. Did his parents' faith mean nothing to him?

She stroked Eduardo's head. One minute Brooks scared her to death, the next he brushed her hair with more tenderness than she'd ever received in her life. Then her temper flared as she remembered their kiss. He was just like all the others. As soon as she let her defenses down, he went after her.

But he stopped, a little voice in her head argued.

Sure, after she bit him.

If he really wanted sex, do you think that would have stopped him?

Regina shuddered as old memories flickered to life.

"Are you cold?" he asked.

Amazing how the man could see her in this inky blackness. He must have eyes like a cat. No, not a cat. His were more like a wolf. Cold and predatory.

"No."

"Is the kid okay?"

"*Eduardo* is fine." She put extra emphasis on his name.

"Sweet dreams, Reggie," he rasped softly and rolled away from her.

Regina lay still, watching his back until his breathing grew slow and even. The man kept her emotions constantly off balance. Just as she'd decide she could trust him, he'd do something to scare her. Then she'd be scared, and he'd do something unexpected and gentle. She couldn't decide what he wanted, and that scared her most of all.

She and Eduardo would be better off on their own, Regina decided. She kissed the top of Eduardo's head, said a prayer for wisdom, and made her plans.

As a tracker, she'd be useless. The woman made more noise than a gaggle of teenage girls. He'd been awake since she started to slither out of the sleeping bag, inching the kid out with her. Trying to make a break for it, was she? He wondered how she planned to get the keys out of his jeans pocket.

Through slitted eyes, Brooks watched her place the baby in the back seat of the car, then creep toward him. Inch by inch, her hand crept closer to where his pants lay beside the sleeping bag. He let her slide her palm in and close around the keys before he grabbed her wrist.

"Going somewhere, Reggie?"

Surprise showed clearly in her eyes. "I-I need something for Eduardo from the trunk."

He took the keys from her, then leisurely rose and stepped into his jeans. "You're a lousy liar, Reg, you know that?"

He walked over to the car and took note of the way she'd tucked everything in. "Weren't planning on leaving me a thing, were you?" he remarked casually as he opened the trunk.

In the predawn light, she had the grace to blush.

"So what did you want from in here?" he asked, bending down to her duffle bag.

Too late, he saw her swing something at his head. Just before everything went dark, he heard her whisper, "I'm sorry, Senhor."

He opened his eyes sometime later and waited for the trees to stop galloping like some crazed merry-go-round. The sky wasn't much lighter, so he couldn't have been out for long. He heard an engine and raised his head, only to drop it back down. Big mistake.

Gingerly, he raised himself to a sitting position and looked around. She'd taken everything. She hadn't left so much as a can of soda to quench his thirst. He probed the back of his head and felt a lump the size of a golf ball. No blood, though, so she hadn't used the sharp end of the camping hatchet he'd bought.

He felt a chill and looked around. She had spread his jacket over a nearby bush. Generous little thing, wasn't she?

Brooks shook his head and cursed his own foolishness. He'd known from the first she was skittish about men, but he'd never expected this kind of reaction. He lurched to his feet and moved slowly over to the jacket. He slipped it on, then fired off a fresh round of curses as he realized she still had his passport. And she'd taken his wallet and cell phone.

Fine. She was on her own, then. He'd walk to the nearest town, call his friend Jax, and have a new passport, visa, credit cards, and cash delivered within twelve hours. He may not officially belong to Uncle Sam any more, but he still had connections. Getting the kid safely out of the country was no longer his concern.

Regina headed to Passo Fundo with one eye on the road ahead and the other glued to her rearview mirror. Her erstwhile companion would not be a happy man when he woke up. At least she hoped he'd wake up. He'd been so still, so quiet, that for a minute she thought she'd killed him. A quick check of his pulse had confirmed he was alive.

Mercy, but his skin had been hot to the touch. And the stubble on his cheeks had been rough against her palm when she allowed herself one quick swipe down his face. In repose, he didn't seem threatening at all. It was when he was awake and trying to control everything and everyone that she couldn't deal with him.

Okay, so maybe, just maybe, bashing him over the head with the hatchet handle had been a little extreme. But desperate times, so the saying went, called for desperate measures. That kiss had rattled her badly. She was just starting to believe that maybe he wasn't like other men. Maybe he wouldn't just take what he wanted. But he had.

But he'd stopped, too.

And she wasn't entirely sure if that was good or bad. She shoved the uncomfortable thought away and concentrated on driving. She needed to stock up on formula and gas. In the back seat, Eduardo stirred. He needed more diapers, too. They'd get what they needed in Passo Fundo, then keep going.

Pulling the cell phone out of her sweater, she quickly dialed the number of the farm outside Porto Alegre where she'd sent the children.

Jorge answered on the first ring. "*Oi*?"

"Jorge, it's Regina. How is everyone?"

"Oh, Senhorita, we have been so worried about you. Where are you?"

Regina remembered something she'd read about cell phones being traceable, so she said simply, "We're fine. Is everything okay there?"

"*Sim*. No problems. The children are all okay after their little adventure. And I called one of the neighbors; they say the fire was kept to the shed. No other damage."

Regina let out a relieved sigh. "I'm so glad. How is the guard?"

"He is recovering nicely, enjoying all the attention."

Regina gripped the phone as a sudden thought occurred to her. "What did he tell Senhor Lopez about the shooting?"

"I convinced him of the wisdom of keeping the incident quiet," Jorge said, then added, "for his job's sake, you understand."

Regina smiled at his resourcefulness. "Good thinking. I'll check back with you in a few days. Give my love to Olga and the children." She flipped the phone closed and tucked it back in her pocket as Passo Fundo came into view. She checked her rearview mirror again and her heart skipped a beat. Was it her imagination, or was that car gaining on her?

Plotting all manner of retribution, Brooks set off toward the highway. With any luck, some passing farmer would give him a lift into Passo Fundo, and he could corner his elusive quarry. She had some explaining to do. And if anyone were leaving anybody, it would be him. She wasn't going to knock him out cold and then leave him without so much as a toothpick. Not bloody likely.

He stood just inside the cover of trees when he heard a car approaching. He'd taken one step toward the road when some sixth sense warned him, and he ducked behind a tree. Far enough back to stay hidden, but close enough to see the road.

His irritation kicked over into fear when the dented brown Fiat came into view. He crouched down so he could get a look at the driver as the car sped past. He didn't have long; the guy was clearly in a hurry, but he saw enough to determine that he was Brazilian, probably in his fifties. Dark hair, average build, determined chin, but the brim on his ball cap shadowed the rest of his features.

Brooks' heartbeat kicked up several notches. Regina and Eduardo weren't far ahead of him. He reached back and congratulated her for having the foresight to take his knife with her, along with her own. She was gonna need both. He reached down, glad to discover she'd missed his boot sheath and the knife there.

Hearing another vehicle, he jumped from the trees and stood in the middle of the road waving his arms. The old farm truck shuddered to a halt, and Brooks jogged around to the driver's side. "*Oi, tudo bem? A Passo Fundo*?"

The driver didn't respond to either his polite greeting or his question, merely gestured to the back of the truck with his thumb. Brooks smiled his thanks and climbed in, adding another transgression to Regina's list of sins. The crates of chickens were stacked three high. The birds were loud, smelly, and clearly unhappy. Whenever the truck took a curve in the road, the whole load shifted and the nearest birds tried to peck a strip off his hide.

By the time the driver dropped him in the center of town his head throbbed—as much from the noise as from the bump on his head—and he stank to high heaven. He spotted a café and headed there before he realized the lovely Regina hadn't left him one blessed *real*.

He scanned the busy street and walked purposefully toward the nearest gas station. His query as to the location of the nearest *mercado* made him smile. Two blocks wasn't all that far. He thanked the man and hurried off, keeping his jacket collar turned up and avoiding eye contact.

Brooks approached the market from the opposite side of the street and stopped to evaluate the activity by looking in the shop window in front of him and watching the reflection in the glass. Pay dirt. Way in the back of the lot was the little Toyota, crammed between two other Toyotas of similar make and vintage. The woman might be vindictive, but she wasn't stupid.

His relief was short-lived. Just as he turned toward the grocery store, he saw the reflection of the brown Fiat, slowly cruising down the street.

Regina clutched Eduardo in her left arm and pushed a small shopping cart with her right. She moved purposefully, but not so quickly as to draw attention to herself. An old woman came up behind her to chuck Eduardo under the chin and Regina almost screamed. She had to calm down.

She'd bashed Brooks over the head. She still couldn't believe it, though this wasn't the first time she'd used violence for self-preservation. Her heart thudded painfully as she realized that she'd well and truly pulled the tiger's tail. If—when—she hastily corrected, he woke up, he was going to make a bear with a thorn in its paw look positively docile by comparison. She planned to be far, far away by then.

In retrospect, this probably wasn't the smartest thing she'd ever done. But she'd felt threatened, cornered, and she'd promised herself no man would ever make her feel that way again. She had to gather her wits about her and decide what to do next. She may not be a country girl, but she was a survivor.

She tossed diapers and a big box of moist towelettes into the cart. Then formula, some canned food and a can opener, crackers, several bottles of Guarana soda for herself, a pot, some instant rice, and boxed milk. She also added a supply of plastic plates, cups, and silverware.

At the end of every aisle, she hunched down and scanned the shoppers in either direction before making the turn. In one aisle, she discovered a display of souvenir ball caps, and grabbed one for herself and a small one for Eduardo.

She paid for her purchases and shoved her hair up under her cap before snugging Eduardo's down on his head. She tried to put her change in her wallet with one hand and hold the wriggly child in the other, but he squirmed and slipped in her grasp like an eel.

Regina's frustration edged up another notch as she left the store. Pushing the cart, holding Eduardo and scanning the parking lot for the terrifying brown Fiat all at once was no small feat, even for a woman who prided herself on her ability to do several things at once.

As she tossed the last bag of groceries into the trunk, a hand came around her neck and gripped it in an iron fist. "Don't scream," an all-too familiar voice growled in her ear.

Sweat popped out on her forehead and under her arms. Moisture made her grip on Eduardo even more precarious as he tossed his head to be rid of the hat.

"I'm going to let you go, and you and the kid are going to get in on the passenger side as though we'd planned this all along. Do you understand?"

She nodded mutely and willed her knees not to buckle. She stood frozen, rooted in place.

"Move," he ground out, giving her a helpful little shove in the right direction.

Regina shook off her lethargy and got in the door he held open.

"Do not even think about making a run for it," he warned.

It wasn't until they were out of the parking lot that Regina risked a glance at his profile. Livid would be too mild a word for the anger raging in Brooks's face. She shivered as she again sensed the raw power he ruthlessly held in check. She did not want to be around when he unleashed it.

Though perhaps she should have considered that before she tried to crack his skull open.

He wove his way up and down several streets, ever checking the mirrors. Every muscle in his body appeared rigid, though his grip on the wheel remained loose and competent. She didn't need to hear his muffled curse to know their pursuer had found them again.

"Brooks, I—" she began, though she had no idea what to say next. "Sorry I bonked you on the head" didn't seem adequate. And in truth, she wasn't all that sorry. He kept pushing her. So she'd pushed back.

She risked another glance in his direction. The lump just behind his ear had swollen up enough that she could see it from here. Oh, dear, maybe she'd been a bit too energetic with that hatchet. She'd wanted to slow him down while they got away, not do him any real damage.

"Don't. Say. One. Word." Each syllable sounded like he'd hurled it with his knife.

She started guiltily as she realized she had that same knife securely tucked in her purse. She twisted around in her seat and glimpsed the Fiat screeching around the corner behind them. If Brooks was going to the trouble of trying to get them away from this madman, the least she could do was make sure he was armed.

Slowly, she pulled his wicked-looking knife from her purse and handed it to him, handle first. He shot her one unreadable glance, then tucked it quickly into its sheath.

Brooks whipped around the next corner on two wheels. He'd jerked the wheel so hard to the left that she and Eduardo slammed into the door. Eduardo began shrieking, but Regina wasn't sure if it were from fright, or if he'd hurt himself.

She planted her feet firmly on the floorboards, braced one hand on the dash and began singing loud enough to be heard above his screams while she checked him over. He seemed to be fine. When Eduardo stopped long enough to draw breath, she lowered her volume, coaxing him to quiet down so he could hear her. But keeping the song going was hard, with Brooks trying to give them whiplash, the Fiat gaining, and Eduardo screaming.

As they wove through the narrow streets, Brooks suddenly uttered an exceptionally harsh word and slammed a hand on the steering wheel. Hard.

"Why didn't you get gas first!" he demanded.

Her gaze shot to the gas gauge. Empty. "I-I planned to, as soon as I got the groceries," she stammered. The fact that he was right only made her more defensive. "How could I know that madman would be this close?"

His expression said more clearly than words what he thought of her. He didn't slow their pace one kilometer, but now he hunched over the steering wheel, scanning the buildings.

Spotting a car repair shop with several dozen cars sitting behind it in various stages of decrepitude, he checked the rear-view mirror, whipped around the block, and darted through the high chain link fence from the opposite direction.

With scant inches to spare, he wedged the car between two rusting hulks and scrambled out the open window. No way could they get the door open in the narrow space.

"Hand me the kid."

She handed him a still-screaming Eduardo and climbed over the console and out the window after them. Brooks was already striding out the gate, and she ran to catch up.

He was in full military mode. Eyes scanning constantly, expression intent behind the mirrored shades, body poised for the unexpected. She reached them just as he flattened himself against the building and took a quick peek up and down the street. Eduardo reached out for her, and she quickly clutched him securely against her chest.

"Let's go. Whatever happens, keep up and follow my lead."

If he said anything else, Eduardo's energetic howling drowned it out. Without giving her a chance to reply, Brooks jogged to the alley, looked both ways, and darted down it.

They crossed one street, then another. Regina's arms were aching from gripping the child, and her ears rang from his screams. Given the stress level they were under, it was no wonder he sensed it, but that still didn't make the howling easier to bear.

"You've got to shut the kid up," Brooks growled as they crouched down and sped across another side street.

As though his screams were directly her fault. "Yeah, well, it's not like there's not a little tension here for him to pick up on," she retorted.

They heard a car, and Brooks grabbed her wrist and hauled her into a dimly recessed doorway. He pushed on the door and it moaned and swung inward, revealing a rickety set of stairs.

"Up," he commanded, pushing her ahead of him.

He swung the door shut behind them, then took the stairs two at a time to catch up. At the top, they found themselves in a warehouse stacked with packing crates. Empty packing crates.

Several of the high windows had been broken and small patches of sunlight highlighted dancing dust motes. Eduardo's screams echoed shrilly in the cavernous room. Regina stepped up her jiggling and crooning as Brooks propelled her between high walls of crates.

They crouched in a dim corner and she tried sticking her finger in Eduardo's mouth. In the brief seconds of quiet that followed, they heard the lower door creak open.

He'd found them. Regina looked at Brooks, but he was scanning, always scanning, looking for other options, other ways out. But she could see that he didn't have much hope as he eased the knife from its sheath and prepared to defend them.

She looked down at Eduardo, who was scrunching up his adorable little face in preparation for another scream. She had to keep him quiet.

In that split-second, she remembered a war movie she'd watched in college. She couldn't remember anything except one horrible scene where the enemy was about to discover a busload of refugees. A baby about Eduardo's age had reacted just as he was—crying pitifully. The full busload of passengers had focused on the mother, begging her with their eyes to somehow quiet him and save their lives. In desperation, the poor mother covered her child's mouth to keep him quiet and ultimately, with silent tears pouring down her cheeks, smothered her own son to protect everyone on the bus.

Right then, Regina knew that same mixture of desperation and love. It strangled her, froze her limbs. She couldn't do it. She couldn't. There had to be another way.

Eyes pleading, begging for another alternative, she met Brooks' gaze. He'd removed his shades, his expression carefully blank, but he looked pointedly at her chest, then back up to her face.

She instantly understood his meaning, but now a new fear gripped her heart. She was afraid, so afraid to make herself vulnerable to any man. Yet with one glance at Eduardo's sweet face, love conquered fear. For him, she would do whatever she had to. But she wasn't taking unnecessary chances.

Regina deliberately turned her back to Brooks and then unbuttoned her blouse and pushed her bra aside with hands that shook and fumbled badly in her haste. She guided Eduardo's mouth to her breast, and he instantly latched on. His tense little features relaxed as he suckled greedily, one plump fist pushing against the curve of her breast. How long before he realized there was no milk and started screaming all over again?

The seconds ticked by as he sucked contentedly. Regina slowly released her pent-up breath and smoothed the damp curls back from his forehead, trying to hold back the mix of emotions rioting through her. His rhythmic suckling sent a shaft of pure agony straight to her empty womb, where no child would ever grow. Her fear of their pursuer faded away as tears slid down her cheeks and she pretended, just for this brief slice of time, that she was his mother. She hugged Eduardo closer, tracing the shell of his ear, stroking his tiny fingers.

When her tears blinded her, Regina forced her thoughts back to the present, to the precarious situation they were in. There was a madman closing in. She strained to hear any sounds from below, trying to stay calm for the baby's sake. For several minutes, she heard nothing. Then, she heard the door creak again and close. Had the shooter left, or was this a trick? Half-afraid to hope, she looked over her shoulder at Brooks and froze.

He hadn't turned toward the sound below as she'd expected. He stared at her, an arrested expression on his chiseled face. Sensing her gaze, his gray eyes met hers, but amazingly, in them she didn't see lust, she saw something that looked like awe. Right now those gray eyes weren't stormy at all, but as deep and quiet as a lake at dawn.

She sucked in a breath and an embarrassed flush crept up her neck. Flustered, she tucked her chin down, pulled her blouse together, and moved farther away, but Brooks's hand shot out and gently stopped her. Trembling with an emotion she could not name, she waited, rooted to the spot, as he turned her back toward him slowly, making sure her oversized blouse was completely closed. He then carefully brushed his finger across Eduardo's cheek.

Slowly, so as not to jostle a now-drowsy Eduardo, he leaned forward and brushed her tears away with his thumb before pressing his lips to her forehead. Never had anyone touched her like this, treated her as if she were made of spun glass and something to be treasured. But in just two days, this man had done it twice. Her heart pounded with something akin to envy and her eyes filled again. What would it be like to be loved by a man capable of such deep emotion, to suckle their child at her breast?

She squeezed her eyes shut against the pain of impossible dreams and willed herself to focus on their situation. But it was hard.

Moments later, Brooks leaned toward her again. "Stay here. I'll go make sure he's gone." His warm breath tickled her ear, then he slipped away.

13

BY THE TIME BROOKS RETURNED WHAT SEEMED LIKE HOURS LATER, Eduardo, thank the Lord, was sleeping the sleep of utter exhaustion. Regina's shoulders ached with tension, and she envied the baby his easy escape.

When she'd first heard that ominous creak of the door, panic clawed at her belly, but she forced herself to remain calm. All she needed was for her tension to transmit itself to Eduardo and for him to start wailing again. Although she really couldn't blame him for it; she felt like howling, too.

Breath held so she could hear beyond the pounding of her heart, she waited, switchblade ready. Her breath came out in a rush as Brooks slid into view. For one absurd moment, she had to fight the urge to fling herself into his arms and curl up against his hard chest with the same abandon Eduardo embraced her. Which made no sense, given she'd almost killed him earlier that day.

She straightened Eduardo's clothes and avoided Brooks's gaze. She had no idea how to react after what had happened earlier. Whatever connection, for want of a better word, had sprung up between them in those few moments was wrong. It didn't belong there. She didn't need or want a man in her life.

All the ones she'd known had brought her grief. And pain. So much pain.

She shot to her feet and marched toward the stairs. In two long strides he had her arm and swung her around, though mindful of the sleeping child she carried.

When Regina looked up into his face, the warrior looked back and their earlier encounter might never have occurred. "Stay behind me. We've got to move fast."

If she'd had a better plan, she'd have argued with him. Since she didn't, she simply nodded, but his constant bossing was wearing thin. True, Irene had been bossy, too, and the self-appointed leader of their little group. But she and Irene had been a team. They'd worked together. Irene always said she supplied the brawn while Regina supplied the brains. But Brooks's dictatorial attitude made her feel about as congenial as a cat petted backward. She wanted to yowl in protest. Eduardo made a sleepy mewling sound and reminded her to pick her battles—and battlefields—carefully.

Brooks could hear Regina's labored breathing behind him and regretted pushing her so hard, but it couldn't be helped. They'd been given a very small window of opportunity, and he intended to make the best of it. Their shooter had left the warehouse, but Brooks knew he wasn't far away. In the other man's shoes, he'd resume driving a grid pattern, hoping to get lucky. Brooks intended to see the man's luck turn south.

Towing Regina behind him, he wove in and out of alleys and doorways and wended his way back to their vehicle. When Regina prepared to climb in the window again, he stopped her and did a thorough check of the vehicle first, inside and out, to be sure the man hadn't left them any nasty surprises.

He guided Regina behind a rusting pickup and then scrambled under the car, checking for a telltale tripwire. He didn't think this was the shooter's MO, but he wasn't taking any chances. The extra time proved worth the risk, because sure enough, he discovered a thin little wire attached to the gas pedal.

"I win this round, pal," he mumbled. He took his time defusing it, making sure the bomb really was as simple as it looked. The guy was obviously an amateur, but Brooks wanted to know his identity. Time to end this hide-and-seek game with an invisible shadow. Somebody wanted this kid dead, and he wanted it badly. Brooks wanted to know why.

When he was satisfied the car was safe, he motioned Regina over and held the kid while she climbed in. He still couldn't make himself refer to the child by name or acknowledge him as his own flesh and blood, but he couldn't seem to turn his back on him and walk away, either.

As for the unpredictable Miss da Silva, he didn't like the feelings she inspired in him any better. He generally knew exactly where he stood and what he felt. But Regina was part mother, part vixen, and kept him agitated as a penned bull.

As soon as they were settled, he hightailed it out of town on the main highway, stopping at an out-of-the-way gas station. Within minutes they were back on the road, hoping to put enough distance between them and the brown Fiat to figure out what was going on.

The man gripped the steering wheel and squinted against the glare. Where were they? He'd thought he heard something in that old warehouse, but his careful search had revealed nothing. He edged closer to the repair shop, but not so close that they'd see him. If they were anywhere close by, they would have run back to the car by now.

He pulled up next to the curb between two delivery trucks and prepared to enjoy the show. From his vantage point, he wouldn't be able to see it, but he figured the flames would be high enough for him to bask in their glow.

He twisted his hands together in his lap and pulled the picture of Teresa out of his pocket. He didn't want to leave it out on the dashboard where anyone could get a glimpse of it.

"I'm sorry, Teresa. I didn't want to hurt Regina, but she wouldn't leave the baby alone. If she'd only heeded my warnings . . ." His jaw hardened. "She didn't want me either. If she had, I could have spared her all this. But now that she's thrown her lot in with Anderson, she'll have to die." He cocked his head as though listening. "I have to do this; you know that. An eye for an eye. Noah must pay for his sins. And since she won't leave, she'll have to pay, too."

Seconds ticked by, then minutes. Still, he heard nothing but the sounds of men working, traffic rumbling several streets away, and a radio blaring somewhere in the distance.

"Come on, come on." The time had come to end this. As soon as he'd taken Teresa's revenge, it would be over. He'd be free to put the past behind him and start his own life. He wanted to drive his own car, live in his comfortable apartment. He rubbed the crick in his neck. He was too old to sleep in cars.

After thirty minutes, he couldn't take it any longer. He slipped out of the car, tiptoeing close enough so he could see the Toyota.

It was gone.

He stiffened in shock and stepped closer. How had he missed the explosion? Several quick steps brought him nose-to-nose with the high fence.

And the empty spot where the car had been.

He pressed his nose against the fence in disbelief and studied the ground. Instead of smoking hunks of metal, he saw the trip wire lying there, tied up in a neat little bow, mocking him.

He gripped the fence so hard he drew blood, but he didn't notice. His entire being was focused on the fact that they'd eluded him again.

"Noooo!"

His agonized howl brought one of the mechanics out of the bowels of the shop, his face concerned.

He held up both hands and assured the mechanic that he was all right.

"You are sure?" the man asked, wiping greasy hands on an even greasier rag. "You're bleeding."

He looked down in surprise, and then waved the man's concern away, carefully hiding his rage behind a bland smile. He did not want this imbecile later to say that he'd met a crazy man who screamed in the middle of the street for no reason.

Back in his car, he wrapped a bandana around his palm and studied Teresa's picture some more. "Which way did they go, Teresa? I need to know."

He cocked his head as though listening. "North?" He kissed the picture before tucking it carefully back in his pocket. North it was.

The Fiat peeled out from the curb. He never noticed the mechanic reach back into the shop and pick up the telephone.

14

THE KILOMETERS CLICKED BY AT A SPEED THAT BLURRED THE SCENERY OUTside the window. Regina settled the still-sleeping baby in the back seat with her rolled-up sleeping bag wedged around him like a giant bolster. She rubbed a weary hand over the back of her neck and rolled her shoulders. For a little guy, he sure got heavy after a while.

Brooks whipped into the opposite lane to pass another slow-moving truck crawling up the hill, and Regina closed her eyes. Brazilians' belief in fate made them entirely too careless with their lives, in her opinion. Brooks was an American, but he seemed to view each hill as a personal challenge to be met. And conquered.

"Hand me the cell phone." He held his hand out.

She bristled at his tone. "How about, please?"

"If you think I'm going to be nice after you stole my phone, lady, think again."

So, they were back to lady. Though she supposed he did have a point, if you wanted to get technical about it.

She fished the phone out of her voluminous handbag and placed it in his palm, careful not to let any of her skin come into contact with any of his.

He scooted back into their lane and checked the mirrors again. Satisfied, he flipped the phone open. "It is time to find out exactly what is going on here." He thrust the phone at her. "Who hired the bodyguard?"

"Francisco Lopez."

His eyes widened. "The same Francisco Lopez who wants to be the next *presidente* of Brazil?"

"Yes." She swallowed hard. "He came to Irene's funeral and said he was a friend of Noah's and had been sent to help and keep an eye on Eduardo."

"You didn't find it odd that such a powerful man got himself involved in this?"

"He came to the funeral incognito. Only two bodyguards, and afterward, when he asked to speak to me alone, I discovered he'd been wearing a wig and fake mustache." She shrugged. "I know Noah has influential friends, and I appreciated him coming and trying to help."

"That's when he offered the guard."

"Yes."

"Call him. He knows more than he's saying."

She hesitated. "I don't know his number."

"So get it. How hard can it be to find one of the most important men in the whole blasted country?"

His impatience flicked over her like fingernails on a blackboard, but she shoved her irritation aside and dialed. It galled her that he was right again. Within minutes, she was connected to Colonel Lopez's aide.

"I'm sorry, Senhorita, but the Colonel is not in his office this week. Would you like to leave a message?"

"*Por favor*, where did he go?"

It was a risk. Logic said if the man was worth the salary they paid him, he wouldn't tell her a blessed thing.

"I am sorry, Senhorita, but I am not at liberty to say," the voice replied stiffly. "Would you like to leave a message?"

"*Um momento.*" She covered the mouthpiece. "He's away this week. Should I give his aide this number?"

In response to Brooks's nod, she said, "Yes, please, tell him that Regina da Silva needs to speak with him immediately about an urgent matter."

Was it her imagination, or did the man suddenly perk right up. "Senhorita da Silva, of Casa de Anjos Orphanage?"

"Yes," she replied uncertainly, watching Brooks, "this is she."

"Is everything all right? The Colonel said to contact him immediately if you were to call."

"Please just have him call me, *por favor*," Regina responded and repeated the number as Brooks dictated it to her.

"You will hear from him right away, Senhorita," the man assured her.

Regina flipped the phone closed and turned a bit in her seat so she faced Brooks. "He says the Colonel will call me right away. Don't you find this sudden urgency a bit odd?" she asked thoughtfully.

"Maybe. Maybe not. Either the man is genuinely worried about you, or he's somehow connected to this."

Regina shuddered and rubbed her arms against a sudden chill, despite the balmy temperature. When he said nothing further, she leaned back in her seat and gazed out at the passing scenery. The farther north they drove, the more mountainous it became. She looked at the peaceful farms and tried to relax. Brooks still checked the rearview mirror regularly and passed slower traffic like a native, but based on his body language, he hadn't seen anyone behind them.

She dozed in the pleasant state between sleep and wakefulness when the cell phone rang. Brooks flipped it open and handed it to her. "*Oi.*"

"Senhor Brooks, *por favor.*"

She handed it back. "For you."

"Brooks. *Sim. Nao.* How long ago? *Obrigado.*"

He pressed the disconnect button and dialed again. "Jax. Brooks. I'm in Brazil." He waited through the other person's response and shot her a rueful grimace. "Yes, still. My errand is taking a bit longer than I thought. Listen, I need you to run a plate and get me whatever you can on the driver—and I need it yesterday." He rattled off the Fiat's license plate number and a detailed description of the driver, then paused to listen. "If I do, you'll be the first to know."

Regina waited for him to tell her who had called. Thirty seconds went by, and when still no information came her way, she burst out, "Who was that?"

"Friend of mine. If anyone can get me a handle on who's after us, it's him."

She huffed out a breath. "That much I got. I meant before that."

"Guy who works at the repair shop. I asked him to let me know if anyone in a brown Fiat came by."

"So he's still back there."

He hesitated. "Probably."

He tried to act casual, but Regina wasn't fooled. He was back to full warrior alert.

Sometime later he turned off the highway onto a narrow little road that seemed to head straight into the mountains.

"I thought we were going to Erexim?"

"Too obvious. Time to lay low for a bit."

Regina watched him and had to admire his ability to deal with this kind of situation as if it were no more stressful than a casual vacation. How would it be to have such confidence, such faith in one's ability? She supposed she'd probably never know, but right now, even though her own neediness galled her, his calm competence provided a safe harbor in a world gone mad.

He drove several kilometers, then turned onto an even narrower road, and finally a dirt track that wound its way deeper and deeper into the woods. When he finally stopped the car and cut the ignition, the sudden stillness was deafening. After a minute though, she could make out birdcalls and the rush of water close by.

Brooks swung his door open and came around to open hers. His unconscious acts of courtesy never ceased to surprise her. "We'll camp here tonight," he said, offering her a hand up.

Her glasses slipped down her nose and she pushed them up again, wondering at the direct way he seemed to be studying them. Because his perusal made her uncomfortable, she raised her chin a notch. "Is there a problem, Senhor?"

He studied her a moment longer, then turned away and began unloading the trunk. "If you want a bath, I suggest you take one now. It'll be too cold to do it later."

The thought of washing, not just her hands, but all of her, sounded delicious. But in the river, in broad daylight, with him nearby?

As if sensing her hesitation, he said, "I'll stay here with the kid. I won't peek." He paused, then added, "Unless you ask nice."

If there'd been even a hint of a smile when he'd said that, she would have shrugged it off as a joke. But he didn't smile, never really had that she could tell. Certainly not around her. She rummaged in her bag for clean clothes, but then realized she had no soap. Only her ever-present supply of moist towelettes.

To her astonishment, he dropped a tiny bar of soap, a mini bottle of shampoo, and a sweatshirt into her hands. "That'll have to do as a towel."

"*Obrigada.*"

He had already turned to lift Eduardo from the car. With a deftness that surprised her, he spread out the sleeping bag one-handed and diapered the boy like he'd done it all his life. When he looked up and saw her watching him, she could have sworn she saw a flicker of embarrassment cross his face. But it disappeared so fast she was sure she'd imagined it. "You going, or not? Otherwise, take the kid and I'll go."

She didn't need any more prompting. She marched in the direction of the rushing water and set her clothes on a nearby rock. The spot took her breath away. The river ran wide here, crystal clear as it tumbled down from the mountain. She scanned both sides as far as she could see and breathed easier when she spotted no one.

A quick glance over her shoulder in the direction of their camp and she tugged her sweater off, then her blouse. Quickly, she slipped off her shoes and skirt, and then debated briefly over removing her underwear. She paused to listen. The quiet reassured her, so she stripped off the rest of her clothes and waded in.

The cold water robbed her of breath and she had to bite her bottom lip to keep from crying out. Goose bumps formed on top of goose bumps and her teeth began an annoying chatter. Clamping them firmly shut, she ducked her head under, and came up gasping. With a speed that would have been comical to watch, she lathered her hair, soaped her body, and ducked under for a quick rinse.

The rock where she'd put her things sat in a patch of sunlight, and his sweatshirt felt gloriously warm. She scrubbed until her skin tingled, then gave in to temptation and inhaled the clean, masculine scent trapped in the cloth. It smelled like Brooks, strong and without pretense. Alarmed at her own reaction, she pulled on clean clothes and then tossed the soggy sweatshirt toward the rock.

As though she was watching in slow motion, the sweatshirt hit the rock, dislodging her glasses. They sailed through the air in a graceful arc and disappeared in the river. "Noooo!" Without thinking, she lunged for them. She had to get them. She needed them.

In her haste, she lost her footing. Windmilling her arms to regain her balance, her right foot had just slid into the water when a strong arm circled her waist, swung her back up onto the river bank and set her on her feet.

The need to cling when he set her down sent sparks flying. "What did you do that for? I needed those!" She advanced on him, poking him in his hard chest with every step.

He stopped and planted both hands on his hips. "Sorry. Could have sworn you yelled for help." He whirled around and headed back to camp.

"I need my glasses." She trotted to keep up with him. "I've got to have them."

"Well, I guess you're going to have to live without them."

He was an odious man. Totally without feeling. Everything was matter-of-fact to him. Glasses got lost? No problem. Do without them. Well, it wasn't that simple.

She was still in high temper when she marched into camp, and judging from how tightly he had his jaw clamped, he wasn't much happier. Fine. He wanted a fight; she'd give him one. It would certainly relieve all this tension.

She checked on Eduardo, who sprawled in the middle of the sleeping bag sucking on his toes; and she then turned to start dinner. Nothing like banging pots together and rattling a few pans to work off some energy.

She was making him crazy. Or maybe she had always been crazy and it was rubbing off on him. Either way, she riled him like no female he'd ever known. He tried to snatch her out of the water, and she left nail imprints in his chest to thank him for his trouble. He crumpled his clean clothes in one fist and headed for the river.

On the way, his eyes passed over her and his temper snapped. She was scrubbing again. She'd just taken a bath and now she raked those blasted towelettes over her hands like they were pots with crud stuck on the bottom. Without considering the consequences, he marched over and snatched the towelettes out of her hands. "Stop it. You're obsessed."

She tried to grab them back, and he shoved them into his jeans pocket.

"Give those back. You have no right."

She reached for the pocket of his jeans and he clamped a hand over hers.

"You don't want to do that," he warned.

Her cheeks were flushed and her brown eyes snapped like a fire ready to explode. "Stop telling me what I do and don't want to do!" she shouted. "You don't know me, and I've had all I can take of you ordering me around."

He spread his arms out at his sides. "Fine. Go ahead and get them. I won't stop you."

Her eyes narrowed as she considered the dare. Head high, she whirled and grabbed several more towelettes. She tore them open with jerky movements, and something about her desperation tugged at his heart in ways he didn't like at all. What was she so desperate to wash away?

Deliberately, he advanced on her. "Are we going to have to do this all over again?" he asked quietly.

"Just. Leave. Me. Alone." Each word punctuated by more scrubbing.

"Can't," he drawled. "Last time I did I got bashed in the head."

That stubborn chin shot up just as he'd known it would, and the flames in her eyes were truly a sight to behold. With her hair shorter and curling around her shoulders, and without those atrocious glasses, Regina da Silva was gorgeous. The thought stopped him in his tracks. Seeing her this way was like looking at a stranger.

She was also madder than a wet hen and ready to peck a strip off his hide. For some absurd reason, he could deal with her temper easier than her earlier desperation. He kept walking toward her, proud of the way she held her ground, even though uncertainty flashed through those delightful eyes. He reached out, stripped the sodden bits of paper from her fingers, and tossed them on the ground. Then, without quite knowing why it mattered to him, he lowered his mouth to hers and offered comfort in the only way he knew how.

15

For an instant, she was too stunned to respond. His scent enveloped her just like the warmth of his worn sweatshirt had earlier. His lips were soft, like the cotton fabric. They brushed over hers with exquisite care, the merest brush of skin on skin. He tasted like he smelled, strong and completely, utterly masculine.

The knowledge of what he was doing, of what she was letting him do, shocked her and she gasped.

He instantly deepened the kiss, but he didn't assault, or try to conquer; he sipped and savored as though she were a fine wine. There was that odd tenderness again, the part of him she glimpsed only rarely, but that always left her shaking and uncertain. She drifted in the haze of sensations, even as a part of her told her she should turn tail and run.

Suddenly, his arms wrapped around her and pulled her closer. In an instant, everything changed. Where the kiss had seemed innocent only seconds ago, now it turned threatening, a harbinger of things to come. Instead of making her feel safe, now those arms felt like cords of steel, keeping her in place.

Her lethargy gone in a flash of panic, she fought him, shoving, twisting. She was ready to take a chunk out of him when he set her away and cupped her face in his hands.

"Easy. You want me to stop, say so. Don't you bite me again," he warned.

She struggled to slow her racing heart and looked into his eyes. She saw temper in their stormy depths, to be sure, but something else she couldn't name, wouldn't even try.

Without warning, he scooped up his clothes and headed for the river.

Regina stared after him for a long time, her emotions roiling. Twice now he'd kissed her. And she'd liked it. At least until he got too intense. Not once had he tried to force her into anything.

She scooped up the towelettes, amazed. For the first time in her life, a man's touch hadn't made her feel dirty and ashamed. Maybe it was because Brooks wasn't like other men. And maybe there was more to this man-woman thing than she thought. A strange anticipation filled her as she opened a can of black beans for their supper.

His dip in the icy cold water cooled his frustration, but not his body. The woman tied him in knots. Coming back into camp and hearing her humming didn't help.

To take his mind off her, he crouched down and built a small fire. She inched over and peered over his shoulder. "What is that?"

"C4." He glanced up and sighed. So much for staying away from her. "It's an explosive."

Her eyes widened in alarm as he struck a match. "And you're going to light it?"

"Yeah, I thought we'd blow up the beans. Heats them quicker."

Gauging his expression, she grinned. "Sure, I'll get the pot so we can catch whatever comes back down."

He couldn't suppress a half smile of his own. "Might make for an interesting meal."

She watched the flame take hold and he saw her worried expression. "I know what I'm doing. Trust me."

The look she pierced him with went straight to his heart. "It seems Eduardo and I have no choice but to trust you, Senhor. You, and God."

She turned back to get the beans, but he stayed where he was, tending the fire with hands that weren't quite steady.

"Don't trust me," he wanted to say. "I'm not worth it." His eyes went to the kid, gurgling and flailing his arms, and then to the woman preparing their meal, and he knew he would protect them both with his dying breath.

He only hoped that would be enough. If not, their only hope was God, and Brooks had lost faith in Him eighteen years ago.

How had they vanished again? He had combed the streets of Erexim for hours, and found no sign of them. They hadn't stopped for gas or groceries either, because as far as he could tell, he'd been to every single gas station and mercado. Since the gas tanks on both their cars were about the same size, they couldn't have gone on without filling up.

Which meant one of two things: Either he hadn't found the right gas station yet, or they had gotten off on one of the side roads and were lying low.

He got back into his car and continued up and down the streets. He'd give it several more hours, then he'd head back south and start looking off the beaten path.

Darkness had settled in by the time the phone rang. Brooks slipped it out of his shirt pocket and flipped it open. "*Oi.*"

Moving over to sit beside her by the fire, he handed it to her and mouthed, "The Colonel."

"Good evening." Regina held the phone so Brooks could listen, too, but his nearness did all sorts of things to her concentration.

"Ah, Regina, is that you?"

"It is. How are you, Colonel?"

"I'm well, but I'm concerned about you. I've been trying to contact you for days, but no one's answering at House of Angels."

Yet she'd left a message at his office only hours ago. "Colonel, the other night, someone shot at the orphanage."

"What? Are you all right?"

She thought his concern sounded genuine. "Yes, we're fine. Did you hear about the fire?"

"Yes, I read about it in the newspaper. I've been frantic, wanting to make sure all was well. Was anyone hurt?"

She looked at Brooks, who gave a negative shake of his head. She prayed God would forgive the small lie. "No, no one. But I've taken the children somewhere else for a few days."

"Excellent. Where are you, so I can drop by and see you?"

Again, the negative shake of his head.

"That won't be possible for a bit, Colonel, but I thank you for your interest in myself and the children."

"I'm not sure I like the secretive sound of this, Regina. What's going on?" His voice had lost its fatherly tone.

"As I said, someone shot at us the other night." She paused to draw a deep breath. "I need to know what you know about it."

"Me? What could I possibly know?"

"You were the one who suggested a guard just before this happened, Colonel," she said quietly. "If I'm to keep the children safe, I need to know what's going on."

"I wish I could help you, Regina, but there's really nothing I can tell you. I'll see what I can find out and get back to you. Will you be at this number?"

"Yes. Thank you, Colonel."

After she hung up, they just looked at each other, and for once Regina welcomed his nearness. "You were right. He knows a lot more than he's saying." She turned to gaze into the fire. "It's so hard to think he could be involved in this."

Brooks turned her face to his with one finger under her chin. It wasn't a grasp, just guidance, without restriction. She could pull away if she chose. "We don't know anything for sure. Yet."

16

Early the next morning, Regina jiggled Eduardo on her hip and watched Brooks with unabashed interest. He must have taken another bath earlier, for his dark hair glistened in the predawn light. But her curiosity about what he was doing had her inching closer. He'd taken their small fire and banked it to a mere smolder and then had taken a map and burned just one edge. Now he'd set it casually near the coals.

"What are you doing?"

He shot her one of those almost-grins over his shoulder. "Setting up a bit of insurance."

At her blank expression, he beckoned her over.

"C4 burns very hot. It will also explode if stomped on." He repositioned the map just so and rose. "We leave it like this, with just the ends smoldering slowly. If our friend happens by and sees the partially burned map . . ."

"He'll stomp on it," she finished.

"Bingo. Let's get a move on."

They wound their way back to the main road via a very circuitous route, and when they reached Erexim, he filled the gas tank with astonishing speed. The elevation continued to climb the farther north they went, and as the day progressed, so did the traffic. Driving the two-lane highways in Brazil would terrify the faint of heart, but Brooks handled them like a pro. More than once, they had to pull over when a truck heading down the hill moved into their lane to pass. The general rules of the road said that the bigger vehicle had the right of way. Never mind in whose lane it actually traveled.

About mid-afternoon, he flipped open the cell phone. "Carol Anderson, please." After the barest of pauses, he said, "Mom. How're things going?" Regina watched his jaw tighten and all expression vanish from his face. "Uh-huh. Well, I wanted to let you know I may be a few days later getting home than I thought." Another pause, longer this time. "Why would Francisco Lopez be calling you?"

Beside him, Regina's eyes widened.

"Uh-huh. Yes, Eduardo is fine. What do you know about this, Mom? It's important."

Regina thought she heard him grinding his teeth.

"Can't or won't?" he demanded, swerving as a car passed him so closely it almost took the side mirror off. "When will you stop defending him?"

He tossed the phone into the back seat and shot around three trucks, almost forcing a lumber truck off the road. The driver's shouting could have raised the dead.

Regina waited for the steam to quit billowing from his ears before she asked, "Is your mother okay?"

"She's fine."

"Noah."

If possible, his expression grew even harder. "He may die."

Regina had to take several deep breaths before she whispered, "What?"

He spared her one quick glance. "Sorry, I thought everyone in the organization knew. Heart attack. Bad one. Lots of damage."

He sounded like they were discussing a stranger, she realized, while her entire world shifted for the second time in less than a week. Noah Anderson had been like a father to her since she was fifteen years old. He had rescued her and Irene from the streets, had taken her to America, had led her to Christ. How could he be ill and nobody have told her?

"How long have you known?" she managed.

He shrugged. "Few days."

Regina looked carefully past his sheen of indifference and wasn't fooled. It was amazing how well she'd learned to read him the few days they'd been together. He was more affected than he was letting on.

"At least you'll get to say good-bye."

He said nothing.

She waited a while longer to screw up her courage. "What happened between you two, Brooks?"

She didn't think he'd answer, but he surprised her. "Doesn't matter anymore. It happened a long time ago."

"It matters to you."

"Back off, lady."

"No. You have a chance I'll never have. My father died in a factory fire years ago, and even if I'd known, I hadn't seen or spoken to him since I was six years old. You have a wonderful father. Don't throw away the chance to make things right."

She saw him struggle against his resentment, and she knew the exact moment he lost the battle.

"You don't know anything about my wonderful father. My wonderful father had an affair that resulted in a child. And then he had the unmitigated gall to ask my mother to raise that child as her own. Even more amazing is that she did. And she loved that child as if she'd borne him herself. Now he's done it again. Knocked up another woman, leaving another baby behind." He shot a look at Eduardo, curled in her lap. "And you want me to forgive him? Not in this lifetime."

Everything inside her went still at his words. Beyond her shock that her idol indeed had feet of clay, she heard the hurt and betrayal of a little boy. Regina groped for the right words.

"We all make mistakes, Brooks. Haven't you made any?" she asked gently. She thought she heard his jaw crack, so she hurried on. "Your mother loves you, and you love her. How the family is formed isn't what matters."

"It matters to me."

Beyond her heartache for his pain and bitterness, the tiny flicker of hope born in the warehouse died in Regina's heart. Brooks would never want a woman like her, someone with a past, who couldn't have children of her own. But maybe she could help to heal the rift between father and son.

It didn't take him that long to find their camp. He'd made another call to his "consultant," who'd told him to check the back roads that went near water. They'd try to make camp there.

He smiled in satisfaction as he looked around and saw a half-buried diaper. Yup, he'd found the right place.

He noticed the fire and his smile widened. The embers were still smoldering. He reached over and carefully plucked the map from the ashes and blew it out.

Then, following his friend's instructions exactly, he carefully kicked sand over the fire and ran for his car. Oh, yes, it was good to have friends.

He spread the map over his lap and studied it. Nothing. No markings, no anything. But he wasn't worried. Teresa was guiding him, and with her help, he'd find them.

But he'd need a bit more cash for his new life. He pulled out the phone and dialed a familiar number, asking for twice his usual fee. It amazed him how much people would pay to keep their dirty little secrets buried. He tsk-tsked and pulled out Teresa's photo.

"We're getting there. We'll have them soon. Then you can rest in peace."

The kilometers flew by and Regina closed her eyes because the combination of curves, hills, and valleys—along with Brooks's determined driving—made her queasy. She heard his teeth grinding and felt as if he cut every curve and pass closer than the one before. If she didn't block out the sight, she knew she would hyperventilate.

She thought of the part of his conversation with his mother she'd heard. Something wasn't quite right. She was still trying to absorb the facts Noah had a heart attack and Brooks wasn't Carol's son, but she pushed that aside for now. Something else nagged at her. The knowledge floated in the back of her mind, just out of reach.

She sat up straight and her eyes snapped open as the little car lurched around a curve. She grasped the door handle, then deliberately focused on the task at hand. She got on her knees, making sure she had tucked Eduardo safely into his makeshift bed. He was wide awake, gnawing contentedly on a knuckle. The slobbery smile he sent her created another crack in her heart.

Regina didn't know how she was going to hand him over when the time came. She didn't doubt Carol would find him a good home and family, but still . . . he was Irene's baby, her last link to her best friend. Oh, how she wished he were hers, that she could raise him as her own. But he deserved better, two parents from good Christian families, who had clean pasts and bright futures and could give him everything she and Irene never had.

Regina rubbed a hand over her heart against the pain there. When she'd held Eduardo to her breast in that warehouse, the love she'd felt for him had been so huge, so deep, so overwhelming, she didn't know how to describe it.

For that one instant, when Brooks had looked at them, her heart had begged for impossible things, for a man to look at her like that. She'd wished she and Brooks were a family and Eduardo their child. But just that quick, the fantasy shattered. Brooks was a loner who swore he'd never marry. And even if he did, he wouldn't want a woman with baggage like hers. No one would.

She couldn't even have children to atone for her past sins. But she supposed that, too, was just punishment, reaping what she'd sown.

Regina ran an unsteady finger down Eduardo's plump cheek and swiped at an errant tear on her own cheek with her other hand. She'd cry later, after he was safely in the States with his new family. Right now, she only had one job: to keep him safe.

With her maternal protective instincts on full alert, a solution occurred to her. She dug around behind her seat until she found the cell phone. One hand on the dash, she buckled back into her seat belt and flipped the phone open.

"Give me your mother's phone number at the hospital."

She saw the question in his eyes, but he didn't ask. Merely rattled off the appropriate digits.

When Carol answered she said, "Hello, Tia Carol. This is Regina, calling from Brazil."

"Regina, I'm so glad you called. How are you?" Regina heard the concern in the other woman's voice.

"Please, we need your help." It was very impolite to jump over the usual niceties, but these were not usual circumstances.

Regina heard the other woman's sharp intake of breath. "Is everyone all right?"

"For the moment," she responded deliberately. "Tia Carol, I'm going to be very frank. Someone is following us, and he has already tried to kill us several times. Without your son's quick thinking and reflexes, the man very well might have succeeded."

"I didn't know things were that serious," Carol gasped, horrified. "Are you sure you're all right?"

"Yes, Tia, please. We know you have spoken to Francisco Lopez. He will not tell us who's behind this, but we have to know. Right now we are fighting a shadow. Please, tell us what you know."

Through the silence on the line, Regina could almost hear the woman's internal struggle.

"Does it have something to do with your husband?" Regina prompted. With an apologetic look toward Brooks, she added, "I know something about Brooks's birth." Following a hunch, she asked quietly, "Does what is happening now have something to do with that?"

Carol's voice shook, and it sounded as though she were speaking to herself. "I can't believe he would do such a thing . . ." Her voice trailed off.

"Tia Carol. Somebody killed Irene. I will *not* let them kill Eduardo, too."

Regina heard another sharp gasp. "But they ruled Irene's death an accident!"

"No, Tia. It was no accident. I was there. Please. Tell us."

"Francisco didn't tell me. Never that it had come to this."

During the pause, Regina heard Carol taking several deep breaths. When she spoke again, her voice had lost its quaver, and in its place Regina heard the thread of steel behind the softly spoken words. "Years ago, Noah, Francisco, and I went to school together in Brazil."

Regina stifled the urge to tell the woman to get to the point, but bit her tongue. Whatever it took to get the whole story. She'd let her tell it in her own way.

"What you probably don't know is that there was another girl there, Teresa. She was beautiful, and we were good friends." Regina heard pain behind the words, old but still able to inflict hurt. "Anyway, she died some years later." Carol paused, and Regina tried to figure out where this was leading.

"Her older brother, Raul, blamed Noah for her death and swore vengeance on our family. Shortly afterward, Raul went to prison for attempted murder. Life went on, and we forgot about the threat." Her voice trailed off.

"Why did he blame Noah?"

The silence stretched. If not for the continuing static, Regina would have thought the connection had been lost.

Finally, Carol said, "I can't answer that."

Regina sighed and changed tactics. "Why do you think it might be him?"

"He got out of prison recently and went to Francisco's office. Said he'd changed and wanted to catch up with his old friends as he made a new life."

"Senhor Lopez believed him?"

"At first. Later he started to have doubts."

The pieces began to click into place. "That explains why Senhor Lopez came to Irene's funeral. Did you know he posted a guard at the orphanage?"

"No. It seems I've been kept in the dark about a lot of things." Regina pictured the woman's chin lifting into the air. "It's time I stopped burying my head in the sand. That's all I can tell you. Is there anything else I can do to help?"

Regina bit her bottom lip. "Do you know who Eduardo's father is?"

"No." The silence stretched out. "You think it might be Noah, don't you?"

"I'm sorry, Tia."

"What makes you think so?" Regina heard defensiveness now.

With another quick glance at Brooks' frozen profile, Regina said, "I found a photograph in Irene's things that was taken while she was pregnant with Noah."

"It might be innocent."

"*Sim*. It might," she agreed.

"Let me speak to Nathaniel."

"Just one more question. Is there really something wrong with Eduardo that requires medical care?"

Regina felt, rather than saw, Brooks's head whip in her direction at the question. But she was more interested in the silence on the other end of the line.

Finally, Carol said briskly, "I said what I did in the best interests of the child."

"I understand, Tia, believe me." Regina handed the phone to Brooks. "She wants to talk to you."

Then she turned her face to the window to give him what privacy she could, even though she desperately wanted to know what his mother said.

Brooks said nothing, merely listened. Finally, he said, "I'll do what I can," and hung up.

The hours crept by as the landscape became more and more mountainous. Regina's nerves frayed, though she wasn't sure if it stemmed from Brooks's silence or the insane pace he had set.

"Tell me who she thinks the shooter is."

She didn't understand him. How could it have taken him three hours to get that one question out? As succinctly as possible, she relayed what his mother had told him about Raul and Teresa.

He nodded once and lapsed back into silence. Regina busied herself entertaining Eduardo, who had turned fussy and unhappy after being in the car all day. She understood the feeling.

Late in the afternoon, shortly after a stop for gas and snacks in Pato Branco, Brooks reached for the phone.

"Jax. Brooks. What did you find out?" He nodded. "That matches what I've learned. Look, I need to get this kid to the States. I'm headed for the Falls. I need a chopper." He paused to listen some more. "Call me when you line it up."

"We're going to Foz do Iguaçu?"

The huge group of waterfalls, with their nearby town, were a major tourist attraction. It was beautiful there, but seemed an odd place for a rendezvous.

"It's easier to cross into Argentina from there."

Regina had no idea what that had to do with anything, but she let it go. She was still trying to figure out why this Raul would blame Noah for his sister's death.

17

RAUL SPED NORTH ON THE HIGHWAY, HIS ANTICIPATION BUILDING WITH every car and truck he passed. Every instinct told him he was gaining on them. He'd propped Teresa's picture up on the dashboard again, and her smile acted like a beacon guiding his steps.

He felt a bit guilty at his eagerness to be done with this. Death was not something to be taken lightly. But it had been so long. He wanted to fulfill his duty to his sister and then move on with his life. He had a nice little nest egg stashed away. All he needed was a lovely lady to share it with. Raul stroked a hand over his smooth face and mused that it was too bad Regina wouldn't be that woman. His life would be quite enjoyable with her in his bed every night—provided she got over her aversion to men. He patted the gun on the seat beside him, allowed himself several minutes to enjoy visions of just how he would convince her. Then he shoved the thought aside.

She was a whore, and he'd have to kill her. She'd left him no choice.

Raul urged the Fiat faster and strained his eyes to get a glimpse of his quarry. But with the twists and turns in the highway, and the lumber trucks with their flapping canvas tops, his view remained blocked.

He picked up his cell phone and dialed the familiar number. "I'm still heading north. If you were Brooks, which way would you go? I just passed Pato Branco."

He heard a rustling noise, like a map being unfolded. "Head for Foz do Iguaçu. The border to Argentina isn't guarded too carefully. It would be the ideal spot to escape with the kid."

Raul smiled. The man appeared to be worth every exorbitant penny he was charging. "Perfect. I think you're right."

"I'll meet you there tomorrow."

The other man's eagerness triggered alarm bells in Raul's head. "I can handle it."

"I'm sure you can. Just thought you might want a hand, that's all."

Raul thought the other man's voice seemed too casual, all of a sudden. "Fine. But they're mine."

"Whatever you say, my friend. I'll just be there as back-up."

"Meet me at Klaus Bier at midnight tomorrow."

"I'll be there with bells on."

"Senhor?" He did not understand this expression.

"I'll be there. Look for a tall man wearing a Miami Dolphins baseball cap."

"*Sim*. Until tomorrow."

Raul disconnected, but he furrowed his brow in thought. When he hired the man, all he'd asked for was information. Insight into how a Ranger thought so he could track Brooks Anderson better. A face-to-face meeting had never been in his plan.

Then he shrugged. Whatever would be would be. He'd deal with it as it came.

Carol Anderson sat by her husband's bedside and waited for him to wake up. Her feelings seesawed between the urge to shake him awake and get whatever information she could from him to a desire for him to sleep a long time. A part of her was in no real hurry for him to open his eyes, because when he did, they would finally have to deal with things she'd avoided for more than thirty years. But her son and the woman she considered a daughter were in danger.

Maternal instincts won out, and she perched impatiently on the edge of her chair. She focused on her short, buffed nails, fighting the unladylike urge to drum her fingers on the arm of the chair. Then she paced the floor, her sensible pumps barely making a sound on the worn linoleum. The clock ticked slowly, and every second plodded by on leaded feet. She walked to the window and looked out at the sparkling sunshine, wincing against the brightness. Winter in Orlando was like nowhere else.

"What's wrong?" he asked hoarsely.

Carol whirled toward the bed, her heart in her throat. "It's okay," she soothed, going to him and smoothing the covers. "How are you feeling?"

His gaze pierced her. "You're upset." After all these years, he knew her well.

"I spoke to Nathaniel. He has Eduardo and Regina with him." She paused, carefully considering her next words. "They asked about the past, about our connection to Francisco." She sighed. "He'd posted a guard at the orphanage." It took all her formidable self-control to speak calmly, with no more inflection than she would if she were ordering dinner in an expensive restaurant.

Noah's eyes widened with alarm. "Are they safe?"

She patted his hand and hoped he wouldn't notice the tremor in hers. "For now. Nathaniel will protect them."

"You told them about Raul." It was not a question.

"I did. And about Teresa." She had to swallow hard. Her cowardice threatened to choke her. "Though I left out the most important facts."

Noah gripped her hand, his sudden burst of strength surprising her. His eyes glistened, but surprisingly, he wouldn't allow the tears to fall. "I was wrong, Carol. So wrong to get involved with Teresa."

Carol looked away, her own tears threatening. "It happened a long time ago," she whispered.

"But you still hurt, and for that I'm sorriest of all. You are far more woman than I deserve, and the way you've loved Nathaniel . . ."

She couldn't help but smile. "Nathaniel is easy to love. He's a lot like his father."

He tugged on her hand, pulling her down beside him on the bed. "I'm sorry, Carol. I'm sorry for Teresa, and I'm sorry for not telling you about my heart problems. I should have told you about both right away, but in my heart, I'm a coward. You were always the strong one."

Carol gazed at him, amazed, because inside, she felt weak as a newborn kitten, wanting to run and hide until it was safe to come out again.

"I thought we were a team, Noah. Why did you hide your illness from me?" She couldn't keep the accusation out of her voice.

"I didn't want you to worry. When it's time to go, I'm ready. I've done what God asked me to do in life."

She flinched from his words, trying to stand up, to run away from the truths spilling from his lips, but he held her fast. She could break out of his hold, but to what end? "I want more time with you," she finally managed.

He smiled then, the wonderful smile that made his eyes light up and made him look invincible. This was the man she'd always loved—the dreamer, the visionary.

Then his expression sobered. "If you can find it in your heart to forgive me—for back then, and for just recently—I'd be grateful."

His pleading look made her want to weep. Her Noah didn't beg. He had always been larger than life, a leader who dwarfed other men.

"I forgave you for the past years ago, Noah. You gave me Nathaniel. I couldn't stay angry forever."

"But I owe it to you to ask for forgiveness," he said, before she could continue.

She looked into his beloved eyes and tears blurred her own. Why did all this closeness come now, when it might be too late? Why couldn't he have said the words then, when she'd desperately needed to hear them?

Carol clasped his hand in hers and said the only thing that mattered. "I love you, Noah Anderson. I always have. I always will."

And in her battered heart, she prayed their son would forgive his father and save them all from this madman.

Night was falling as they approached Cascavel. Regina felt so tense she wanted to scream. She was stiff and sore from sitting for so long, and Brooks's silence had almost worn through her last nerve. She glanced at his profile periodically, but his lean features told her nothing of what he was thinking or feeling.

Suddenly, they heard a grinding noise and the Toyota began slowing down. Fast.

Brooks gripped the wheel and filled the car with some phrases even she'd never heard. She stifled a smile at his creativity and glanced nervously out the back window when he pulled off the shoulder of the road. Thankfully, there were trees along the roadside and he'd stopped behind them. At least they weren't sitting out in plain view.

"What's wrong?"

"I don't know." He reached under the seat for the flashlight. "Sit tight. I'll see what I can find out."

He poked around under the hood for a long time. Regina took the opportunity to lean over the back seat and change Eduardo. She'd fed him, burped him, and sung three lullabies when something made her look up.

The traffic had thinned as night approached, but it was still light enough to make out the make and model of approaching vehicles.

A scream lodged in her throat as she looked through the rear window and saw a farm truck moaning up the hill. Directly behind it, unless her eyes were playing tricks on her, was the brown Fiat. She prayed he wouldn't see their hiding place even as she leaned lower to see his face.

He seemed to be studying something on his dashboard and never glanced in their direction. In the deepening twilight, Regina could see only his profile and a ball cap. She shivered and tightened her hold on Eduardo.

Brooks jerked her door open. "Grab the kid. We've gotta get out of here."

He leaped for the trunk, while she snatched Eduardo and however much of his gear she could grab, and hustled out of the car. "Did you see him?" she asked.

"Yes." He had their bags in one hand and grasped her elbow with the other as he steered them deeper into the woods. "Stay here," he said, directing her to the shadow of a huge old tree.

He turned and headed for the edge of the road, thumb out in the universal signal.

"Come on, come on," Regina mumbled. "Please let someone stop."

Finally, a pickup truck that had been ancient in 1950 slowed to a halt. After several hastily exchanged words with the driver, Brooks beckoned her over.

The back of the aging truck contained crates of fruits and vegetables, but there was enough room for them to squeeze in.

"Hand me the kid," he commanded.

She wanted to tell him again to stop referring to Eduardo as "the kid," but decided to bide her time.

He handed her up, tossed her the bags, and then nimbly leaped up after her, Eduardo tucked under his arm like a puppy. She reached her hands out for the child, but Brooks surprised her by saying, "Take a break. I'll hold him for a while."

Surrounded by all this fresh fruit should have been pleasant, but some of it had been out in the sun too long. The pungent odor of rotting produce made her slightly queasy, so she concentrated on breathing through her mouth.

Beside her, Brooks leaned against a sagging crate, Eduardo propped on his raised knees. The baby kicked and smiled, and Brooks grabbed his feet and tickled his toes.

As she saw the tender way Brooks handled his brother, Regina's heart constricted and she fought against another round of those dratted tears. Don't think about it. Don't wish for what you can't have. Hadn't Tia Carol always said, "If wishes were horses, beggars would ride"? When would she learn to ignore her heart's foolish dreams?

Regina's bruises had bruises by the time the old truck rattled into the heart of Foz do Iguacu. The bustling tourist town, cleverly named after the nearby waterfalls, was thronged with people, even on a weeknight. Her stomach let out a growl, and Brooks quirked an eyebrow at her. "I'm hungry. So shoot me."

His eyes watched her mouth in a way that sent funny little tingles shooting through her. Though whether she hoped he'd kiss her, or dreaded that he might, she wasn't sure.

After several more blocks, the driver pulled into the parking lot of a *churrascaria,* and the smell of barbecued beef made Regina's stomach groan in anticipation. Brooks shot her an unexpected smile, making her toes curl. Maybe it was because he smiled so rarely, but he turned her to complete mush with that potent glance.

"Guess this is where we'll eat," he commented as he swung down from the tailgate and reached a hand up to assist her down. After thanking the driver, they ducked behind a van and scanned the parking lot and those nearby.

No brown Fiat.

Brooks hitched Eduardo higher on his hip and curled his arm protectively around her. Dimly, Regina registered that his nearness didn't make her jump anymore. In fact, it made her feel seductively safe. It was a false feeling, she knew, and wouldn't last past the next twenty-four hours. But for now, she decided simply to enjoy it and pretend, for this one night, that they were a family out for a nice dinner together.

Brooks scanned the restaurant's occupants in that lazy way that wasn't lazy at all, and took in everything and everyone in the space of several heartbeats. With a guiding hand at her back, he led her to a table, and surprised her by keeping Eduardo on his lap.

She took that opportunity to duck into the ladies room to wash her hands. She washed them to her satisfaction and then, without thinking, raised her head, startled to see her reflection in the mirror. Normally, she avoided mirrors, combing her hair without looking. She didn't usually like what she saw.

Looking at herself now, surprise widened her eyes. With her hair shorter and without the glasses, she looked different. Softer, somehow. But most arresting was her eyes. They had lost their haunted look.

Which amazed her, considering they were on the run from a lunatic with a silencer on his gun.

Brooks watched her approach the table and saw her bewildered expression. His anxiety jumped up a notch. "Everything all right?"

She nodded and slipped in across from him.

Before he could censor the words, they slipped out. "You look beautiful. Especially without the fake glasses."

He expected a sharp retort, but instead she smiled, a slow, sensual smile that fried his brain and made him shift uncomfortably. Did the woman have any idea what she did to him?

She lowered her eyes shyly, and he realized she didn't. Which was just as well. They had no future, and she wasn't the kind of woman who'd go for a casual relationship. He'd heard enough horror stories about the street children of Porto Alegre's *favelas* to have an inkling of what she had faced in her childhood. He completely understood her wariness of men; her acceptance of him a gift he didn't deserve. He suddenly found that a casual fling was not what he wanted either.

Soft candlelight fell over her cheeks and the urge to tear limb from limb whatever nameless piece of trash had hurt her and taken advantage of her had his fists clenching until Eduardo squealed.

She looked up and blanched at his expression, even as he loosened his hold on the boy and crooned in apology. "I won't hurt you, you know," he said.

She met his gaze directly. "Yes, you will, but it is unavoidable."

Her calm acceptance made him see red. "I'm not talking about physically." What kind of man did she think he was?

"I know."

"Or sexually," he felt compelled to add.

"I know that, too."

In that moment, he understood, though he wished he didn't. This feisty, tough woman, who didn't like men, but had gotten used to him, cared for him. Even after the childhood she'd suffered, she still had enough softness in her heart to care.

Something inside him shifted, loosened. The cold, hard knot in his heart eased a fraction as she gave him her sad smile. He wanted to warn her off, to tell her he was no knight in shining armor, no hero who would sweep her away. He was a failure, a burned-out soldier without a future. The most he could offer was to try to keep her and the kid alive. After that, he'd be gone and she'd be alone again. She deserved better.

But the waiter appeared before he voiced any of it, and the moment was lost. They ordered the buffet and filled their plates. Eduardo happily gummed crackers while they feasted on various cold salads and more meat than Brooks had ever seen.

Every few minutes another server appeared at their table with a long skewer of meat. If they turned the little sign on their table green side up, servers kept coming and offering slices until either Brooks or Regina turned the sign to red.

Brooks watched as Regina tucked into the food like a farm hand after a long day. The beef was saltier than he preferred, but it was so tender you could cut it with a fork.

When neither one could eat another bite, they pushed back from the table, paid, and left the restaurant.

At the door, Regina hesitated. "Um, I need to stop in the ladies room."

When she came back out with her hands still slightly dripping, he pretended not to notice. He couldn't decide if this obsessive hand washing was something she did when she was nervous, or, and this next option made him scowl, a holdover from the way she felt about her early life. He hoped it was the former, but decided he could deal with the latter if it came to that.

Then he remembered that he and the kid were leaving in another day, two at most. Whatever hang-ups and foibles Regina had would be some other man's to deal with. The thought made him inexplicably and explosively furious, and he clamped his jaw to contain it.

Keeping Regina behind him, he stepped out of the restaurant and scanned the parking lot. Still no brown Fiat. Turning back inside, he asked the host to call a taxi.

When it arrived, he quickly stashed Regina and the kid inside and ducked in beside them. He didn't bother stowing their bags in the trunk, simply pushed them inside in front of him. "Take us to *Parque Nacional do Iguaçu*," he growled.

"The National Park is closing soon, Senhor."

"We're staying at the *Hotel das Cataratas* at the Falls.

"*Sim.*" The driver nodded and stomped on the gas pedal.

Brooks tried to ease up on his resentment and think about other things. How had he never noticed how nice she smelled? Casually, so as not to alarm her, he stretched his arm along the seat back and then slowly lowered it to her shoulder. When she didn't shrug away, he increased the pressure just enough to pull her against his side. Something inside him relaxed when, instead of pulling away, she snuggled closer. It was a simple matter to gently press her head to his shoulder.

He found he liked the feel of her too much, so he pulled the brim of his ball cap lower and whispered, "Keep your head down in case our friend is around."

He immediately regretted his words. The slack went out of her shoulders, and she stiffened like a broom beside him.

"Relax. It's dark. This is just a precaution."

Since it made his palms itch not to, he slid his fingers through her dark curls. He loved the way they wrapped around his fingers. "I love your hair," he whispered, so as not to wake the sleeping Eduardo.

Regina didn't respond, but she didn't slap his face either, which he took as a positive sign.

The remainder of the trip passed in silence. When the cabbie delivered them to the front steps of the elegant pink hotel, Brooks kept his face averted as he paid the fare, then hustled them quickly up the stairs. Bypassing the check-in counter in the lobby, he maneuvered them down several richly appointed hallways and out a side door. Regina was a quick study, he decided, for she waited for him to check out the area before she quickly followed him across the grass and into the cover of the trees.

According to the map he'd studied, if they went back into the trees for about half a mile, the cover became dense enough to provide a good place to spend the night. And then, if all went well, Jax would have everything set up and send a bird for him and Eduardo.

He scowled as he imagined the coming confrontation with the man pursuing them. He didn't question that there would be one. In fact, he was determined to create one. He'd been examining the angles all day and didn't have it all worked out just yet, but he would. It had to be away from innocent bystanders, and Regina and the boy had to be safely out of harm's way.

"Slow down," Regina whispered.

He stopped and turned, shining the flashlight this way and that, surprised to see her several yards behind him. "Sorry."

"You're walking like we have to get there in the next two minutes."

"Lot on my mind, that's all. You okay?"

She grimaced, panting slightly. "It's not easy to hike in here in the dark."

He forced himself to take it slower. From somewhere up ahead, they heard a screech that sounded almost human. Behind him, Regina gasped.

"It's okay, just a bird. We're not far from the *Parque Das Aves*. They have all kinds of birds in there."

Maybe it was because she was tired, and all the good food and the *cerveja* she'd allowed herself with dinner were relaxing her, but to Regina it seemed they were hiking to Argentina. It took all she had to keep up with Brooks's long stride. He sped up again, but pride prevented her from asking him to slow down. She stumbled over yet another protruding root and bit back a few choice comments. In her arms, Eduardo slept. Near as she could figure, the child had put on several kilos in the past few days. He got heavier with every step.

Finally, Brooks stopped in a small clearing. Efficiently, he pulled both sleeping bags out, zipped them together, and spread them out. When he held out some toilet paper and a moist towelette, she wasn't sure if he was being helpful or making fun of her.

"I'll put him down while you go do your thing." He handed her the flashlight. "Remember to watch for snakes," he said to her retreating back.

After the tangled-in-the-tree episode, Regina went far enough to hide behind some thick underbrush, but still close enough that she could hear Brooks murmuring to Eduardo.

When she scampered back into camp, she gaped at finding Eduardo tucked into his jammies, sound asleep on one side of the sleeping bag. Without a word, Brooks turned his back on her, shucked his boots, and climbed into the bag, scooting Eduardo farther to one side. Which put Brooks squarely in the middle of their makeshift bed.

Right next to where she'd sleep.

18

HE MUST HAVE SEEN SOMETHING IN HER FACE IN THE REFLECTION OF THE flashlight, for his voice drifted quietly to her. "I just want to be near you tonight."

Her fingers shook as she fumbled with her shoes and then climbed in beside him, fully clothed. She had no idea how to interpret that statement. Confused and uncertain, she switched off the flashlight and lay still, her switchblade providing the courage she lacked and a measure of security in case she'd misjudged him. Her heart knew she could trust him, but . . .

He propped himself on an elbow and looked down at her. As her eyes adjusted to the darkness, she tried to make out his expression, but the deep cover of trees blocked out the moonlight.

"I'm not going to attack you, Reggie. Not tonight or any other night."

Though his words were reassuring, she felt duty bound to point out, "After tonight, there will be no other nights."

His hand snaked out and brushed her cheek. Though there were calluses, he was gentle. "Your skin is so smooth."

Suddenly wary, she blurted, "I'm not interested in sex, Senhor."

Even in the dark, she could see his eyebrow shoot up. "Was I asking?" he queried lazily. "Now a little kissing, I could probably suffer through."

"You're teasing me."

He brushed his lips over hers so lightly she wondered briefly if she'd imagined it. "You looked like you needed it." Then his voice turned serious. "Don't be afraid of me, Reggie. I won't force anything on you, ever."

She wanted to believe him, she really did. She wanted to be lulled by the sincerity in that wonderfully masculine growl. Since the moment they'd met, he'd been nothing but honorable in his treatment of her. But past pain still had the ability to wound, and a lifetime's habits were not erased in a matter of days.

"I want you to move away from me."

She expected a protest from him, but instead, his thumb slowly caressed her bottom lip, back and forth. "Are you sure?"

"Yes." *No. I don't know.* She squeezed her eyes shut, swamped with indecision. She wanted more of that safe, yet fluttery, feeling his touch ignited.

Without another word, he scooted over toward Eduardo and rolled onto his side, turning his back to her.

She immediately missed his warmth.

"If you change your mind, just reach out and touch me. I won't mind." His voice sounded indifferent, lazy, as if it didn't matter to him one way or the other.

But as she lay there and listened to the wind rustling in the trees and the screech of birds, she replayed his words in her mind. Suddenly, she realized he'd made them deliberately bland. For her sake.

Bunching her lumpy sweater under her head, Regina curled on her side and studied the man beside her. For years, in her mind, men had simply been big, formless threats to be avoided at all costs. She'd never taken the time to study one.

His even breathing convinced her he slept deeply, so she made a leisurely study of him. One hand tucked under her head, she looked her fill. His neck was strong; his ear well-formed.

As if it had a mind of its own, her hand reached out, then she snatched it back before she touched him. She'd never willingly put her hands on a man in her life. Well, except for the occasional peck on Jorge's cheek and the lavish attention she gave Eduardo and the orphanage boys, but those touches didn't count.

Regina studied the night sky overhead a while, then turned back to him again. Drat the man for putting the thought in her mind. She hadn't had the least interest in touching him until he'd mentioned it.

Liar.

Would his hair be rough or soft? she wondered. His breathing had leveled out as he drifted into sleep and its slow, even cadence calmed her nerves, though a flicker of . . . something shimmered in her belly.

She tucked her knife under her pillow and screwed up her courage before her hand snaked out again, using two fingers to lightly brush his nape. His dark hair was soft, so soft she had the urge to run her fingers all the way through it. She stopped, suddenly wary, but his breathing hadn't changed.

She knew it was absurd, but the fact that he was asleep gave her courage. Drawing a deep breath, she moved three inches closer and this time cupped the back of his head in her palm. Was it her imagination, or had his breathing hitched? She waited.

When he didn't move, she ran her fingers through the hair on the top of his head, delighted with its rich texture. Bolder now, she trailed her fingers over his ear, down his neck, and outward to cup his strong shoulder, avoiding the bandage. She measured his biceps in her hand, but instead of being alarmed at his obvious strength, it gave her an odd sense of safety. She'd seen his strength, yes, but she had also seen him keep it under control.

He made a muffled sound, and she froze. When he turned onto his back, she veiled her eyes with her lashes and feigned sleep. He settled back into sleep, eyes closed, hands at his sides. Amazing how much less big and threatening he looked this way.

Brooks figured he just might lose what was left of his mind if she didn't touch him again. He scrambled for a mental distraction, some way to remain motionless while she worked up the courage for a bit more exploring. When one of his Ranger checklists flashed through his mind, he grabbed it with both hands, desperate. This wasn't survival behind enemy lines, but it came close.

S—Size up the situation. From Reggie's point of view, Brooks knew thinking he was asleep gave her control. Since he figured this was the only way she felt safe enough to touch him, he vowed he wouldn't react if it killed him.

U—Undue haste makes waste. He clenched his teeth when her hand snaked out. *That's it, Reggie. Do it again. Take your time.*

R—Remember where you are. He forced his breathing low and deep. No sudden moves.

V—Vanquish fear and panic. This was about her fears. Still, her tentative touches stretched his control to the breaking point.

I—Improvise. She'd surprised him again. He hadn't expected such hard-working hands to be so soft and gentle, so welcoming.

V—Value living. Though he wanted to look into her deep brown eyes, find out what she was thinking, he wouldn't risk it. *Stay focused, man. This isn't about you.*

A—Act like the natives. He ached to kiss her, to bury his hands in her hair. But he wouldn't. She'd dealt with enough "natives" to last a lifetime.

L—Live by your wits. This was her show, a way for her to overcome her past. He couldn't give her any tomorrows, but maybe, just maybe, he could help her get beyond yesterday.

Regina's nervousness seeped away with every passing minute, every slow, even breath he took. He felt wonderful under her hands. Strong and masculine, but not mean. She didn't doubt his capacity for violence. She had seen glimpses of it several times. But instead of disgusting her, knowing that he took care of his own filled her with gratitude. She still wasn't sure what had changed his mind about walking out on them, but she knew beyond the shadow of a doubt that he would protect them with his life. It was a staggering thought.

As the moon rose higher in the sky, she propped herself up on one elbow and traced her fingers over his face. He had a great face. Not model pretty or movie star handsome, but rugged. Solid. Attractive in a don't-mess-with-me way. His nose looked like it had been broken sometime in the past, and his cheeks were heavy with dark stubble. She loved the way it rasped against her palm.

She ran her thumb over his lips. Odd, she'd never have expected such soft skin in such a masculine face. She did it again and the strangest urge to taste him caught her. But on her terms.

Careful, so as not to wake the sleeping dragon, she leaned over and slowly brushed his lips with hers. It felt just as it had before, only better. Safer, because she knew she could pull back at any time.

Oh, this was wonderful. Never had she imagined kissing could be like this. This had no resemblance whatsoever to the nauseating rush of drunken breath and stabbing tongues of her childhood.

She wanted to kiss him again, fairly shook with the need to do it again, but a lifetime's caution held her back. Instead, she focused on learning his face, slowly stroking her fingers over its rugged contours, until she gradually noticed a heat coiling in her belly. Startled by her own reaction, she raised her head and froze as she looked down the length of Brooks, who was wide awake and had obviously been so all along.

Scooting backward, her eyes flew to his. He was watching her, completely motionless. Heat flooded her face, and she turned to leap from the sleeping bag. One of those strong hands flashed out to stop her in a grip that was painless, but effective.

"Shh," he crooned. "I didn't mean to scare you."

She ducked her head, embarrassed. "I'm sorry."

"Never be sorry." She heard the smile in his voice. "I enjoyed every second of it."

"Good night," she whispered and prepared to turn away.

The hand on her arm stopped her, but somehow she knew he would let her go if she tugged.

"I asked you to sleep next to me tonight, but that's all. I won't ever force you, and I won't let things go too far." He let go of her arm and looked her right in the eye, his blunt words shocking. "But I also like your touch."

She looked into those gray eyes and saw desire burning there, but behind that she saw compassion . . . and caring. To give him back a bit of the comfort he'd given her, she bent her head and kissed him again. She expected his hands to come up and touch her, but he kept them firmly at his sides.

She looked at him and her curiosity got the better of her pride. "Why didn't you put your arms around me?"

"Because you didn't ask."

Her eyes widened as she realized the gift he was giving her. He was letting her have total control, allowing her to set the pace and the limits. The thought was freeing.

It was also terrifying.

"Would-would you put your arms around me?"

"Only gladly," he growled, curling her into the curve of his body. "Anything else you'd like?"

"Would you kiss me?"

"With pleasure."

And he did. This time, he feathered kisses over her lips, nose, and eyelids, then the slope of her cheeks, before leisurely returning to her mouth. Once there, he took his time, until their hearts were racing, and her world had gotten blurry around the edges.

"Please." It was all she could get out.

"Please what?" he asked softly, eyes tender.

She couldn't find words, so she simply stroked his lean cheek, her hand shaking. Would he understand what she was asking, what she couldn't explain even to herself?

He went still for a moment, and Regina sensed the control he was keeping himself under.

Slowly, he leaned over her, his eyes locked with hers. Touching her with just his thumb, he repeated much of what she had done earlier. Cheeks, nose, ears, hair, none of it escaped his careful attention. With a touch as light as a butterfly's wing, he lingered at her lips, stroking softly.

Slowly, giving her time to call a halt, his palm drifted down over the slope of her shoulder, down her arm to her hands. He lifted one hand and kissed the tip of each finger before placing a soft kiss in the center of her palm, watching her.

Regina's eyes filled with tears. She'd had no idea things could be like this between a man and a woman. He treated her as though she was beautiful and precious, her body something to be adored, rather than conquered. His touch sent her floating in a haze of new and wonderful sensations, aware of herself in a way she had never been before.

His wonderful mouth returned to hers then, and he kissed her as if he had nothing more important to do for the rest of his life. Regina's mind went slightly fuzzy, and she wanted him to slow down, to give her time to sort out all these new feelings; but they were coming too fast to analyze, too bone-melting to think about.

To anchor herself, she gripped his upper arms. Instantly, Brooks changed the angle of the kiss, his mouth suddenly hungry, impatient.

Like a lightning bolt from the blue, everything changed. His weight pushed her hard against the ground, his hands gripped with too much force, and his kiss made her gag. She couldn't breathe.

Memories swirled in front of her eyes, blocking out his face. Nameless, faceless drunks with thick tongues and hurtful hands, grabbed, and pulled, and squeezed. *Dear Father, no, not again.*

She stiffened and then let herself go limp and pliant, just as Irene had taught her when she was no more than a child. It would be over faster if she didn't hinder him. Tears of betrayal leaked out from under her closed lids and ran down into her ears. He was just like every other man. She was simply a convenient means to an end.

Regina forced every thought of what was happening from her mind and drew herself into her safe place, where there were no grasping hands and no pain. She shut out the sound of Brooks's thundering heartbeat and pictured herself walking in a sunny meadow, a toddler running alongside chasing butterflies, a baby securely tucked in the crook of her arm. Instead of Brooks's weight pinning her down, she dreamed of a wonderful man walking beside her, looking at her with loving, accepting eyes. There was no real spot like that for Regina, of course, but in her dream place she could escape when reality was too painful.

He'd lost her. The knowledge sliced through his sensory fog like a bullwhip. One minute she was right there, and the next she became a rag doll. He instantly released her and rolled over, running a hand through his hair, trying to figure out what had happened. His heart still hammered like a runaway train, and it took a minute to slow his breathing.

He studied her in the moonlight, and comprehension and regret slapped him from either side. Her eyes were squeezed shut, but tears dripped down her face, each drop like a sharp spike piercing his heart. He'd scared her to death.

He knew he shouldn't touch her right now. But how could he not? He reached over and brushed at the wetness with nothing more than the tip of one shaking finger. He knew it was absurd to soothe with the same hands that had frightened her to begin with, but he had to try.

"Don't cry, Reg. I'm sorry. So sorry." He drew a ragged breath and studied her face, begging her to look at him. "I got carried away. You tasted so good, I wanted more . . . too much more."

He was no different than every other scumbag who had ever used her. He knew he was making excuses, but couldn't seem to stop. He hated seeing her cry. More tears ran down her face, and again he brushed them away, utterly disgusted with himself, and frustrated beyond measure at his inability to fix the hurt he'd inflicted.

When she opened her eyes briefly and looked at him, he almost wished she hadn't. They were filled with such betrayal, the pain was worse than any gunshot wound. She'd given him her trust, and he'd let her down. He watched her, filled with self-loathing, and waited for some response from her. Anything.

Regina didn't say a word. She turned her back on him and curled into a little ball, shivering.

Even though she didn't make a sound, the echo of her tears followed him into the woods and reverberated in his head as he sat on a fallen log for the rest of the night.

He couldn't undo what had happened, but he could keep her safe while she slept.

19

Francisco Lopez sat in the leather chair behind the desk in his den and thrust his fingers through hair that was usually impeccably groomed. He ran a finger under the starched collar of his shirt and hoped it would help him draw a deep breath. Sweat pooled beneath his armpits, and the tangy scent only twisted his gut further.

He had done all he could to keep the boy safe. Hadn't he? Eduardo was in the care of a well-trained Army Ranger and a woman he knew would protect the boy with her very life. Then why did he feel like such a coward?

Because he was. He should have told Brooks and Regina exactly who they were up against, right from the start. And after his conversation with Carol yesterday, he also knew with sickening certainty that Brooks thought Eduardo was Noah's son. His stomach turned over as he realized the betrayal Brooks must be feeling, thinking his father had not once, but twice, fathered children out of wedlock.

Francisco swiveled his chair and stared out the darkened window, but what he saw wasn't the night sky of Porto Alegre. In his mind's eye, he saw his dreams of becoming the *presidente* going up in flames. He was a good man. He could be a big help in bringing needed change to his beloved Brazil.

The door to his den swung open with a slight creak. He whipped his chair around and glimpsed his youngest daughter poking her head around the corner. Dark curls bounced, but her expressive eyes widened when she saw his face. "*Pai*? How come you are in here all alone?" she asked softly.

With one hand, he waved her over and patted his lap. The six-year-old dashed across the room and hopped up, wrapping her sturdy little arms around his neck. He held her tight and thanked God for this wonderful treasure.

"I love you, *Pai*."

His heart ached at her innocent words, and he slowly set her aside. "Go play for a bit before bed, all right? Daddy has some work to do."

When she scampered from the room, he picked up the telephone. He should call Brooks, tell him whose child Eduardo was. His palm was so slick with sweat, the receiver slid from his grasp and clattered to the floor.

After rubbing his palms on his slacks, he picked it up and set it back in its cradle before burying his head in his hands. God forgive him; he couldn't do it. It would mean the end of his political career. He would have to trust that Brooks's training would overcome his animosity toward his father and that he would do right by Eduardo.

It was his only hope.

Raul woke slowly and stretched, enjoying the feel of crisp sheets against his body. His hotel wasn't quite on par with the Hotel Cataratas, but it would do nicely. The big pink hotel would be too obvious; there would be too many chances for someone to remember him. Odd that Brooks had chosen to stay there. He pushed the thought aside. This morning he would scout out the town and make his plans. The time had come to take action.

He reached over and felt under the other pillow for his gun. The weight of it in his hand reassured him. Excitement began to build, but he did his best to slow it down. For now, he needed to take it easy. Play tourist. Blend in with the crowd. Fine-tune his plan and find the best place to tree his quarry. It was time to end their little game. He was tired of the chase. He wanted to pounce, enjoy his meal, and be on his way to other things, other mice.

He smiled at his clever image. His sister had often accused him of being stupid. Well, now she'd know for sure that he wasn't. He'd avenge her death, make those responsible pay.

Maybe then she'd finally stop tormenting him.

Regina woke the next morning and reached for Eduardo, but he wasn't beside her. Heart pounding with fear, she scrambled up, knife in hand, and scanned the clearing. Brooks sat on a fallen log several feet away, calmly feeding Eduardo as though it were something he did every day of his life. She willed her heartbeat to slow down and slowly closed her switchblade. He hadn't taken the boy and left her alone. He was still here.

That thought should have reassured her, but instead it reminded her of what had taken place last night. She wrapped her arms around her middle as the fear and sense of betrayal washed over her again. Like all men, he took what he wanted.

Her conscience and sense of fair play brought her up short. In reality, he hadn't hurt her, certainly done nothing approaching force. He'd triggered awful memories, but that was all. Most importantly, he'd stopped.

He wasn't the problem, she was, and the knowledge made her feel foolish and uncertain. In the harsh light of day, she didn't know what to say to him, how to behave. She tried civility. "*Bom dia,* Senhor."

His eyes narrowed fractionally, but his face remained impassive. "Good morning to you too, Senhorita," he returned. "Did you sleep well?"

She nodded and moved to take Eduardo.

"I've got him. Go take care of whatever you need to." He gestured toward the woods.

When she returned, he had the boy on one shoulder and was setting out bread and jam with the other. Why did the sight of all that rugged maleness cradling a tiny boy make her eyes tear and her knees go weak?

His cell phone rang, and he handed her the baby with what seemed obvious reluctance. "Brooks."

Regina buried her nose in the curve of Eduardo's neck and inhaled the wonderful baby scent of him, trying to commit it to memory so she could pull it out and savor it again throughout the lonely years ahead. This was reality; not foolish dreams.

"What?" she heard Brooks growl into the phone. "No. You've got to do better than that."

Moments later he tossed the phone onto the sleeping bag and shoved his fingers through his hair. He whirled away and Regina saw him battling his temper under control. His hands balled into fists, the muscles in his arms bunched, but after no more than a minute or two, he turned back, completely under control again.

His voice, when he spoke, was so totally without inflection that Regina realized the effort of holding himself in check had stripped all emotion from it. "We're going to have to lay low for a day. Jax can't get a chopper here till tomorrow morning."

He marched over to the sleeping bag and began unzipping it with quick, efficient motions. "We'll head back into town and get you on a plane back to Porto Alegre."

Everything inside her went still. "Today or tomorrow?" she asked carefully.

He shot her a direct look, daring her to argue. "Today. As soon as we can arrange it."

She met his look with a stubborn one of her own. "Not until I'm sure Eduardo is safely away."

"It's too dangerous. You'll do as I say."

She huffed out a furious breath, and her underlying horror that he could and would do just as he said spurred her on. "I've been with you from the start, and I'll see my promise to Irene kept. I'm not going anywhere until *after* you and Eduardo are gone." Her voice wobbled on the last word, but she steadfastly ignored it. Later. There'd be time for grief later.

20

BROOKS CLAMPED HIS JAW UNTIL HIS WISDOM TEETH ACHED. THE WOMAN was making him crazy. He stared at the angle of her stubborn chin and the light of battle in her beautiful brown eyes. Without the glasses and with her hair pulled off her face, she was astonishingly pretty. Her high cheekbones and deep-set eyes shocked him every time. Especially since the mere sight of her face made him want to stroke the curve of her cheek and ease the lingering worry and doubt he saw in her eyes.

He stepped closer and she took a wary step back. His eyes narrowed and temper flared. Did she still not realize he wouldn't hurt her? Because he couldn't seem to stop himself, he cupped her cheek and slowly turned her to face him, which wasn't easy, since she wasn't cooperating.

"Reggie, look at me," he commanded softly.

With obvious reluctance, she slanted him a quick glance before tilting her chin in the air again.

"I'm sorry I scared you last night, but I'm not sorry for touching you."

Now her head did snap in his direction. "You don't think manhandling an unwilling woman deserves an apology,

Senhor?" Amazingly, she was even more enticing when she was spitting mad. He hid his appreciation and cupped both her cheeks, as much to keep her still as to make sure she understood.

"I think there's no excuse for manhandling." He saw the satisfaction in her eyes. "But that wasn't what happened last night, Reggie. And the lady in my arms wasn't unwilling. She was warm and welcoming." Honesty forced him to add, "At least at first."

She turned her head away.

"For that I am sorry, Reg. I scared you. I should have stopped sooner. I got carried away, and that's no excuse."

"I am sorry I disgusted you," she returned stiffly, a dull flush creeping up her neck.

Her words caught him like a sucker punch, slackening his grip and allowing her to slide from his grasp. "You don't disgust me, Regina. You never have," he said quietly to her back.

She slowly turned to face him again, and he saw the tracks of tears on her cheeks. "*Sim.* That's why you spent the night deep in the woods. Because I don't disgust you."

Again he closed the distance between them, but this time she didn't back up. She held her ground until he stood almost on her feet. The woman was tying him in knots, so he gave her bald honesty.

"I left because if I hadn't, I might have scared you again. You deserve better than that." He used his thumb to dry her tears and met her gaze squarely. "And I won't be around long enough to make the commitments you deserve."

She shoved hard against his chest. She moved so fast he didn't see it coming and almost sprawled butt-first in the dirt. "Who says I want anything from you, Mister."

He looked past the crossed arms and haughty expression and saw confusion swirling in those brown eyes.

"No matter who the man is, it'll always be your call, Reggie." Maybe if he kept saying it, she'd eventually believe it. He met her gaze. "Will you tell me what happened?"

Regina bit her lip and looked away. "I grew up on the streets. What do you think happened?"

"I think you did what you had to do to survive. There's no shame in that, Reggie."

"What do you know about it?" she shouted, then turned away and wrapped her arms around her middle.

He wanted to go to her, but sensed that wouldn't help. Instead, he turned and began to break camp. "We need to get moving."

Maybe if he kept his mind on his mission, he could let go of his rage at those who'd hurt her. And maybe, he could forget how she'd looked with her eyes dreamy and focused only on him.

"What if I want you to kiss me?"

Stunned, he stopped and slowly turned to look at her over his shoulder. Her shocked expression said she hadn't expected the words either.

"All you gotta do is ask, darlin'."

She opened her mouth, but no sound came out. He wanted to sweep her up in his arms and kiss her until she begged for mercy, but he didn't. This move was hers. Just like all the others. He wouldn't scare her again.

"Will you . . . ?" she squeaked.

He stood. "Will I what?" He crossed his arms over his chest and waited.

She must have seen his expression, for her eyes narrowed. "You're enjoying this, aren't you?"

"Yes and no. Waiting for you to work up your courage is killing me." He grinned wryly. "But I'm hopeful." He wanted to add that she'd done just fine last night, but didn't dare.

She took a step in his direction. Then two more, her eyes locked with his.

Come on, Reggie. That's it. You're doing fine.

Finally, she stood before him. She went up on her tiptoes and slowly wrapped her arms around his neck. This was progress. He kept his arms firmly at his sides.

After drawing a deep breath, with her eyes wide open, she barely bumped her lips against his before jumping back. He waited and saw her muster up the courage to try again. The second attempt wasn't much better than the first.

She looked up at him, puzzled. "How come you're not helping?"

He hid a grin. "This is your show, Reg. You lead. You set the pace." She needed safety; he'd make sure she got it.

Her face flamed and she looked down. "I don't know how."

"Sure you do," he said firmly. "Just kiss me the way you want to be kissed." He'd almost said *the way you did last night*, but again caught himself in time.

Her eyes widened and locked on his lips.

Brooks's heartbeat picked up speed, and he tightened his hands at his sides. *Patience.* He felt like the spider trying to coax the fly into his web. He frowned. Bad analogy. He didn't plan to make a meal out of her. Better to focus on the here and now.

With the speed of hair growing, Regina inched her lips toward his, one agonizing millimeter at a time. This time, when her lips touched his, she didn't pull away, but rubbed softly, gently. Once, twice. Three times.

He shivered, and she pulled back to look at him. He thought he could look into those lovely brown eyes for the rest of his life. "You're doing fine, darlin'."

She frowned. "I-It's not enough."

Brooks heart cracked at what she couldn't put into words. Sadly, she knew all about sordid sex, but nothing of physical affection. He wished he'd be the one to teach her the wondrous difference. The idea of someone else, like a prissy boyfriend, putting his hands on her made him see red, but he forced the thought away. She was a marrying kind of woman, and he wasn't a marrying kind of man. Still, he could give her a taste of what it could be—with the right man.

"Would you like me to hold you?"

Red flags of color appeared on her cheeks, but she nodded, head down.

"Then come here."

Eternity passed in the space of two heartbeats. The sound of birds chirping in the trees, monkeys chattering, and macaws screeching faded until all he could hear was the beating of his heart. And hers.

His arms gently wrapped around her, holding her close, but not tight. He held himself motionless as she cupped one hand behind his head and pressed her lips to his.

Sweat slicked his palms. The temptation to bury his fists in her wonderfully wild hair and devour her mouth was almost more than he could stand. Almost. But this was what she needed—simple affection and a sense of power and control. To give her that, and more, he would walk through the very fires of hell.

The thought sobered him and cut through some of the sensual haze surrounding them. He was on a mission, and he was getting dangerously sidetracked.

Sidetracked, my butt, he thought. He had stepped so far out of line, if one of his men pulled such a stunt, he'd have his backside on the next flight home.

When Regina curled deeper into him, all thoughts of duty and mission fled. "Don't you want to kiss me back?" she asked.

He hated the uncertain note in her voice. "More than anything I can think of right now."

She bit her lip nervously and looked up at him. "Then why aren't you?"

He raised an eyebrow. "Because you haven't asked me to."

Regina regarded him suspiciously. "Are you going to make me spell out every little thing?"

He nodded. "Yes."

Anger sparked. "You're just playing games with me."

She moved to turn away, but his arms shot out and clasped her shoulders, lightly. "This is not a game, Reggie. It's killing me. But I want to convince you—once and for all—that you have nothing to fear from me. You can touch me all you want, and wherever it ends, that's your choice."

"You'd be okay with that?"

"I'd be grumpy as a grizzly and swim eight miles in the river, but that's where it would end."

She regarded him solemnly for a long moment. "And if you were in charge, what would you do?"

He ground his back teeth. "You don't want to know."

"Yes, I do."

This is what honesty got you. Stretched tight on a rack of your own making.

He took a deep breath and looked right into her eyes. "If I was in charge, I'd ask you to undo that thingy in your hair so I could bury my hands in those amazing curls."

She reached up and sent the rubber band flying, then fluffed her mane until it swirled around her shoulders. "Like this?"

"Yes." He ran his fingers through the mass and marveled at how it sprang back at his touch. He brushed a wayward strand off her forehead and then he saw something that stopped him cold.

There, just below her collarbone, was a small round circle, a scar, faded, but still plainly visible. He pushed the collar of her blouse aside to get a better look, but she put her hand over his to stop him. He tried to meet her gaze, but she looked away. "Reg, is that what I think it is?"

She nodded. "Cigarette burn," she whispered. "Long time ago."

He wanted to kill whoever did this with his bare hands. Instead, he kept his voice level. "Is this the only one?"

She shook her head.

He tucked a finger under her chin. "Will you let me see?"

She met his eyes then, hers so filled with shame and uncertainty that he would have moved mountains with his bare hands to erase that look. Slowly, with trembling fingers, she undid the buttons, turned her back to him and let the blouse slide off her shoulders.

Brooks had seen many unspeakable things in his life, but he was not prepared for the neat row of small round burns that marched over her collarbone and shoulder, down her back, and disappeared underneath the waistband of her skirt.

Air hissed between his teeth, and she grabbed for her blouse. For her sake, he banked the fury that burned in him and tenderly brushed her hand aside.

"May I touch you?" he asked.

Her nod was almost imperceptible, but it was there. Slowly, reverently, he stroked the back of his hand down the terrible line of scars. Her skin was warm, soft to the touch and fired his blood, but this wasn't about him and it wasn't about lust; this was about acceptance and self-esteem. It was about healing. About letting go and feeling whole.

He could sense her obvious agitation, so before she pulled away he bent his head and placed a tender kiss on her collarbone, another on her shoulder, and a third in the middle of her back. His rage that someone would hurt her this way he would deal with later. For now, she needed to know how he felt about her. Slowly, he pulled her blouse up, wrapped his arms around her from behind, and rocked her gently back and forth. "I'm sorry, Reg, so sorry."

When he finally let go, he waited until she'd buttoned the blouse before he turned her to face him. Then he cupped both cheeks in his palms, desperate that she read his expression as well as his words. "If I ever find the man who did this, he'll rue the day he was born. But what that animal did to you has no effect on who you are. Not only do you turn me on like nobody I've ever met, but I care about . . . I'm glad I've gotten to know you."

Fearing he'd said too much—or not enough—he set her firmly away from him. "Now, get a move on. You have a plane to catch."

"Why?"

He looked into her tear-filled eyes, cautious. "Why what?"

"Why do you care about me?"

"Because you are an incredible woman, Regina da Silva, inside and out. Warm, caring, giving. Everything a woman should be."

The tears came faster now, making her voice thick. "But what about . . . you saw the slums, my scars," she sniffed, "and all I've done lately is be a burden, a problem."

He laughed at that last part; he couldn't help it. "Yeah, you're a real pain, but it goes with the territory." Seeing she still didn't get it, Brooks took a deep breath and plunged into the kind of emotional quicksand he'd always avoided. "I care about you because you're you. Not what you've done, or what you look like, but who you are. Okay?" At her nod, he said, "Now let's get moving."

21

REGINA WAS PACKING THEIR FOOD SUPPLIES WHEN SOME HIDDEN SIGNAL made her turn toward Brooks. She hadn't been able to look him in the eye since he'd set her away from him, but she couldn't avoid it now. He crouched on the ground where he'd been rolling up their sleeping bags, a finger to his lips, reaching for his knife with his other hand.

Regina cocked her head to listen. At first, she heard nothing but the usual sounds of the forest: birds cawing and flapping their wings, trees rustling overhead, and in the distance, the underlying hum of the water pounding over the falls. But after a few seconds, the birds fell silent, as if they, too, were listening.

Hardly daring to breathe, she strained for some sound. Yes, there it was. A footfall. She froze, every sense on high alert, her heart pounding in her chest. Brooks had heard it, too, for he turned toward the sound. With his knife, he signaled her to move back into the woods behind her, opposite the approaching figure.

Hugging Eduardo to her with sweaty hands, she inched backward, her gaze darting back and forth between the threat approaching them and the tree roots and rocks scattered behind her. When she was safely under the cover of the trees, she moved behind the biggest one she could find. With one hand, she felt around to make sure her knife was in her skirt pocket. Then she peeked out and saw Brooks give her a quick thumbs-up before turning all his attention to the intruder. Regina's blood pumped faster, and she crooned softly to Eduardo, afraid he would pick up on her fear and begin screaming.

When she looked up, she realized that Brooks had melted into the shadows. Regina scanned each tree near where he'd been, but couldn't find him.

The seconds dragged by. Suddenly, she heard a thump, a muffled cry, and then sounds of a struggle. Regina crouched farther behind the tree and sank down on her haunches, shaking with fear. With hands that trembled, she rubbed Eduardo's back and whispered a quick prayer for Brooks's safety. "Please Father, protect him."

Eduardo had fallen asleep, and every nerve in her body ached from holding herself motionless by the time Brooks finally called her name. Relief flooded her, and she scrambled to her feet, prepared to burst into the clearing. Just as she turned in that direction, caution asserted itself and she stopped. What if their intruder had captured Brooks and this was a trap to catch her and the baby as well?

Inch by inch, she leaned around the tree until she could see Brooks heading out of the trees. He had his arm around another man's shoulders and suddenly threw his head back and laughed out loud. The sound was so unexpected, so rich and carefree, for an instant she wondered if it was the same man.

Her knees threatened to buckle as relief and another, more complex emotion, swamped her. This was a side of Brooks she'd never seen, but one she wanted to see again. Just like the tender side he'd shown her earlier. She'd thought him appealing before, but these unexpected glimpses made him even more devastating to her heart.

She watched as Brooks thumped the man on the back and said, "I could have killed you, man."

The huge blond man beside him slanted him a look and quipped, "I'm not that easy to kill."

They laughed companionably and then Brooks looked directly at her. "Come on out, Regina. It's all right."

When she walked out into the campsite, she automatically swept her gaze over Brooks from head to foot, checking for injuries. He seemed fine, relaxed.

Laughter lurked in his gray eyes when he said, "Regina, meet Jax, my good friend and general pain in the butt."

"I should be offended, but he's right," the blond man said, reaching for her hand.

He was almost as tall as Brooks, but broader, thicker in the neck and shoulders. Regina took an instinctive step back, but it was the look in his eyes that worried her most. He took her hand, gallantly kissing her knuckles, but then, just as she let her guard down slightly, he turned her hand over and licked her palm. Her gaze collided with his, and he held tight while he subjected her to a very thorough, very carnal perusal. Revulsion clogged her throat, and she yanked her hand away.

Brooks apparently didn't like what he saw in that exchange, for he suddenly appeared beside her, wrapping his arm around her shoulders in a decidedly proprietary manner.

With something close to awe, Regina watched as the two men took each other's measure, like two hunters after the same prey. Tension hovered in the air, and Regina fought the urge to squirm. She wanted to protest that she was nobody's prize or pawn, but something kept her silent. She sensed more going on here than what was obvious on the surface. And if she was honest, at some deeper level, the very feminine depths of her were secretly pleased that Brooks had come to her defense. It was a totally new sensation, and she found she liked it, though she probably shouldn't make more of it than it was.

After a long moment, Jax dropped his gaze. "So it's like that, is it?"

Brooks gave one quick nod and then let his arm drop as the two men moved off together, out of earshot. From the way their voices murmured together, their standoff might never have happened.

They also acted like she didn't exist. Regina's emotions came to a rolling boil as the two men talked, oblivious, and Regina noisily packed up the camp. She couldn't decide if she was more angry or hurt. After telling her he cared about her, now he was shutting her out. She thwacked the lid onto the coffee pot. His big bad buddy shows up and *poof*, she's not part of the team anymore. Well, he was in for one heck of a surprise.

She nearly jumped out of her skin when Brooks said quietly from behind her, "I know that's my head you'd like to be bashing in, but maybe you could make a little less noise. We don't want any unexpected company."

Regina whirled around, poking him in the chest with a large metal stirring spoon. "Well, we've already got that, now don't we?"

"I asked him to come."

She fairly sputtered at that. "Listen, you, we've been in this together from the beginning. You're not going to get rid of me now."

He gently pried the spoon from her grasp and regarded her intently for a long moment. Regina studied his gray eyes and saw regret, mixed with something else she couldn't name, in his expression.

"Jax will take you and Eduardo to the airport in fifteen minutes. You'll be back in Porto Alegre by lunchtime."

Her mouth opened and closed, but no sound came out. Had he not been holding onto her arms, her legs would have given out and she'd have crumpled in a heap. He was sending her away. Despite what he'd said earlier, he didn't want her anymore. The bald truth slammed into her and stole her breath. This was it.

Part of her wanted to fling herself at his feet and beg to stay, but pride raised its head to shield her from the slap of rejection. Finally, she latched onto the first question she could pull from the haze of pain. "What about Eduardo?" she whispered.

The expression in his gray eyes turned fierce, implacable. "I'll come get him when this is over."

"No!" she cried, breaking free of his hold. Pride and panic evaporated like water on a hot stove, vaporized in the heat of loyalty to Irene and Eduardo. "This is not how this is going to go. I'm not leaving until this is over. I told you that. Until the threat to that child is gone, you're stuck with me. Like it or not, you need me."

His jaw hardened, and she saw his warrior face slide into place. Instantly, all clues to what he was thinking were wiped away. Regina couldn't guess at his emotions; nothing of the man she'd come to know remained but a rock-hard expression and immovable stance. "Don't fight me on this, Reggie."

Her chin shot into the air and she planted her hands on her hips. "You're not making a decision like this without me."

His voice was flat, emotionless. "I just did."

"Well, it's not going to happen like that." She sat down on one of the fold-up camping chairs. "I'm not leaving."

"You're only making this harder on yourself. Collect your stuff and the kid's."

"And if I won't?" she taunted. She wouldn't go back to being a spineless victim now. Too much was at stake.

"I'll do whatever it takes." His voice was quiet, but his intent deadly clear.

Regina studied his face and knew that in this battle of wills, he would prevail. He had decided on his course, and nothing and no one would be able to sway him. He was not above bodily hefting her onto a plane, unconscious, if necessary. Brooks wanted her and Eduardo in Porto Alegre, and that was that.

Defeat seeped into her and all the fight left her. After all they'd been through, all they'd shared, he still didn't consider her a real partner, didn't want her around. She was just part of a job he was doing, a warm body to take care of the baby until the real help—in the form of his friend—arrived. He had deemed her qualified to babysit as long as there was no imminent danger, but nothing more. Whatever foolish dreams she'd conjured up, he was just doing his duty. And now she'd outlived her usefulness.

She forced her shoulders back and walked to the blanket where Eduardo sucked on his toes, socks and all. Tenderly, she picked him up and showered kisses on his forehead, his tiny ears, his button nose. "It's okay, Eduardo," she whispered, her voice suddenly clogged with unshed tears. "I'll take care of you." Regina nuzzled his neck, committing the sight of his lopsided grin to memory, hoarding it with all the others, so she'd have it later—when she was alone again.

She wouldn't think about that now. Carefully, she set Eduardo back down on the blanket so she could pack. An errant tear ran down her cheek as she reached for her bag, so she wiped it quickly away. She would not leave with her tail between her legs, like a sniveling coward. She would leave with her dignity intact.

She finished putting all of their things into her bag and then stood. With what she hoped was a bright smile, she turned to

Brooks and stuck out her hand. "Thank you for your help in this matter," she said formally. "I'll look forward to seeing you when you return to Porto Alegre."

That he would succeed against their pursuer, she didn't have the slightest doubt. At first he'd been reluctant, but now she knew he wouldn't rest until the threat was "neutralized," as he called it. A shiver swept over her, but another part of her acknowledged that violence might well be necessary to secure Eduardo's future.

A fierce scowl on his face, Brooks closed the distance between them in two steps. "Don't do this, Reggie," he growled, just before he hauled her into his arms.

He slanted his mouth over hers and kissed her with all the desperation of a soldier going off to war. This kiss was different than all the others; he took everything she had to give. Regina gave back all he took. Their mouths met, advancing and retreating in a conflict where there were no winners or losers. There was only a desperate wanting for more. More time. More words. More chances to see the other's heart.

Abruptly, Brooks pulled away and cupped her face in his palms. "I can't risk it," he groaned, then set her firmly away.

The agony she'd glimpsed in his expression sliced her heart to ribbons. *What can't you risk?* she wanted to ask. Numb, she watched as he scooped Eduardo into his arms, gave his forehead a quick kiss, and then gave her the baby and motioned for her to go with Jax.

Feet heavy as cement blocks, she stumbled after the man, who set a relentless pace out of the clearing. At the edge she stopped, wanting one last look, a final glimpse to relive in the days ahead. She turned, but Brooks wasn't looking at her. He had his back to her, dialing his cell phone.

He'd already forgotten her.

Brooks sensed her stop and almost turned around. But he forced himself not to. It was better to make a clean break. Besides, it was the only way he knew to get them both out of harm's way. He already felt empty without her.

He ran a hand through his hair. Now he was getting maudlin. He'd made a smart, tactical decision. His enemy would want them at the meeting; he'd make sure they weren't. Jax had promised to see them safely back to the orphanage and speak with the guard about stepping up security for a few days. Brooks wasn't taking any chances with their lives.

The image of Beatrice Simms and her son wanted to intrude on his thoughts, but he pushed it from his mind. He had no time for emotion now.

It was time to hunt a killer. And to hunt, you had to know your prey.

He dialed and paced. This time he would get the information he needed, hurt feelings or not. He had to know what he was dealing with. And he knew the one person who could tell him.

Carol answered on the first ring, so he assumed Noah was asleep in his hospital bed. Brooks shoved the disturbing image away. "Mom, it's Brooks."

"Nathaniel, how are you?" She didn't try to hide the concern in her voice.

"I'd be a lot better if I knew exactly what was going down here," he said baldly.

"I'm sorry." She drew a deep breath. "We—no, I—should have told you sooner."

"And now?"

He heard a shuffling noise, as though she had moved away and was cupping the phone with her hand. "We got a photo yesterday, by cell phone, of you, Regina, and Eduardo."

His worst suspicions were realized. This had everything to do with Noah and the past. "Did he see it?"

"Your father? Yes."

"When were you going to tell me about it?"

"I-I wasn't sure how."

He reigned in his impatience and commanded, "Tell me now. It's important. Who sent it?"

The image of the ambush flashed into his mind again, but this time, the woman and child lying on the ground bleeding were Reggie and Eduardo.

There was a long silence, punctuated only by the bleeping sounds of hospital machinery.

"I need to know," he prodded.

"I'm not sure where to start."

"Just give me the high points. Who is this guy?"

"Your father and I knew his sister when we were in school in Porto Alegre together. We were all friends. His name is Raul."

"Right. So, what happened?"

"Raul's sister, um, died, and he blamed your father for it. He swore vengeance on him and our family. But then Raul went to prison, and we forgot all about it."

Brooks reigned in his impatience. "You already told me that. Now tell me why this Raul blamed Noah for his sister's death."

"I-I'm not sure."

"Don't lie, Mom. You're lousy at it," he growled.

He waited, wondering if she'd finally get the truth out. She'd preached honesty all his life, but he supposed some truths were harder to tell than others. This one, apparently, had been hidden a very long time.

When she spoke, her voice had gone flat, devoid of emotion. She might have been reciting pages from the telephone book. "Teresa is—was," she corrected, "your biological mother. She died when you were eighteen. Raul blamed your father for her death."

Brooks reeled back as though he'd been slapped. Of all the scenarios he'd painted in his mind, this one never crossed his scope. The man trying to kill them was his uncle? It boggled the mind, but it was also distant, as though they were discussing someone else.

"How did she die?"

Another pause. "She killed herself."

He decided he'd think about that later. "What do Irene and Eduardo have to do with this? Why kill her, if he's after our family?" Even as he asked, he thought of the photo of Noah and Irene.

Another long pause. "We believe Raul thinks Eduardo is Noah's son."

Brooks steeled himself. "Is he?"

The silence stretched. "No." Carol's voice sounded tentative, unsure.

Brooks didn't buy it. "Then who is?"

"That I can't answer."

He growled in frustration. "Can't or won't?"

"In this case, both." Her crisp tone let him know this was all he was going to get from her. At least at this point.

He heard a quiet sniffle and realized what this had cost her. His whole life, he'd watched his mother worship Noah, doting on him and, like an eager puppy, hoping for some scrap of affection. Noah cared for her, but he treated her with the sort of distant affection one showed a visiting aunt. Beloved, but not somebody you wanted to spend all your time with.

"Thank you for telling me," he said. "I know it wasn't easy."

"Just keep them safe. Don't let anything happen to them, Nathaniel."

The weight of responsibility settled like lead. He fought the urge to hang up and head for the nearest bar and oblivion. Let someone else handle it. But then he remembered Reggie's face as she'd said good-bye.

"I'll do my best," he promised.

Regina followed Jax through the woods, Eduardo balanced over one shoulder, the bag with their belongings over the other. You'd think the man could at least carry the bag for her. But as she watched him moving ahead of her, she decided maybe it was better that he ignored her. The way he'd licked her palm earlier coiled a tight knot in her belly and made her wish for a baby wipe, washcloth, anything to wash the smell and feel of him off her hands. Jax might be Brooks's friend, but she didn't like him. Something about him put all her self-protective instincts on alert. She'd only ignored that instinct a few times in her life, and each time had bitterly regretted it. *Father, show me what to do, how to act.*

She slowed her pace to put more distance between them. Jax noticed immediately and scowled over his shoulder.

"Keep up, Miss da Silva. We have a plane to catch."

She increased her speed slightly and shifted the bag higher on her shoulder. The darn thing got heavier with every step. Without a word, they tramped through the trees, finally coming out behind the elegant hotel at the falls. Regina blinked at the sudden change from the dimness of the forest to the bright sunlight. Eduardo squeezed his little eyes shut and yowled a protest. Regina smiled. "Tell me about it," she murmured.

Just as she was wondering if Jax planned to march them all the way to the airport, he casually approached a parked car and pulled what looked—at first glance—like a key from his pocket. Having hot-wired a car or two in her life, she was impressed with the speed at which he got the door open.

"Get in," he ordered brusquely, holding the passenger door open.

She met his ice blue eyes and stifled a shudder. Then she reminded herself that Brooks wouldn't have sent her with his friend if he didn't trust him. Reluctantly, she handed Jax her bag and then climbed in with Eduardo.

He started the older model Mercedes and drove casually out of the parking lot, down the winding road and out of the national park. Regina kept her attention on Eduardo, hoping that Jax would forget her presence.

From a purely objective standpoint, the man was undeniably attractive. He had that all-American look about him: football player's build, blond crew cut, blue eyes. She figured he made female hearts pitter-patter when he walked by. He just made her nervous.

Regina breathed a sigh of relief when they arrived at the airport and she could move out of Jax's reach. She relaxed further when they boarded the two-and-a-half-hour flight to Porto Alegre, and Jax took a seat across the aisle. With him at arm's length, exhaustion set in and she finally felt safe enough to snooze, Eduardo cuddled against her chest.

Meanwhile, Brooks paced the campsite, frustration clawing at his gut. Every instinct told him that a) time was running out, and b) he was still missing some vital clue. He again replayed the conversation with his mother. What had he missed? When his cell phone rang, he snatched it up, annoyed.

"Good morning, Senhor Anderson," a mechanical voice greeted. "How are you enjoying your tour of Brazil?"

Brooks stopped short as frustration and rage found their target. He'd had enough. "When and where, Raul?" he snapped. Then he added quietly, "Or should I say, Uncle?"

The mechanical voice chuckled as though he'd made a joke, but Brooks wasn't listening. He focused on the background noise, searching for a clue to the other man's location. Based on the absolute silence, Raul must be calling from a hotel room.

"You impatient Americans, always in a hurry." Raul paused as though making a decision. "In this, however, I find I must agree with you. It is time to end our little game."

Brooks waited, every nerve stretched tight. Let Raul think he called the shots.

"We will meet tonight. I left a map to our little rendezvous in the lobby of the Hotel Cataratas. Don't be late."

By the time the other man disconnected, Brooks was almost halfway to the hotel.

A very short time later, by South American standards, Regina stood in the doorway of House of Angels and thanked Jax for escorting them home. Just before she closed the door he leaned close and whispered, "If you ever decide you'd rather have a real man, look me up."

Regina slammed and locked the door, then leaned back against it, shivering. As soon as the taxi pulled away, she rushed into the washroom to scrub Jax's ugly words away with a fingernail brush. Finally, as the lather disappeared down the drain, she took a deep breath, then another, before she deliberately shifted her thoughts to Brooks. He never made her feel dirty and used. Just the opposite, he made her feel clean, cherished, even loved.

She looked up and stopped short, her eyes landing on the picture of Christ that Noah had hung there in the washroom years ago. It showed a smiling Christ surrounded by laughing children. "Jesus loves you, Regina," Noah had said. "So much that He died for your past and every one of your hurts." Noah had held up a bar of soap. "This won't make you clean, but His blood and His forgiveness will. His love is a gift, not something we deserve and certainly not something we can earn. But the gift is meaningless if we don't accept it."

Regina stood there a long time, tears streaming down her cheeks as those words finally, finally made sense. By his actions, Brooks had shown her their meaning. She had done nothing to earn either Brooks's acceptance or God's, yet both had given it anyway. Despite her past.

Regina set down the bar of soap and looked at Christ's picture again, stunned by the realization. "Will you make me clean? Forever? Because I can't do it myself."

There in that tiny washroom, a Bible verse Olga taught her years ago sprang to mind and answered her plea. *Though your sins be as scarlet, they shall be as white as wool.*

Regina wasn't sure how long she stood there before Eduardo's cry roused her. She murmured a quick, "Thank you," before she hurried out and tucked Eduardo into his crib.

Then she called the airport. Both commercial and charter flights ran back and forth to the Falls all day long. She checked the clock on the wall. If she hurried, she could be back at the Falls by nightfall.

Slowly, she replaced the receiver. Who was she kidding? She had a baby to protect. She couldn't lose sight of that. Eduardo's safety was her number one priority. Besides, and it stung to admit this, what help could she provide two of Uncle Sam's finest? She retrieved her knife and slipped it back into her pocket. She could fight if the situation warranted it, but she didn't have the training or skills those two had.

She hated Brooks's easy dismissal of her, but had to admit it was a practical decision. Whatever was—or wasn't—between them, Brooks also had Eduardo's best interests at heart. He would be safer somewhere else. Brooks trusted her to take care of that much, at least.

What if he needed her help, though? It was always good to have extra hands and eyes. She should be with him, by his side. Why wouldn't he admit it?

When the doorbell rang, Regina's eyes widened at seeing an impeccably dressed Jair standing on the threshold.

"You are back!" he exclaimed, kissing both her cheeks. "I've been coming by every day, hoping to find you here."

Before she could politely turn him away, he'd maneuvered his way in and led them both into the office. He turned and pulled her down beside him on the couch, his gaze intense. "Tell me where you've been. I read about the fire. Was anyone hurt?"

"No. Just one of the sheds burned down."

"But where did you go?" He looked around as though just now noticing the silence. "Where are all the children?"

The location of the farm hovered on the tip of her tongue when some inner warning held her back. "They're having a little holiday away from the city. It's good for them."

"But why aren't you with them?"

She thought fast. "Eduardo was overtired, so we came home." Which was true.

He took her hand, and Regina forced herself not to flinch. This was Jair, a very nice, very attractive businessman she'd met at church. He was old enough to be her father, but had always been kind and attentive. A nice man, even if she hated the way he crowded her and proposed every other week.

Even Olga who, like most Brazilians, harbored deep pity for any woman still single at the ripe old age of twenty-eight, was thrilled with the attention Jair paid Regina. The sweet woman had taken to humming love songs on a regular basis.

"I brought you a present," he announced, grinning like a schoolboy.

Regina refused to think about how differently she'd responded to Brooks's touch. She folded her hands to keep them from fluttering nervously. *Please, no jewelry. Nothing that bespoke commitment.* "You didn't have to do that."

He laughed. "Of course I didn't. I wanted to." From his superbly tailored jacket, he produced a small bottle of red wine. "I visited a vineyard this week and thought you would enjoy this."

As he stood and walked toward the kitchen, Regina stifled her annoyance at how comfortable he was making himself in her home. She stepped ahead of him and removed two glasses from the cupboard, allowing him to pour.

Jair raised his glass in a toast. "Welcome home, *meu amor*," he said.

Regina opened her mouth to protest his use of the endearment, then decided it wasn't worth the effort. Instead, she touched her glass to his and took a sip.

"Do you like it?" he asked.

"It's lovely. Thank you."

"Well, drink up, my dear." Twelve-thirty seemed a bit early in the day for wine, even in Brazil, but she didn't want to offend him. Regina obediently drained her glass and then noticed he'd barely touched his.

"Let's go back and sit down," he said. "I want to hear all about this holiday you've taken the children on." He steered her back down the hallway.

Regina hadn't been sitting for more than a few minutes when the room took a slow spin. She gripped the arms of the sofa. That wine must have been more potent than she'd thought. Jair's voice seemed to echo from far away.

"Are you feeling all right, Regina?" he asked.

She tried to respond, but her tongue filled her entire mouth. She couldn't get any words around it.

The last thing she remembered was Jair whispering, "Sweet dreams."

22

THE AFTERNOON SHADOWS WERE LONG AND BROOKS'S TEMPER SHORT BY the time Jax sauntered back into camp.

"Where have you been?" he barked.

Jax' negligent shrug only added fuel to the fire. "Relax, man. The flight left late. Everything took a little longer than I thought, that's all." He walked toward the small fire and sprawled in one of the folding camp chairs.

Brooks was too keyed up to sit. Anxiety prickled his skin as though ants marched just below the surface. He punched in the numbers again and then listened to the phone ring and ring on the other end before he snapped it shut. Regina still wasn't answering the orphanage phone. Every time he called, the churning in his gut increased. He couldn't get through to the guard or Jorge, either.

The sense of impending doom, of being part of his nightmare, increased. He leveled a sharp glance at his friend. "You took her all the way to the orphanage?"

Jax had been known to cut a few corners in favor of his own comfort. It wasn't impossible to think he dropped Regina off at the airport and then spent the day at a bar.

"Isn't that what you asked me to do?" Jax shot back.

"Everything looked okay there?"

Jax crossed his arms defensively. "Far as I know."

"Then where is she?"

Another shrug. "I don't know. Maybe she went to buy diapers. Quit worrying. She can take care of herself."

"I won't stop worrying until they're both safe. For good."

Jax looked up then and grinned, the same foolish grin he had worn the day they met at boot camp. It reminded Brooks of a mischievous little boy who'd just performed some dastardly deed and had the spoils of war in his pocket. "You should get your wish before long."

"I found out who our friend is," Brooks tossed out.

Jax sat up straight. "Oh?"

"Name of Raul Carvalho. Old friend of the Anderson family, according to my mother."

"Motive?"

"Revenge, apparently."

Jax's eyes widened. "Against your parents? Why?"

Brooks looked away for a moment, then back to his friend. "Raul blames Noah for his sister's death."

Jax shook his head. "You lost me, buddy. What does your fath—I mean, Noah—have to do with this guy's sister?"

"His sister was my mother, and she killed herself," Brooks said bluntly. He recited the facts without embellishment, with no hint of the turmoil they caused. Emotions could wait. They had a job to do. No distractions.

Regina's big brown eyes and stubborn chin came to mind, and he shoved the image aside. No distractions, he reminded himself sternly—of any kind.

Brooks studied his friend a moment, then tossed him Raul's map. "I'm supposed to meet him in little over an hour."

Jax picked up the map, studied it, and then nodded before he fed it to the smokeless fire. "Let's do it."

Brooks retrieved a simmering pan of beans. "Have some chow first. You bring everything we need?"

"Got it. No problem."

Five minutes later they doused the cook fire and went over their plans, outlining all possible scenarios. Casually, Brooks flexed his gun hand, gratified he could do it without flinching. He checked the clip on the Berretta Jax had brought him and double-checked his ammo before changing into black jeans, shirt, and jacket. Mentally, he went over everything one more time, firmly blocking everything else from his mind. He hefted his backpack and headed out. Time to catch his prey.

At his signal, he and Jax split up, each approaching the meeting place from opposite directions.

Near his destination deep within the national park, Brooks stepped off the path and melted into the trees. At least their quarry hadn't chosen one of the open pathways that hugged the sides of the gorge and hung out over the river. They were too public, too crowded with tourists. This spot wasn't far from the falls, though, because the sound of thundering water increased with every step.

The falls themselves were beyond description. Two hundred seventy-five separate waterfalls spread across just under two miles. While most of the falls were on the Argentine side, the Brazilian side had the more spectacular view. At this time of year, runoff swelled the river, forcing park rangers to close some of the catwalks. He knew some of them had washed away several years earlier.

Just before one of the more impressive lookouts, an enterprising young man had set up a booth where he rented towels, ponchos, and umbrellas. At this time of year, he did a brisk business since nobody could get near the falls without getting soaked.

Brooks had reconnoitered earlier and knew the small clearing in the rainforest Raul had chosen was just ahead. He stopped and listened. They weren't too far from the borders of the bird park. Myriad screaming birds competed with the deafening roar of the falls.

Brooks checked his watch, though he didn't need to. Since childhood he'd had an instinctive sense of time and could generally pinpoint it within five minutes. Their meeting was scheduled for thirty minutes from now, which meant he was right on time. Always know the lay of the land and what you're getting into. Before you get there.

If only he'd followed the rules, listened to his training, that other morning.

"Time to go. Roll out." Brooks had nudged his men awake with the toe of his boot.

"Aw, c'mon, man," Woody groaned. "I just got to bed. We've got time."

In one smooth motion, Brooks hauled the man up by his shirtfront. "Up. Now." Then he abruptly let go, and Woody sprawled in the dirt. Behind him, the other men scrambled up, lacing their boots with comical haste.

Jax eyed him quizzically and Brooks met his look with an implacable one of his own. Something about this whole rescue mission bothered him. Some might call it instinct, but he didn't believe in that. He believed in facts. He was missing something. Maybe it was nothing, maybe it was important. The sooner he got the two hostages safely out of there, the better he'd feel.

Brooks went over the plans with his men one last time, then their team of seven sanitized the camp until no one would ever know they'd been there. Brooks grabbed his gear and called, "Move out." Instantly they melted soundlessly into the predawn darkness, mere shadows floating past.

And walked right into hell.

Brooks gave his head a violent shake. He cocked an ear and listened, blocking everything from his mind but the here and now. With the approach of darkness, the forest floor started coming to life, daytime animals bedding down for the night and nocturnal ones stirring.

A slight rustling to his left put every sense on high alert. He whipped in that direction, gun ready. A haughty raccoon glared at him and continued on its way. Brooks relaxed his grip on his weapon, adjusted his pack, and inched closer to the meeting place. He moved in a crouch, slowly zigzagging from tree to tree. For one brief moment he wondered what he thought he was doing here. How had a simple transport mission turned into this? And why did he think he could handle the job?

He knew there would be bloodshed before the night ended. His only comfort was that Regina and Eduardo were far, far away. They were safe. His grip tightened on his gun. Even if she wouldn't answer the phone. Everything in him wanted to call one more time, just to make sure she was okay, but he wouldn't risk it. Sounds, especially voices, carried too well out here. No distractions, he reminded himself.

The night sounds increased around him and Brooks fought a nauseating wave of déjà vu. The predawn night his team was ambushed had been eerily like this one. Deep in the jungle, with only the wildlife for company. A chill rippled over his skin, though the night was not cold. Four-footed creatures hadn't been the only ones about that night. The bullets had come from the weapons of the two-legged variety.

Again, he thrust the images aside. Nothing but the job at hand. Everything else could wait.

Roughly ten yards from the small clearing, he stopped. The low murmur of voices made the hair on the back of his neck stand on end. He couldn't see what was going on because of the thick foliage. He had to give Raul credit. If he'd been choosing the location, he'd have picked this little glade, too. Or one just like it.

"Senhor Brooks, show yourself," a male voice called. "I know you are there. I know you would not want to be late for our little appointment."

Brooks didn't answer. Responding would give away his location. He waited, wondering why that voice sounded so very familiar. Where had he heard it before?

"I have a small surprise for you, Senhor Brooks." The sing-song intonation sounded childlike, cajoling. "Two surprises, actually." The man paused. "A big one and a small one." He laughed at his own joke.

When Brooks still didn't respond, his voice turned sullen. "You Americanos are very rude. You won't even acknowledge my gift." He made a tsk-tsking sound with his tongue. "Perhaps you just need a bit more encouragement."

Brooks heard a brief shuffling and then the voice continued.

"Have I told you that I asked Regina to join us tonight? Underneath all those drab layers, she's really quite a lovely woman. But I'm sure I don't have to tell you that, do I?"

Violence leaped behind Brooks's eyeballs and terror momentarily blinded him. His muscles strained with the effort of holding still as every instinct urged him to charge the clearing.

Regina. She was safely home. Raul was bluffing, as lunatics often did. *Wait him out. Don't give yourself away.*

The silence dragged on and sweat ran off his body. He refused to let the man play mind games with him. Regina and the baby were safe. All Brooks had to do was wait for his chance, and he and Jax could take this guy down. His opportunity would come. He just had to be ready to leap into action when it did.

When the man's voice came again, all pretense of civility had disappeared. "I'm tired of this game, Senhor. So I'm going to make your choices very easy. Either you show yourself in the next five seconds, or your lovely girlfriend gets a bullet between the eyes. One."

Brooks didn't hesitate. He charged for a gap in the foliage, years of practice making his approach swift and soundless. He was done with games, too.

"Two."

In a crouch, Brooks parted a thick curtain of leaves with the barrel of his gun.

"Three."

For an instant, he wished for his night vision goggles, but he didn't have time to get them out of his pack. He saw a shadowy form separate itself from the shadows and take careful aim.

"Four."

Brooks put his finger on the trigger, gun pointed, arm rock steady. But he waited one heartbeat longer. Never take a shot in the dark when a hostage could be in the line of fire. He knew Regina was safe, but what if he was wrong? What if this lunatic had taken some innocent tourist hostage? He strained to see, determined to hit the right target.

"Come on, man, show yourself," he muttered. Shooting Regina—or someone else—by mistake was not a risk he was prepared to take.

Suddenly, the figure's arm shot up, gun pointed. Brooks heart leaped, and the familiar jolt of adrenaline slammed him like a fist. He aimed. Fired. Everything around him slowed, each second stretched out and hacked off into separate chunks of time.

Just as his bullet cleared his gun, he heard another shot. A muffled groan. The telltale thud of a body hitting the ground. Knowledge knocked him like an unexpected blow.

He hadn't been quick enough.

Brooks clamped his jaw to keep the scream of outrage locked inside. "No!" his mind screamed. This couldn't be happening. Not again. He couldn't be too late. *Not Regina, please God, not Regina.*

With one lunge, Brooks rolled and burst through the brush, gun pointed with deadly accuracy at the man standing in the center of the glade. The man clasped his bloody shoulder in one hand, the gun in his other pointed squarely at a body lying on the ground. Brooks swept the scene, and his heart came to an abrupt stop. His gun wavered as he fought to stay upright.

His nightmare, the one no amount of alcohol could help him escape, had come to life. And he was living it. Only this time, it was worse, much worse.

The woman lying dead on the ground wasn't a stranger; it was Regina. The way she was lying, thrown down and discarded like a child's rag doll, was so much like that other time, he blinked. The two scenes were so eerily similar a Hollywood director could have staged them.

Brooks wanted to run and hide, lose himself in the sweet oblivion of alcohol where he wasn't responsible, didn't have to be accountable. But his eyes were drawn to Regina's face, obscured by her wildly curling hair. Once he'd thought it an unruly mess; now he knew the beautiful face she hid behind it. He glanced down at her ratty cardigan, the one she was almost never without. He'd bought her another one, but she insisted on wearing this one. It was torn and dirty, one sleeve torn at the shoulder, testimony of the struggle she'd waged against her captor.

Rage pounded through him. Only the barest thread of control kept him from rushing forward to straighten her limbs from their uncomfortable position. He ached to check her pulse, just to be sure, to put a pillow under her head, stop the bleeding.

The blood. Dear God in Heaven. Brooks blinked as the scene swam before his eyes and images from the past superimposed on the present. For one suspended moment, he couldn't tell reality from memory.

Then, like a lightning bolt, past and present split in two. His vision cleared until all he saw was Regina, broken and bloody. His wanted to howl and smash everything in his path. His heart screamed for retribution, for relief from the excruciating pain. Acid churned like bitter poison, bringing up the truth. He was too late. Again. Someone made the fatal mistake of trusting him. And once again it cost her her life.

Regina, who trusted no man, had finally come to trust him. His thanks for that priceless gift was to get her killed. It was over. He was done. He would never let something like this happen again.

Brooks raised his gun, prepared to kill the shooter, prepared to die himself. It was the only way he'd ever find relief.

He tensed, his finger on the trigger, bracing for the impact of return fire. He allowed himself one final glance at Regina's still face and regret swamped him. He'd never told her what he felt for her, never dared to put his complicated feelings into words. Never even allowed himself to name them.

Now he'd never have a chance. Her death was his fault. He had arrived too late.

Again.

As he stood there, poised at the brink, Brooks's training slapped him, hard. What if Regina wasn't dead? Never give up, because it's not over till it's truly over.

Like a dunk in an icy stream, his head cleared. Brooks the man let Brooks the soldier take control. He swept grief and retribution from his mind. No time for that now. Seconds could mean the difference between life and death. He heard his instructors bark commands in his ear. Focus on your mission. Don't get distracted. Evaluate the threat. See about the victim.

Brooks looked up and found himself eye to eye with their pursuer. Shocked recognition slammed him. Raul Carvalho and Regina's boyfriend Jair, the man he'd met at the orphanage, were one and the same. How could he have been so stupid, so blind?

"Let me check on her," he demanded.

Raul gave a negative shake of his head and sighed. "She's dead, though I hated to kill her. I rather hoped she and I could come to some agreement, but . . . well, you know how she feels about men touching her." His eyes narrowed. "Or did she respond differently with you?"

Brooks gritted his teeth. "Regina da Silva is a lady. She came with me to take care of Eduardo." He scanned the clearing with his peripheral vision, but the encroaching darkness hid everything outside the small area in which they stood. "Where's the baby?"

"He's not far from here."

Brooks pierced him with a hard look. "Is he alive?"

"For the moment."

Brooks inched closer to Regina, his stance deliberately relaxed. He couldn't see any blood from this vantage point.

"Why are you doing this?" he asked conversationally, every nerve cell on high alert. He employed an old tactic: get the perp to talk while your backup gets into place. Regina and the boy were still alive. They had to be. He pushed any other possibly firmly out of his mind.

"Do you read the Bible much, Senhor Brooks?" Raul asked, as though they were seated at a dinner table, sharing casual conversation.

"Not much," he admitted, though it had been different during his youth. He looked closer at Regina. No visible gunshot wound that he could see, no telltale pool of blood beneath her.

"But you are familiar with some of its tenets, no?"

Brooks nodded, taking a step the other way so he could see her other side. That mane of hers completely covered her face.

"Are you acquainted with the passage in Exodus 21 that talks about 'an eye for an eye'?"

Brooks nodded. "So it's revenge you're after. I can understand that." He pointed his chin toward Regina, taking a gamble. He worried if he paid her too much attention, Raul would shoot again. "But she has nothing to do with this."

"I hadn't planned to kill her. I even tried to get her to leave it alone, but she wouldn't. As I'm sure a man of your background knows, sometimes in war, the innocent die."

"Some would say all of us here are innocent. It's Noah you want." Brooks avoided the temptation to scan the surrounding trees again, searching for Jax. Frustration gnawed at his gut. Regina could bleed out while he stood here making small talk.

"Ah, so someone has told you the whole story. Was it Noah, I wonder?"

"Carol told me." *What was Jax waiting for?*

Raul smiled. "Your mother. Such a lovely woman. Tell me, is she still trying to get her husband to notice her?"

The too-accurate description of his parent's relationship stung like salt in an open wound. "I'm not discussing my family with you." He glanced from his gun to Raul's and asked, "So what happens now? We seem to be at an impasse." *C'mon, scum, give me a chance to take you out.*

"Oh, not really," Raul said. Keeping his gun carefully pointed at Regina's heart, he casually reached down, picked up a small rock, and tossed it into the trees. Eduardo's indignant cry erupted.

Brooks breathed a prayer of thanks, trying to pinpoint the boy's exact location.

Suddenly, Regina moaned, whispering Eduardo's name. Brooks snapped his head around and relief flooded him. That had to be the sweetest sound he had ever heard.

He turned to his opponent, eyes narrowed, trying to anticipate the man's next move.

"I thought it would be much more effective if you watched me kill them both," Raul announced.

Not good. Sweat poured down Brooks's back in an icy stream, but his gaze never wavered. "Let them go. It's me you want."

"Actually, it's your father I really want. But I understand he may die." He made that tsk-tsking sound again. "This way, he can spend his last days thinking about all he's lost."

Brooks shrugged nonchalantly even as he saw Regina move ever so slightly. His insides turned to ice and panic rushed through his veins as he realized what she had planned. But he kept his voice calm, encouraging confidences.

"I'm no great loss to him, you know. We haven't spoken in years," he told Raul.

In his peripheral vision, he saw Regina's hand inch carefully into the pocket of her skirt, where she kept that blasted switchblade.

"Yes, I know," Raul admitted. "Did you like your eighteenth birthday present, by the way?" he asked, his eyes wide, curious.

Everything inside Brooks went still, but he forced his voice to sound only mildly curious. "You sent that?"

Fourteen years ago, Raul had sent him the photo—the one of Noah and Teresa—that had forever changed the course of his life. And now, unless Brooks acted quickly, Regina was going to get herself killed. He had to stop her.

Brooks chanced a quick glance at Regina, gave an almost imperceptible shake of his head. *Don't do it. Just. Don't. Do. It.*

Regina's muscles screamed with the effort of holding perfectly still. Sweat poured from every inch of her skin, making her grip on the knife slippery. A breeze rustled in the treetops, raising gooseflesh along her arms. Tonight would be cold, and her sweater no defense. She waited patiently for the right moment, just as she had as a child, waiting for stronger scavengers to finish plundering her favorite dumpster. It all came down to timing. Confront them head on, and you might not live to eat again. But wait awhile and they'd wander off, their attention on other things. Then you could sneak in and make your move.

She sensed Brooks's anger. His tension rolled over her in waves, raising the tempo of her own heartbeat. He had no way of knowing her skills with a knife. She wanted to tell him, to reassure him that she had this under control. She met his gaze, putting all the confidence she could muster into it. He gave a firm, negative shake of his head. She barely refrained from tossing her head. Such a masculine approach, he had. Do it my way, or else.

Of course, he was a trained soldier and now that she looked a bit closer, she saw his blank warrior face. Tension coiled as tightly in him as in her. He waited for his chance, too.

Regina looked up at Raul, at the hideous black gun he had pointed squarely at her heart. His eyes gleamed with some unholy light, and he kept muttering to himself. He had been running his hands through his hair until it stood up in disorganized tufts. How odd to see him this way, so rumpled and out of control, so very different from the man who'd devoted months to his courtly romance.

Self-recrimination swamped her. How easily he'd fooled her, how willing she'd been to see only what he wanted her to see. Now that he'd removed his mask, she saw the madness he'd kept so carefully hidden. While the drug had worn off, she'd listened to his explanation for all this. He wanted revenge, but his desire for it had marked him, twisting his soul into something ugly and fearful.

She didn't want to die. She'd heard Eduardo cry out and that, together with Brooks's voice had brought her back to consciousness and reignited her dogged determination to live. It wouldn't end like this. She wouldn't let it. She and Brooks had unfinished business, and she had a promise to Irene to fulfill. Eduardo was still a long way from safety.

So whether Brooks liked it or not, she planned to help him. She let go of the knife just long enough to wipe her hand on the inside of her skirt pocket. Then she moaned loudly and used the sound to cover the little snick the knife made as the blade extended to its full length.

Brooks wasn't fooled, though. He must have heard the sound for his eyes cut to hers and he redoubled his message: *No, no, no. Let me handle this.*

Regina considered doing just that, then changed her mind. This was all her fault. If she'd heeded what Brooks had told her, she'd never have let Raul into the orphanage. Then none of this would be happening. *Help me, Father.*

Carefully, lest she draw Raul's attention, Regina tested her limbs to make sure she hadn't broken any bones. Her head ached—probably from whatever drug he'd given her—and there were abrasions on her palms. Her hip ached, but nothing else. She had to be sure everything worked before she leaped up. She'd have mere microseconds before Raul shot her.

She firmly shoved that thought away. She would not fail. She would get them out of this; she had to. Irene trusted her to keep her son safe. Since Brooks had done all he could to keep her out of this mess, it fell to her to end it. She listened to the conversation between the two men and her blood turned to ice.

"I thought it would be much more effective if you watched me kill them both," Raul announced to Brooks.

Rather than terrify her, that statement sparked her anger like a match to gasoline. No way would she allow Brooks to deal with that. She wasn't sure exactly what had made him withdraw from life, but she'd learned enough to realize it had to do with a mission gone wrong. Not only did she have no plans to die, but she refused to let her death and Eduardo's wind up on his conscience.

It was almost full dark now. Time had run out. If she planned to do something, she'd better get to it. With Eduardo's plaintive wail giving her purpose, she breathed another quick prayer for help and accuracy.

Knife clenched in her fist, Regina reared up from the ground, launching herself at Raul, knife aimed at his heart. She kept low and lunged, her gaze on him, watching his eyes to see what he'd do next.

He twisted right and made a grab for her arm. She feinted left and buried the knife in his midsection, recoiling instinctively at the howl that emanated from his throat. His feral roar sounded like a wounded animal, and every instinct screamed at her to retreat.

But she didn't. She grunted, struggling to stay with him as he jerked and tried to throw her off. Blood flowed from the wound, over their grasping hands. It smelled coppery, warm, and made her want to retch. But she didn't let go. She had to do this, had to keep the men she loved safe.

She loved them; loved them both.

The thought so shocked her that her attention wavered for the barest instant; then she forced everything from her mind.

Brooks had every cell focused on the writhing figures in front of him, locked in a macabre dance. Together they moved, one step forward, another back, but Regina still had her back to him. His gun hand shook as he followed their every move, the newly healed muscles in his forearm shrieking. He barely noticed, every muscle focused on finding his chance—just one—to get off a clear shot.

Come on, come on. He wanted to shout at Regina to duck, but feared his voice would distract her.

He inched to his left, trying to get between Raul and Eduardo, and at the same time, find an opening for a clear shot. Raul immediately noticed and swung Regina around to put her between them again.

He could see her tiring, but so was Raul. Brooks refused to think about how he'd gotten her into this predicament. He'd have plenty of time to deal with his guilt later. For now, he had to end this.

On soundless feet, he inched to the left again, and took careful aim.

Regina wondered how much longer this could go on, when suddenly, everything changed. While Raul fought her for the knife with one hand, he raised his gun with the other and she realized her mistake. She should have aimed for his gun hand, disarmed him. Too late.

She hung on and looked into Raul's eyes, resigned, waiting for the blast. At least she'd given Brooks time to get away and save Eduardo. Brooks would take care of the baby, she knew.

I'm sorry, Irene.

Brooks saw Raul's gun come up. Regina must have seen it too, for she tensed and moved just the slightest bit to the left. Perfect. Finally, the chance he'd been waiting for. *That's my girl, a little more. That's it.*

His finger slowly squeezed the trigger, eyes locked with Raul's. Brooks had one split second to wonder about the smug look on the other man's face before a shriek rent the night air above his head.

Brooks instinctively flicked his eyes upward. One glance told him the screech came from a huge tropical bird, diving right at his head.

In that instant, he knew he'd failed. Fire flashed from the muzzle of Raul's gun as he squeezed off his own shot.

The world went black.

Regina heard the shot, then another, and braced for the pain. Instead, she heard the sound of movement behind her and the thud of someone hitting the ground.

"NO!" she screamed, the sound echoing eerily through the trees. *He'd shot Brooks. Dear Father, he'd shot Brooks.*

Eduardo set up a terrified wail from somewhere behind her and propelled her into action. She couldn't check on Brooks, couldn't go to Eduardo, until she disarmed Raul. She'd been given another chance, and she wouldn't blow it.

Overconfident, Raul took his time raising the gun to her temple. Regina saw her chance and grabbed it. Using a maneuver Irene had taught her years ago, she brought her knee up into his groin with all the power she could muster. As he doubled over in instinctive reaction, she yanked the knife from his belly and brought it down into his right forearm. He screamed and dropped the gun.

When he collapsed on the ground, moaning in agony, Regina kicked the gun out of his reach and fell to her knees beside Brooks. *Don't let him be dead,* she prayed. *Please, Father, don't let him be dead.* Hope died within her as she took in his still features, the frozen cast to his face. Tears poured down her cheeks, momentarily blurring her vision.

She reached a shaking hand toward Brooks's neck to check for a pulse then yanked it back and scrubbed it down the front of her skirt. Her hand came away covered in blood. She looked down at herself and swayed dizzily. Blood smeared the front of her body. Raul's blood.

She had to calm down. Regina shot a glance over her shoulder to be sure the man hadn't moved, then touched Brooks's neck, searching for a pulse. She jumped at the feel of his skin. His body felt cold; too cold. *No, oh, no.* She couldn't find a pulse.

Frantic, she swiped at her tears with one hand, and pressed down on the side of his neck a bit harder with the other. She shook so hard it was no wonder she couldn't tell a thing.

Regina waited, heart pounding. *Please, please, please,* she pleaded. He had to be alive, he had to be. She leaned closer, but still couldn't find the telltale rhythm.

Memories of the night in her childhood when she'd found a drunk dead in her favorite dumpster raised gooseflesh on her skin. He'd been this cold and still, too.

Fierce denials poured from her lips as she groped both sides of his neck with shaking fingers, hoping, praying for some sign of life. But she found none.

She put her cheek by his mouth, desperate to feel his breath, but when she couldn't find that either, she started CPR, pumping his hard chest with everything she had. "Come on, come on," she muttered. She kept up the chest compressions until her arms gave out, but when she checked his vitals again, there was still nothing.

He was gone. Because of her stupidity, she'd cost this wonderful man his life. She should never have let Raul in, never have reached for her knife.

Sobbing, she fell across Brooks's prone form, hugging his broad chest, "I'm sorry. I'm sorry."

23

I'M SORRY. I'M SORRY."

Brooks fought his way back to consciousness, unsure whether the voice was his or someone else's. It must be his; who else had anything to be sorry for? Details floated just out of reach, but his failure shone clear as the night sky above the trees.

His chest felt like a boulder was crushing his lungs, but the need to apologize forced words from his throat. He had to tell her he was sorry. Was she close by? Could she hear him?

"I'm sorry, Reggie," he croaked.

He heard a gasp and then the weight on his chest shifted, sending waves of pain radiating all the way to his toes. He tried to open his eyes, but they wouldn't obey.

"You're alive," Regina cried.

He felt her hands cradle his head, felt droplets hit his face and wondered when it had started to rain. She babbled incoherently in Portuguese and then something smashed into his wounded side.

As his eyes rolled back in his head, he realized he'd been shot.

Regina could barely see for the tears of joy pouring down her face. *He was alive. Oh, thank you, Father, he isn't dead.* She cupped his beloved face between her palms and placed a gentle kiss on his lips.

When she shifted her weight to check his injuries, he slid back into unconsciousness. Looking down, Regina bit back a word she hadn't said in many a year. *Idiot*, she mumbled instead. She must have bumped his wound.

Scrambling to her knees, she peeled back his leather jacket. Her stomach roiled, but she ignored it. Blood welled from a wound in his side, but she'd treated street children in worse shape than this. *Think, girl. Now is not the time to fall apart.*

Ever mindful of Jair—no, Raul—she cast a worried look in his direction. He posed no threat at the moment. He lay still, eyes closed, hugging his knees. Farther into the woods, Regina heard Eduardo's fretful cries.

"I will be there in a moment, little one," she called, gratified when the baby lowered his volume to listen to the sound of her voice.

With deliberate calm, Regina called to Eduardo, making soothing noises and singing softly while her hands grappled with the hem of her skirt. She needed a bandage, fast. She tore off a wide strip, then another. She folded one piece and carefully placed it over Brooks's wound to staunch the flow of blood. Then she looked at her patient. She would need to tie the other strip around his middle to hold the bandage in place while she went after Eduardo.

Biting her lower lip, she gripped Brooks by the shoulders and tried to roll him onto his side. He weighed far more than she thought. Her shove had no effect other than to illicit a mumbled groan.

"Roll over, Brooks, please," she cajoled, leaning over to speak directly into his ear. She pushed again, stunned when he moaned and rolled onto his side. *Praise God,* he'd heard her. "That's it. Good."

She spread the strip of fabric on the ground and then gently rolled him back to his original position. Gathering up both ends of the fabric, she wrapped it snugly around his middle, using the ends to secure the makeshift bandage firmly in place. Then she buttoned his leather jacket all the way up. She hoped that would be enough to keep him from going into shock.

Before she headed for Eduardo, Regina brushed a gentle hand over Brooks's forehead, her panic returning at the sweat beading there. She leaned closer. He needed to be in a hospital. Now.

She scanned the clearing, torn. Where had Jax gone? Hadn't he come to help? Several grim pictures flashed into her mind, but she pushed them away. She had more important priorities.

Brooks labored for every breath. She didn't want to leave him, even for a minute, but Eduardo had resumed his crying in earnest. He was a defenseless baby, out in the jungle. She had to get to him.

With a last check on the still-unconscious Raul, she sprinted toward the sound of Eduardo's screams.

Brooks slowly opened his eyes and tried to focus. Everything faded in and out, like someone adjusting the lens on a camera. He had to think. He heard a moan and slowly turned his head, gritting his teeth against a wave of nausea. As the world gradually righted itself, he saw that Raul lay on the ground near him, curled up in the fetal position. But where was Regina?

He tried to sit up and a wave of dizziness sent him back down. Pain shot through his side, burning as though flames leaped under his skin. He propped himself on one elbow and looked down. Blood seeped from under the edge of his leather jacket.

Ignoring the way the ground seemed to tilt and whirl, Brooks searched the tree line, straining to hear Regina's voice, the kid's cry.

Finally, after what seemed an eternity, he heard it. Her soft crooning wafted over the lazy clattering of the leaves. She and the kid were okay. *Thank you, God.* The instinctive prayer shocked him, but he'd deal with that later. Right now they had to get out of here.

Brooks turned to his left, pain slicing through his right side. Eyes closed and jaw clamped tight, he rode out the wave. He had almost reached the other side when movement near him snapped his eyes open. Still sweating, he focused on the clearing and froze.

Raul inched his way toward his gun, one hand stretching as far as he could, the other cradling his middle.

Way to go, Reggie, Brooks thought.

He scrambled to his feet, but before he managed to get completely vertical, the world started rocking and he stumbled like a drunk aboard ship, listing to one side. He dropped to one knee before he fell face first in the dirt.

Eyes trained on Raul—both of him, since his vision was decidedly blurry—Brooks crawled over to the gun, scuttling like a crab when Raul realized his intention and made a lunge in that direction.

"Not on your life, pal," Brooks grunted.

By the time he reached the weapon, Raul's fingertips just barely touched the barrel. One more little scoot and he'd have it in hand. Brooks lunged, landing with his knee on Raul's forearm, effectively breaking his grip. His arm, too, judging by the ominous snap and spate of curses streaming from the other man's lips.

Brooks squinted and shook his head to clear his vision. He tried to blend the two Rauls into one, but his mind wouldn't cooperate. He knew he had a concussion, and the timing couldn't have been worse.

Feeling his way between shifting images, Brooks scooped up the gun and then inched backward, out of Raul's reach. To steady his aim, he pulled his knee up and rested his gun hand on it. As far as he could tell, Raul hadn't moved, but had curled farther up into a ball and lay holding his injured arm close to his chest.

Brooks listened for Regina and Eduardo and heard nothing. Panic returned and he closed one eye, hoping that would help his vision.

"Regina?" he called. "Are you okay?"

No response.

He waited a beat. "You can come out now. I've got the gun and it's trained on Raul."

Still no response. Either she was in trouble or waiting to be sure this wasn't another setup. The first option didn't bear thinking about, so he assumed she was simply being cautious.

Brooks slowly pushed himself to his feet and stepped to the middle of the clearing, careful to keep the gun trained on Raul.

"Reggie, I need to know you're okay. I'm up, and I have the gun. If you're okay, let me know." He paused. "Otherwise, I'm coming after you."

He stood still and waited. His side throbbed, and he wondered how long before he dropped like a stone. Just as he began swaying, he heard a slight rustling to his left.

Brooks turned his head and saw Regina crawling out of the thick underbrush. His pulse rate kicked up another notch. Where was the kid?

He squinted and then realized she had tied Eduardo in front of her with her sweater, like a papoose. As soon as she gained her feet, Regina launched herself at him, skidding to a stop just short of smacking into him. He reached out his arms to stop her and braced himself. For a moment he didn't say a word and neither did she, both content to simply look at the other. His relief that she and Eduardo were all in one piece almost buckled his knees. But then her face came into focus and he saw the bruise purpling one side of it. His grip tightened and she flinched.

He loosened his hold and stepped back. "He hurt you," he growled, resentment burning the back of his throat.

"I'm okay. Now," she assured him.

His relief disappeared under a surge of temper like nothing he had ever felt. He wanted to strangle the idiot woman. Slowly. One centimeter at a time. With what he considered remarkable restraint, he shouted instead.

"You almost got yourself killed with that fool maneuver!" he shouted. "Give me that knife."

Her chin came up at that infuriating angle. "I helped you, in case you've forgotten. And I'm not giving you my blade."

Brooks' anger *whooshed* out of him and he yanked her into his arms, pain or no pain. "I thought I lost you," he murmured into her hair. "I thought I lost you." He held her until the panic eased enough to let her go.

Over her shoulder, he saw Raul lying on the ground scowling at them. Brooks realized his burst of anger had weakened him and the ability to stay upright slid from his grasp. He stumbled over to Raul and sank down opposite him, gun again propped on his knee.

Without taking his eyes from the other man he said, "Take off your belt, Raul. Nice and slow. One-handed."

"As if I could use both," the other man shot back.

Brooks merely raised one eyebrow. "Now."

Beside him, Regina said nothing, merely watched as Raul struggled to remove his belt with one hand, while lying on his side in the dirt.

When he finished, Brooks said, "Toss it over here. Gently."

Raul did, with obvious reluctance.

"Reggie, untie my boots and take the laces out," Brooks said.

Regina didn't comment, but he could see the question in her eyes as she bent over his legs. When she had them out, he addressed Raul. "Stand up, turn around, and put your hands behind your back."

Raul snorted, his expression malevolent. "This isn't over, Senhor. Not, as you Americanos say, 'by a long shot.'"

"Oh, I think it's pretty much over," Brooks responded casually, then barked, "Do as you're told."

As Raul struggled to his feet, Brooks rubbed a hand over his face, grateful the two Rauls had merged back into one, but concerned about the cold sweat beading his forehead. He needed to secure this lunatic and then get Reggie and the baby out of here before he collapsed. Adrenaline could only take him so far.

He risked a glance down and lifted the edge of his jacket. Reggie's makeshift bandage had slowed the flow of blood, but he still felt like someone had lit a campfire in his gullet and was roasting his flesh over a spit.

"Regina, put the baby down. Then take Raul's belt and wrap it around his wrists. As tight as you can make it." He saw Regina's gaze dart to Raul, and then drop to the arm that hung at an odd angle by his side. "It has to be done," Brooks added quietly, for her ears only.

She nodded once, unwrapped Eduardo from his makeshift carrier and set him down next to Brooks. Taking a deep breath, she marched over to Raul, belt in hand. Brooks admired her more at this moment than ever before. This woman looked fear in the eye and still did what had to be done.

"Raul, you make a single move I perceive as threatening to Regina, and you're a dead man."

The other man nodded once, but said nothing.

When Regina sent a frightened look over her shoulder, Brooks sent her an encouraging nod. She returned the nod and Brooks stood and moved closer to Raul, so that the barrel of the gun stopped less than two feet from the man's head.

"You even think about grabbing her, your brains will be splattered on the ground." Brooks saw Regina flinch at his choice of words, but he ignored her. He'd do it in a heartbeat.

Regina grabbed the man's uninjured hand in one of hers, then reached for the other. Raul moaned when Regina brought both his hands together behind his back and wrapped the belt around both wrists. Sweat poured off Raul's forehead and his breath came in quick pants.

Regina sent Brooks another beseeching look. He understood her unwillingness to inflict deliberate pain on another—even if the scum had tried to kill them—but sometimes it couldn't be helped.

Brooks eyed the belt, then met Regina's gaze. "Tighter."

She did, and Raul gasped. "For the love of God, man. Have mercy," he choked out.

There was still a gap between the belt and Raul's wrists he could slip a hand through if he worked hard enough. Brooks couldn't take that chance.

"I'll leave the mercy to God." To Regina he said, "Tighter. Make sure there's no way he can slide his hand out."

With gritted teeth, she did as he asked. Just as she tied off the ends, Raul gave one last gasp and melted to the ground in a boneless heap. Regina reached to catch him as he fell, but Brooks yanked her back and out of Raul's reach.

"Why did you do that?" she demanded.

"Might have been a trick to grab you."

She looked at the unconscious man on the ground, then planted her hands on her hips. "Grab me with what? His nose?"

Brooks led her back to where Eduardo lay on the ground, investigating his toes. With one hand still on her arm, Brooks looked her right in the eye. "No. With his feet."

Annoyance radiated off her in waves, but he didn't care. "I'm not taking any chances."

He opened his mouth to tell her to tie Raul's feet with his shoelaces when a familiar birdcall pierced the silence between them. Brooks listened for a moment, then returned the call with one of his own. Seconds later, Jax strolled into the clearing, limping slightly.

Brooks abruptly released Regina and turned toward his friend. "Where have you been?"

Jax sent him a sheepish look and pulled a clump of leaves from his blond hair. "Got caught in the spider's web, so to speak." He angled his chin toward Raul.

Brooks eyes widened a fraction. This was not like Jax. "What kind of web?"

Jax's ears reddened. "Net. Very simple trap any new recruit would have spotted."

"So how'd you get caught?"

"This really pretty macaw flew overhead, and just at the second I looked up, I stepped into it. Took me all this time to cut myself down." He turned his attention to Raul. "How is he?"

"Unconscious, for now. I need to get Regina and the kid out of here."

Jax turned back and studied him. "You look like you've been keelhauled."

"Bullet. Side. It'll be okay." Even as he spoke, telltale spots started dancing across his field of vision.

Jax summed up the situation and took charge, for which Brooks would forever be grateful—though he'd bite off his tongue before he said so.

"Let me finish tying up this carcass and then we'll go," Jax said, bending to tie Raul's feet securely with the shoelaces. Then he examined the knife wound in the man's side and tore a strip from his shirt for a temporary bandage, much like the one Regina had wrapped around Brooks.

While Jax tended to Raul, Brooks gingerly lowered himself to the ground, resuming his position as guard. He shook his head several times to keep his vision clear. Beside him, Regina folded Eduardo back into her sweater and tied him snuggly across her chest, eyeing him all the while.

After Raul had been secured, Jax turned to Regina. "You all set?" At her nod, he eyed Brooks. "Can you walk out, or do I need to carry you?"

Brooks heard the challenge in the words and responded as his friend knew he would. "I'll walk," he ground out, levering himself up like an arthritic old man.

Jax checked Raul's bonds one last time, then swung Brooks's good arm over his shoulder and reached around his waist with the other. Brooks locked his jaw against the pain and then blocked it from his mind. One foot in front of the other. Nothing else. Just one foot in front of the other.

24

REGINA HURRIED THROUGH THE JUNGLE BEHIND THE TWO MEN, CROONing softly to an increasingly restless Eduardo. Anything to keep her mind off the way Brooks leaned more heavily on his friend with every step. She knew if he didn't lie down soon, he would fall down. Jax must have sensed the same urgency, for he suddenly stepped up his pace, half-carrying Brooks by the time they reached the asphalt path leading to the Hotel Cataratas.

Thankfully, he'd parked in the hotel lot. He tossed Brooks into the back seat of the car so quickly, the other man groaned.

"Have a care, Senhor," she snapped as she climbed in beside Brooks. She twisted sideways so that Eduardo remained strapped to her chest and Brooks's head lay in her lap.

Her words didn't seem to faze the other man. He simply climbed behind the wheel and cranked the engine.

"That wound needs checking," Jax said. "And I need to get our friend out of the woods before some well-meaning park ranger finds him and sets him free."

Jax roared out of the parking lot and raced down the gravel road leading to the national park's exit. Brooks muttered softly, and Regina smoothed the hair from his brow, murmuring the same soothing nonsense to him that she did to Eduardo when he fussed. She couldn't have told anyone what she said, but the tone of her voice had the desired effect. Both her charges dozed as Jax sped through the crowded streets searching for a hotel off the beaten path.

Fifteen minutes later, he pulled up to a nondescript two-story older hotel. It looked clean, though unpretentious. Regina glanced at the neighborhood. Not the best, but the bars on the windows were a good sign. At least they wouldn't have any unexpected company.

Jax left the engine running and returned minutes later with a room key in hand. He drove around to the back of the building, parked, and moved to help Brooks out of the car.

"Let's go, my man. We're here."

"Where's here?" Brooks asked groggily.

Jax gave him a minute to get his legs under him, then wrapped his arm around his shoulder again. "Hotel. You're upstairs. Can you make it?"

Brooks eyed the rickety stairs and took a determined step forward.

Regina brought up the rear, casting worried glances over her shoulder and keeping one hand out in case Brooks fell backward. Without laces, his boots slid on his feet and made walking that much more difficult.

It seemed to take forever, but they finally made it up the stairs and into the last door at the end of the corridor. The room's damp, musty smell confirmed that it had not been used in quite a while. In the feeble glow of an overhead bulb, Regina eyed it askance. At least it had a bed, even though it sported a mighty sag in the middle. The bath fixtures were old and rusted, but it still beat an outhouse. She'd need running water.

Jax helped Brooks sit on the edge of the bed, and then turned to go.

Regina blocked his path. "I need you to pick up a few things right away."

Jax tried to move past her. "I have to get back to the woods. Anything you need, dollface, I'll be happy to give you when I get back."

The insinuation behind the words made Regina blanch. Before she'd come up with a suitable retort, Brooks bit out, "Do as she says."

Jax immediately held his hands up, palms out in a gesture of surrender. "Hey, it was just a joke." He tried to leave, and again, Regina stepped into his path. Knowing Brooks supported her gave her courage she might otherwise not have had.

She lifted her chin. "I saw a small market at the corner. I need formula—milk at the very least—a baby bottle, diapers, wipes, some whiskey, cheese, and sugar." She waited a beat. "Do you need to write it down?"

Jax glanced at the bed where Brooks sat, then back at Regina. "I'll be back in a few minutes."

Regina merely nodded and bent to unbutton Brooks' leather jacket, but Eduardo got in the way. She grabbed a wool blanket and quickly made him a bed on the floor.

Turning back to Brooks, she saw that he had stretched out on the bed and lay with his eyes closed. Careful of the sagging mattress, Regina sat on the edge and pulled his jacket aside. His eyes opened, and she paused to look at him, unsure what he was thinking.

"How bad is it?" he asked.

"I'm not sure yet." Carefully, she pulled his black T-shirt farther out of the way, ignoring the way that muscular chest did funny things to her insides. She checked his bandage, relieved to find very little fresh blood. Her pressure bandage seemed to have helped. "I don't want to tear open the wound again, but unless I uncover it, I can't tell how bad it is."

"Did the bullet go through?"

Regina could have kicked herself. With all the confusion, she'd never even considered that it might still be lodged inside him. She should have, though. This was basic stuff.

Brooks must have sensed her frustration. "It's okay. If I roll onto my side, you can check for an exit wound." He did just that, sucking air between his teeth as he shifted his weight.

Regina lifted his shirt and gasped. Blood covered his back. Before her panic ran away with her, she realized the blood was dry.

She ran her hand down his back, but still couldn't tell if the bullet had gone through, so she closed her eyes and used her sense of touch, instead. His skin felt hot under her fingers, and she worried that he'd started a fever.

Inch by inch, she checked his back and side, finally coming to an area just above his hipbone. When he flinched, Regina's eyes flew open. She leaned closer, frustrated by the lack of light. Yes, there it was, a jagged hole where the bullet had gone out. Blood welled steadily. She looked around for something to stop it, and finally tore another strip from her skirt.

"Did you find it?" Brooks demanded.

Regina clamped down on her worry. "Yes. Stay like that so I can get the rest of you cleaned up. It's hard to see what's going on." She hurried to the bathroom and wet a dingy once-white towel, carefully wringing it out.

Then she sat beside him again and gently but quickly washed the area around the wound. She had to hurry. She put one hand on his smooth flesh and jumped when he sucked in a quick breath. "I'm sorry," she said, instantly contrite.

"It's okay. Keep going."

Regina used careful, efficient strokes, studying his back as she did. He really had a very nice build, from a purely clinical standpoint. No extra fat collecting around his middle, just lots of smooth skin and sleek muscles. Sort of like a cat, only without fur. She smiled, picturing his reaction if she compared him to a pussycat. No, a gray-eyed wolf maybe, but never something as common as a house cat.

She had almost finished when Jax burst through the door, a sack in each hand. He thumped the bags down on the scarred dresser.

"Did you get everything?"

"Yes. I'm going back for our package." At the doorway he paused, hand on the knob. "You okay here?"

Regina didn't look up. "I'll be fine. Thank you."

"You know how to doctor a gunshot?"

This time she did look up with a grimace. "Actually, yes."

She saw a smidgeon of respect in his expression. "I gotta ask, though," he said. "What's with the sugar?"

"Helps with clotting and to prevent infection."

Jax nodded briefly. "Take good care of him," he said, and left.

Regina turned back to her task with determination. She gathered up all the towels in the bathroom, then used the minuscule bar of soap to scrub out the small plastic trashcan. She'd need that to hold water. After she'd washed it out, she poured a bit of the whiskey into it, sloshed it around, and poured it out. As a disinfectant, it would have to do.

She returned to the bed with her supplies and finished washing the area around the exit wound. Brooks seemed to be hovering somewhere between sleep and unconsciousness. "Brooks," she said quietly. When he didn't respond, she laid a hand on his shoulder. "Brooks, wake up. I'm sorry."

Still on his side, he mumbled and then opened his eyes to look over his shoulder.

"I have to disinfect the wound, but I wanted to give you fair warning."

He eyed the liquor bottle in her hand and gave a curt nod.

"Would you like a swig first?"

He shook his head, no.

"I'll be as quick as I can, but it has to be done. We don't want—"

"Just get it over with," he ground out.

"Right. Okay." She held a dry towel below the wound to catch the liquid, and then slowly poured a generous amount of whiskey into the wound.

Brooks' whole body tensed and his breathing came in short pants, but he didn't make a sound. "Again," he said.

She complied, then waited, holding the towel against his side, while whiskey and blood poured out of the wound. She wanted it to bleed some; that would help cleanse it. But too much wasn't good. She watched, totally still, to see if the bleeding slowed. Brooks face turned ashen and drops of sweat beaded his brow. She blotted them away, then returned her attention to his side.

Still too much blood.

She would need Olga's remedy. In her years at the orphanage, she and the housekeeper had doctored many a gunshot or knife wound. When the bleeding wouldn't stop, Olga had taught her to pour granulated sugar into the wound. It helped the blood clot and, amazingly, acted as a sort of antibiotic at the same time. Beat anything she'd learned during her nurse's training.

Once that was done, she ripped a pillowcase into a bandage and guided Brooks's hand over it to hold it in place. "Keep the pressure on here, while I take care of the entry wound." She paused. "You'll have to roll over, though."

He eased over onto his back, muttering unintelligible words the whole way. She saw the pain glazing his gray eyes and worked faster. Pour in the whiskey. Wait while he caught his breath. Do it again. Let it bleed for a few minutes. Check the bleeding.

Still too much. Pour on more sugar. Wrap it in clean bandages. Then wrap a piece of the sheet around his middle to hold both bandages in place.

By the time she finished, Regina's hands were shaking. She hated to inflict hurt on anyone, even when it was necessary. Thankfully, Brooks had dozed during some of it. Equally amazing, Eduardo had not needed her attention.

As she quietly collected blood-soaked towels, his voice broke the silence, startling her. "You don't like Jax."

Regina looked up to find his eyes boring into hers. She looked away. "He just makes me uncomfortable, that's all."

"Why?"

What to say? She shrugged. "He just does."

"Did he make a pass at you?"

"They always do." Suddenly, she was tired, so very tired. She had no idea of the time, but she was utterly drained. As soon as she cleaned up, she'd feed and change the baby and then collapse.

She eased off the bed, but his hand stopped her. "You're not like that," he insisted.

At first, she didn't know what he meant. But then understanding dawned, and with it, more tears flooded her eyes. No one but those associated with House of Angels had ever treated her as though that was true. Most assumed she deserved whatever she got. And then some. That Brooks would worry about her at a time like this both humbled and flustered her. Embarrassed by her tears, she wiped them away and chalked the whole thing up to complete exhaustion.

She looked back at Brooks and saw that he'd fallen asleep. Even now, his jaw clamped tight, he looked ready to leap from the bed, completely awake at a moment's notice. He hadn't let go of protective warrior mode, even though the danger had passed.

Eduardo stirred quietly, so she rinsed the towels, washed her hands and poured him a bottle of milk. Sitting in the room's one rickety chair, she cradled the baby close, stroking his sweet-smelling head, caressing his soft cheeks.

Tomorrow she'd have to give him up.

The realization hit like an unexpected blow, the pain burning like fire. She wasn't ready. In truth, she'd never be ready. She'd touched Irene's belly and felt him move even before he was born, and she'd been there when he drew his very first breath. She'd held him when Irene died. How could she send him away to strangers who didn't know that he loved to have his tummy tickled, or know his favorite lullaby?

But she'd promised Irene. Carol had said she'd found a wonderful couple anxious to love him and give him a place within their family. She couldn't deny him that.

How would she let him go?

Carol had often admonished Regina with a quote from her father: what cannot be changed, must be endured. This was such a time. *Father, help me. I can't do this.*

As the moon slowly tracked across the sky and traffic in the street below thinned, Regina created more memories to cherish of this tiny, precious link to her best friend. She cradled Eduardo close to her heart and softly sang all his favorite lullabies, oblivious of the tears pouring down her cheeks.

A soft sound woke him. Brooks's senses sprang to attention, though he didn't open his eyes. He took inventory of his surroundings first, listening for whatever had awakened him. When he heard the soft singing, he relaxed. It was Regina, humming to the kid. Eduardo. His half brother. Maybe.

He moved slightly and white-hot pain flashed up his side, searing him with its heat. Teeth clamped together, he breathed through his nose until it receded. The events of the night flooded back. He opened his eyes, seeking Regina in the dimness.

His vision had cleared, he noted with relief. She sat in a straight-backed chair, holding the baby close. Light from the street pierced the crack in the drapes and reflected off the tears tracking down her cheeks. "Come to bed," he said into the stillness.

Her head snapped up. "Brooks? Are you okay?" She hurried over to the bed and reached out to touch his forehead. "No fever." He couldn't miss the relief in her voice. "How about some water?"

After he'd swallowed some, along with a hunk of now-warm cheese, he said again, "Come to bed."

When she hesitated, he inched over to the nightstand and grabbed his gun. She froze when he turned toward her holding it, so he flipped it around, butt first. "Here. You hold the gun. And your switchblade. That way, if I ever act stupid again, you can shoot me."

Regina made a shooing motion toward the gun with her hand, a smile on her lips. "You keep the gun. I'll be fine with my knife."

The tension inside him eased. "Put the boy down and come lie down. You can't spend the night in that chair."

She bit her lip. "I don't want to hurt you," she whispered.

"Just come to bed, Reggie."

Her hesitation annoyed him. He wanted her next to him, needed the reassurance of her presence.

And not just tonight. Every night.

He stiffened in surprise at the unwelcome thought, denial flooding him. Instead, he pretended to be asleep and waited.

The way the bed sagged in the middle would definitely work in his favor.

When nothing happened after several minutes, he opened one eye and ground his teeth. She clung to the edge of the bed like a limpet to keep from rolling toward him.

He raised his head off the pillow and held out his good arm. "I need you. Please. Come here."

The surprise in her eyes matched his own. He never begged. Not for anything. But with this woman, he seemed to do all sorts of things he didn't usually do.

One eye on his wound, she inched toward him. When she was within reach, he settled her in the crook of his arm, her head on his chest. She hadn't stopped crying, for her tears immediately soaked his shirt. His male ego would love to think she cried over him, but he'd been shot in the side, not the head. She knew as well as he did that tomorrow he'd be leaving with the boy. They'd caught Raul. The time had come to take Eduardo to his new family.

She needed comfort tonight. It was the least he could do after all she'd done for him.

"How's your head?" she asked quietly, carefully touching the bump.

The question jerked him back to the moment he burst into the clearing and saw her crumpled on the hard ground. He bit out the words. "It's fine. Don't worry about it."

That should never have happened. Never. It was a miracle she wasn't dead. It sure wasn't because of anything he'd done to prevent it.

Defeat hammered him, dragged him down, until he almost pulled away from her. She deserved better, far better than a man like him. But he was the only warm body around tonight, and she needed arms around her like a plant needs sunshine.

He could give her that much, at least. Even if it was only temporary.

Brooks tenderly brushed the tears from her cheeks with his palm. "I let you down today," he admitted quietly. "I'm sorry."

She tensed and he berated himself for saying too much. Should have held her close and kept his trap shut.

"What?" Regina raised her head to get a better look at his face. She took in his expression and snorted. "No, you didn't let me down. You saved my life. And Eduardo's. God took care of all of us today."

His grip tightened as he thought of his own stupidity. But his code demanded honesty. "I should never have let you leave."

"And I should never have opened the door to Raul."

"You had no way of knowing he was behind this."

Her brown eyes gleamed with triumph. "And neither had you."

"I should have. It's my job to consider every possibility."

She twisted around as though looking behind him.

"What?"

Regina shook her head sadly. "No wings. The way you were talking, I thought maybe you were God—who knows everything. Or, at the very least, an angel. But you're not. You did your best today. That's all God requires of us."

"Sometimes, that's not enough," he growled. "If we don't do it right, innocent people die."

She didn't say anything for several minutes. "What happened to make you quit the Rangers?"

Brooks hesitated, but finally told her the whole story. "Ultimately, Ambassador Simms didn't give a rat's behind that we had tried to save his wife and child. The end result was still the same: they died. And it was my fault. I still don't know who set us up, but I'm going to find out."

Regina cocked her head to one side. "What if you don't find the answers?"

"I won't stop until I do. I have to know."

When Regina lapsed into silence, Brooks thought she'd finally fallen asleep.

"If I'd only suspected—" Regina began reflectively.

A laugh burst from his throat, and he held her tighter. "No wings on your back either, so let it go."

"You look good when you laugh. Less threatening," she said.

His smile vanished like it had never been. "Will you forgive me for yesterday? I never meant to hurt you."

The resigned look she sent him broke his heart. "I know you didn't. But it is the nature of things between men and women."

Brooks had no idea what to say, because she was right. At least partially. Even though he had no choice, he was going to rip her heart out when he left with Eduardo in the morning. Instead, he coaxed her head back onto his shoulder, and brushed the hair back from her face, loving the way it curled around his fingers.

"How come you've never married? You're wonderful with Eduardo, a natural mother."

She stiffened, and he feared he'd wandered too far into dangerous territory. But he wanted to know.

"Besides the fact that nobody wants to marry a former prostitute who doesn't like to be touched?"

He traced a hand down her arm. "Yeah, besides that. And you seem to be getting over the touching part." Brooks sensed her indecision. "You don't have to answer," he added.

She finally met his gaze, a world of sadness and regret in her eyes. "I can't have children. That wouldn't be fair to a man, even if I found one who wanted me."

"Because of your childhood?" he asked.

Regina nodded and moved closer, biting her lip before she answered. "I was raped when I was fourteen," she began, and he stiffened.

"I became pregnant and after the shock wore off, I fell in love with that unborn baby. I had a focus, a reason to live. But something went wrong, and I started bleeding. Noah took me to House of Angels, but while he tried to save my baby, a man came in and attacked him." She swallowed hard. "The man attacked me, too, and killed my baby. Surgery saved my life, but I'll never have any more children."

"I'm sorry, Reggie." His arms tightened around her and he kissed the top of her head, offering what comfort he could. "It shouldn't matter, you know. If the man loves you, it won't. Besides, there's always adoption."

She nodded, but he felt fresh tears soaking his shirt. "Go to sleep. Tomorrow will be another long day."

Eduardo snuffled in his sleep, but other than that, the room was quiet.

"Will you tell me what happened between you and Noah?" she asked.

"You should sleep."

"Is that your way of saying you won't answer my question?" she probed.

"I couldn't forgive him," he finally said.

"Noah?"

"After I got that photo from Raul on my eighteenth birthday, I left home and joined the Army. I haven't spoken to him since."

"That's a long time to carry a grudge."

"He treated my Mom lousy."

"But she loved you."

"No question. And I love her."

"You have to let it go, Brooks. Some things we won't ever understand, but we have to forgive."

He shifted so he could see her face. "Have you forgiven the man who raped you? The one who killed your baby?"

Her gaze was steady but sad. "The bitterness and uncleanness tries to creep back in sometimes, but I'm learning to push it back. God knows what he's doing, even when I don't."

Brooks rubbed her back and eased her head back on his shoulder. His mind was fuzzy with pain and too many thoughts. It was time to sleep. They fell silent, the weight of shared confidences draining them both.

The first fingers of dawn were poking between the drapes when Regina asked, "You'll make sure they're good people, the ones adopting Eduardo? Not that I'm doubting your parents, of course," she added hastily.

He cupped her cheek and looked into her eyes. "I'll make sure. I promise." As if it was the most natural thing in the world, he leaned forward and kissed her tenderly.

She didn't pull back, but leaned into the kiss. She tasted so sweet, sweeter than sugar, with a flavor uniquely her own.

If only the circumstances were different . . . if only *he* were different.

Deliberately, he pushed everything from his mind except the woman in his arms. The pain in his side, he'd worry about later. The coming good-bye could wait. Right now, he had one chance to cherish this woman, and he wasn't going to blow it.

"Kiss me back," he whispered.

Time spun out as she slowly, gradually, inched closer. First one hand began stroking his hair, then his face. After a heart-stopping while, the other cupped the back of his neck. He was humbled, thrilled. And determined to keep himself in check if it killed him. He wouldn't blow it again.

It was the only thing he could give her—a good memory to hold on to. And selfishly, he wanted the same for himself—the memory of holding the most amazing woman he'd ever met. That she cared for him was humbling, thawing the ice around his heart. That she trusted him enough to show him how much amazed him. He cradled her close and soaked up all the warmth and affection she offered, hoarding it against the cold days ahead.

Suddenly Eduardo let loose a terrific wail. The sound pierced the quiet with the suddenness of an air raid siren. Regina instantly pulled away, but he brought her back to steal one more quick kiss.

"One for the road," he quipped, but it fell flat. They were leaving soon. Too soon.

Without a word, Regina got up and tended to the baby. She had him fed and diapered when a knock sounded on the door.

"It's me. Open up."

Regina looked to Brooks, who picked up his gun before nodding for her to open the door. He recognized Jax's voice, but he wasn't taking any chances.

"What happened?" he asked, as soon as Jax strolled into the room, toting what looked like a bakery sack. "Everything taken care of?"

Jax met his direct look. "Everything's under control." Brooks knew Jax was trying to keep the ugly truth from Regina. *Under control* meant the uncle he'd never known was dead.

Jax turned to Regina and asked, "How about some breakfast?" He set out coffee, rolls and jam, then turned to Brooks. "You look a sight better than you did last night. Let's see." He examined both wounds, ignoring Brooks's hissing breath. "You did a good job," he said to Regina, though his tone sounded grudging.

She responded with a nod.

Brooks searched his friend's face, looking for any clues that he'd tried to hurt her before, done more than issue the same invitation he offered every female on the planet. He saw nothing beyond Jax's usual happy-go-lucky grin.

"I found a doctor last night and persuaded him to give me a few antibiotics." He reached into his pocket and pulled out a handful of pills. "Should keep you covered until we get Stateside. We can catch a flight out later today."

"Jax, would you take me to the airport this morning?" Regina asked.

Brooks snapped his head in her direction, but she wouldn't look at him.

"I need to get back to the orphanage. The children need me."

"Sure. No problem. Soon as you're done with breakfast, grab your things and we'll go. The kid should be fine with this big lug until I get back."

"Eduardo." Both Brooks and Regina said together.

Jax's confused glance bounced back and forth between the two of them.

"His name is Eduardo," Brooks said.

"Right. Whatever. We'll go as soon as you're ready."

Regina quickly gathered her things, and Brooks watched her trying to hide her tears. He looked up at his friend. "Give us a minute, would you?"

Jax nodded once and then walked out of the room.

"I'd walk you out, but that's a bit tough today."

"It's okay." She kept her back to him, holding Eduardo close.

"Reggie. Come here."

"I have to go."

"I know. But come here." He patted the empty side of the bed.

She perched on the edge, her face buried in Eduardo's neck, sobs muffling her voice until he had to strain to make out the words. "I don't know how to say good-bye to him. I don't know how to let go."

He reached his arm out as far as it would go and brushed his fingers down that awful sweater. "I'll make sure they're a good family. If they're not, I won't let him stay there. I promise."

She nodded and sniffed.

"You'll never forget him, but someday you'll adopt a slew of your own." If anyone deserved to be a mother, it was Reggie. She had more love to give than anyone except maybe his own mother. And that was saying something.

She shook her head sadly and straightened Eduardo's little jumpsuit. "Thanks, but women like me don't get to be mothers. I'm lucky enough to be a guardian angel to the precious little ones God sends our way."

"Bull." He shifted closer to her and winced as pain momentarily cut off his breath. He couldn't let her leave thinking that way. "You'll be a mother," he insisted. "And a wonderful wife to a very lucky man."

She snorted. "You must have hit your head harder than we thought. Nice men don't marry women like me. As soon as they find out my past, all they see is how many men I've been with."

"That's not what I see."

She raised a skeptical brow. "No?"

All those men had crossed his mind, but not in the way she thought. He reached out and cupped her face. "When I look at you, I see a warm, caring, beautiful woman—inside and out—who has so much to give a man."

There went that stubborn chin again. "But I'm not the kind you'd want as a wife."

He was struck dumb. Marry her? Dear God. What to say? He'd be lying if he said the thought had never crossed his mind, because it had. But it could never work. False hope was a pain all its own, and he desperately didn't want to hurt her. She'd had enough of that to last a lifetime. Several lifetimes.

"With the kind of work I do, I'll never get married. I'd never ask a woman to wait and wonder if I'm coming back in a flag-draped coffin. That's not fair. I decided that long before I ever met you, Reggie. It has nothing to do with you."

"I thought you quit."

He hesitated. "I did. But I'll probably go back. It's all I know."

She stood up, her back to him. "Of course. I see."

"Don't leave like this."

She turned back to him, puzzlement momentarily overshadowing the pain in her eyes.

"Kiss me." He couldn't let her leave thinking any of this was her fault.

"I don't think that's a good idea."

He sent her a lopsided grin. "You're probably right. But do it anyway." It was the only way he knew to tell her what he felt.

She resumed her seat at the edge of the bed.

"Put the baby down and come here."

Hands twisted in her lap, she slowly leaned toward him. But this time, her shyness fled and her hands crept up to cup his cheeks. Their mouths met like they'd been doing this their whole lives. Like they belonged together, a perfect fit.

Right then, he wanted to beg her to stay with him. Forever. They'd find a way to make it work. But before the words rushed out past rational thought, he swallowed them and focused on the present.

It took him a minute to realize her tears had begun again. “Shh, don’t cry. It’s okay.” He shoved his own impossible longings aside and brushed at her tears.

She buried her face against his neck and placed a soft kiss there. Then, before he could react or respond, she whispered, “I love you,” tore from his grasp, and bent to kiss Eduardo’s forehead.

“Please tell me wh-when you get him settled with his new family.”

With her hand on the doorknob, back to him, she said, “Thank you for everything. For Irene and me, thank you for helping me keep Eduardo safe.”

Then she was gone.

25

REGINA CLOSED THE DOOR FIRMLY BEHIND HER AND SLUMPED AGAINST IT, dropping her bag at her feet. Inside, she could hear Eduardo begin to fuss, then Brooks's deep voice soothing him. Fresh tears poured down her cheeks. She'd never cried so much, and if she kept this up, she'd likely drown. *What cannot be changed; must be endured,* she reminded herself again. Using the sleeve of her sweater, she wiped her eyes, then grabbed her bag and marched down the stairs, head high.

The threat of Raul was gone. Eduardo was safe and would be on his way to his new home in the United States before nightfall. She'd kept her promise to Irene. She could go back to House of Angels where she belonged and give her love to the other children who needed her. *Oh, Father.*

Had she remembered to tell Brooks about the baby's favorite sleeper? She turned, ready to head back upstairs, then stopped. She had to stop stalling. Hadn't the man saved her life? Eduardo would be fine.

Jax lounged against the side of the car, smoking a cigarette. "Ready?" he asked, then flicked the cigarette into some bushes.

Regina nodded and climbed into the car, careful to stay as far away from him as possible. Friend of Brooks or not, she couldn't relax around him. She stared unseeing out of the window as the buildings flashed by, her mind numb with grief.

Her arms ached to hold Eduardo close once more, and every fiber of her being wanted to curl up next to Brooks, just for a little while. How ironic that the one man who had finally gotten past her defenses had no room in his life for a woman.

Or maybe, he simply didn't want her, but was too much of a gentleman to say so. He wouldn't be the first person repelled by her past. And she couldn't really blame him. Her past nauseated her, too, when she allowed herself to think about it.

Though your sins be as scarlet, they shall be as white as wool.

The verse learned long ago filtered through her mind, and Regina wiped her tears. *For Brooks, I wish I could have been clean and pure, a woman without a past.* She knew he cared for her. Maybe if she'd been a different kind of woman, he would have allowed himself to love her.

She brushed the futile thought away and looked up, startled to realize they were in a heavily forested area. When had they left the main road? Apprehension gnawed in her belly. She looked around, but there was no airport in sight. "Where are we?"

"Almost there."

She forced herself to look at him. "Where's there?"

He reached a hand out and wrapped it around the back of her neck. "I thought you and I should take a little time to get better acquainted before your flight."

Panic rose in her throat and sweat popped out all over her body. She tried to keep her voice steady. "I have a plane to catch."

"It's not for a while yet. I checked. There's plenty of time." He ran a hand over her cheek and she jerked away. "Figured you could give me a little taste of what you've been giving ole Brooks all this time."

Regina's revulsion congealed into terror as the truth dawned. She watched in growing horror as his casual good-ole-boy demeanor slid away like the mask it was. This man was no friend of Brooks. Did Brooks know what kind of man Jax really was? She didn't think so.

Jax pulled the car to a stop in front of a dilapidated cabin. "Get out," he ordered.

Regina slowly climbed out of the car and faced him across the roof. "Brooks will kill you when he finds out," she said. That much she knew. He might not love her, but he'd protect her.

Jax threw back his head and laughed. "Kill me? No, I don't think so. I think he'll buy me a beer, and we'll talk about what we each liked best."

Too late, she realized her mistake. This man was capable of anything, but she knew Brooks. The man she'd fallen in love with would never force a woman. She had to keep that in mind. Jax lied. Mentally steeling herself, she got out of the car. She could get through this. A quick check assured her that her knife was safely in her skirt pocket.

But some sixth sense screamed to be heard. Something wasn't right about this whole situation. She was suddenly afraid she was never supposed to leave this place. Heart pounding, she forced herself to put one foot in front of the other and deal with whatever came. Brooks and Eduardo were safe. Nothing else mattered. *God, help me.*

He shoved her up the rickety stairs ahead of him and once they were in the one-room shack, he turned and shoved a chair under the doorknob at his back.

"Let's get a move on."

Regina eyed the dirty floor, littered with dead cockroaches and animal droppings. She sent him a haughty look. "This place is filthy."

Jax looked around the bare room. The only furniture was a sagging bed with a straw mattress, one chair, and a table that listed heavily to one side.

"It'll do, doll, for what I have in mind."

Head high, Regina stood in the middle of the room and glared at him.

He stepped closer and she shrank back when he ran a blunt-tipped finger down her cheek. "Take off your clothes."

Regina swallowed hard to keep from throwing up on his shoes. She couldn't do this. Never again. *You're a beautiful woman, Reggie,* she heard Brooks say. *You deserve better.*

Heart pounding, she lunged for the door. Jax spun her around, hard, and she cried out.

"Where do you think you're going?" he snarled.

"I am not doing this. If Brooks is really your friend, you won't do this. Take me to the airport and we'll forget this ever happened."

He shoved her back against the wall and laughed in her face. "That's rich. The whore is going to tell me no? Not a chance, doll." He leaned closer. "But in case this still isn't enough to convince you, let me put it this way. Either you cooperate, or your precious lover boy and the brat won't live to make their plane."

A scream lodged in the back of Regina's throat, but she refused to give it voice. Not Brooks and Eduardo. One look at Jax's face and she knew he wasn't bluffing. He would do exactly what he said he would. She nodded, once.

His grin was pure evil. "I thought you'd see things my way. Now, get those clothes off."

She shrugged and tried to act like she did this sort of thing every day. *Please, God. Help me through this.* Ensuring Brooks and Eduardo's safety would be her last gift to those two men she loved. She wouldn't let them down. Slowly, she bent and untied one shoe, then the other. She slid them off, then rolled her socks down before slipping them off as well.

Even though revulsion coiled in her gut, her mind raced. How could she keep her knife nearby if she was naked?

"Hurry it up. I haven't got all day," he hissed.

Regina straightened and deliberately moved closer to him. If she dropped her skirt near the bed, she might have a chance. It was the best she could come up with. His hot breath on her face threatened to gag her, but she forced all emotions away.

Right now she had to think clearly. Eduardo and Brooks were the only ones who mattered. Somehow, she'd get to her knife, but if she couldn't . . . she swallowed hard. She'd done this before; she could do it again. For Brooks and the baby.

Slowly, she reached for the buttons on her blouse and prayed her hands wouldn't shake. She undid first one button, then the next, making sure she had his complete attention.

Apparently, his impatience got the better of him because he snatched the fabric from her hands and ripped it all the way open.

Instead of fighting him, she worked her hand slowly into the pocket of her skirt. As soon as her hand closed over the knife, she forced a moan from her throat to cover the sound of it flicking open. She ignored Jax's fetid breath and grasping hands, only one goal in mind: getting away and back to Brooks to warn him.

When he pushed up against her, Regina seized her opportunity. Her hand shot from the pocket and she made a lunge for his back. He must have been more aware than she gave him credit for, because his big fist shot out and deflected the blade, so the knife merely grazed his shoulder.

A vicious curse hissed from his throat.

Wrenching free of his grasp, she whirled away. She could make it. She had to. She yanked the chair out from under the knob. Her fingers had just touched the rough wood of the door when Jax grabbed her from behind.

Hand in her hair, he muttered, "Guess we'll do this the hard way."

Regina fought with everything she had, knowing that if she didn't get away, Brooks and Eduardo were dead. She couldn't fail them. She kicked backward and heard Jax yelp. She fumbled for the doorknob as Jax's beefy arm came around her neck. Without thought, she bit him as hard as she could.

She only had seconds to savor his furious roar. Before she could form another thought, another plan, everything went completely black.

I love you.

Brooks tried to find a comfortable spot on the lumpy mattress and replayed her whispered words over and over in his mind. She loved him. The thought was astounding. Amazing. Humbling.

So how did he feel about her? He didn't even want to think about it, because it made him squirm. Feelings were such unpredictable things, slippery as eels, refusing to be neatly categorized and analyzed. Besides, it could never work. She lived in Brazil, in an orphanage with a bunch of kids. And when he wasn't injured, he went wherever Uncle Sam sent him, always knowing he might never come home. Well, he used to before he quit. But hadn't he known all along, on some level, that he'd be going back? The realization made him uncomfortable.

But do you love her? An annoying little voice prodded.

He ran a hand through his hair and groaned, the movement jarring his side. How could he think about something like love? His mother loved his father, and look what that had gotten her. Irene loved Noah, too, and she was dead. Regina loved Eduardo and had to give him up. From where he sat, the odds for love working out were too low to consider it a safe risk. And yet . . .

Beside him, Eduardo stuck one foot in his mouth, and Brooks chuckled, glad for the distraction. "How do you do that, kid? It looks painful."

He tickled the boy's tummy and turned his mind to yesterday. Something about what happened at the Falls didn't sit right. He mentally replayed the scene, but he couldn't put his finger on it. He knew he'd suffered a mild concussion, but still, he had missed some obvious clue, some important piece of the puzzle.

He'd just given the baby one of the full bottles Regina had left when his cell phone rang. He looked around, grateful Regina had put it within reach on the bedside table. Maybe that was her, calling from the airport, saying she'd come back to the States with him. Even as he thought it, he called himself three kinds of fool. Yeah, right. As though she would.

As though he'd asked.

"Brooks."

"Good morning, Senhor. I trust you slept well."

At that voice, Brooks' insides turned to ice and the hair on the back of his neck stood up straight. Raul wasn't dead. Regina and the baby were still in danger. Hadn't Jax said he had everything under control?

Jax.

Brooks didn't want to believe it, but like lock tumblers clicking into place, the various inconsistencies of the past few days suddenly lined up with military precision. The picture they painted chilled him to the core.

Jax had Regina.

"What can I do for you, Raul?" Keep it casual. Don't push. Find out what he wants and what he knows.

"It seems you and I did not finish our little discussion yesterday." He made that annoying tsk-tsking sound. "Senhorita da Silva interrupted at such an inopportune time."

"That's not quite how I remember it," Brooks returned mildly.

"Nevertheless, I find I'd like to continue our little chat. In person."

Brooks discovered he was more than ready to end this never-ending cat-and-mouse game. "Where and when?" he returned immediately.

"Today, on the Argentine side of the falls. Twelve o'clock." Raul laughed as though he'd made a joke. "Like your John Wayne and his shoot-outs in front of the saloon at high noon. Fitting, don't you think?"

Fitting would be shoving the man's impeccable teeth down his throat, among other things, but Brooks swallowed the words. Instead, he made a noncommittal noise as his mind sorted and discarded multiple scenarios in rapid-fire sequence. He could (a) get the baby out of the country and come back for Raul, or (b) finish this once and for all. With option B, what would he do with Eduardo during Raul's little John Wayne fantasy?

Even as he formulated and sorted his options, one thought clanged in the back of his mind. Where was Regina? He remembered her aversion to Jax, and his jaw clamped shut with such force his back teeth rattled. Jax had her. Panic sent a burst of adrenaline spurting through his system. He needed two plans. A way to keep both Regina and the baby safe.

"Where's Regina?" he demanded.

"Isn't she with you?" Raul asked innocently.

"Cut the crap, Raul. Where is she?"

"From what I understand, she and your friend Jackson were planning a little picnic before her flight."

The last of Brooks's doubts were ripped to shreds, and the heaviness of betrayal settled over him. Jax and Raul were in this together. Brooks ran his hand over his face as another certainty assaulted him. Regina was no more with Jax willingly than he would suddenly sprout wings. He cursed his blindness. The man he'd known for years, faced death with more times than either could count, considered a friend—Jax had betrayed him. And he hadn't seen it coming.

And now, Jax had Regina. Brooks didn't need Raul to spell out what that "picnic" entailed. The knowledge boiled sickeningly in his gut.

"I'm not meeting you anywhere, scumbag, unless you prove to me—beforehand—that Regina is safe and completely unharmed," he spit the words out, placing special emphasis on the last two.

"What kind of proof?"

"I want to see her, and I want to hear from her lips that she's okay."

"You want too much."

"Take it or leave it, Raul."

The other man chuckled, an evil sound. "You forget that you're not calling the shots here, Senhor." He chuckled some more, then stopped abruptly. "You will show up at noon—with the baby—or I'll make sure you get to watch your girlfriend die a very slow, very painful death. I'll call you later to give you the exact location for our meeting. The catwalks over the falls are lovely this time of year, don't you think?"

Then the line went dead.

Brooks tossed the phone onto the bed beside Eduardo and levered himself to his feet, hunched over and gasping. His wound still burned like fire, but the dizziness wasn't as bad as last night. He stood completely upright and slowly began pacing the room, the pain in his side burning off the haze in his brain. He needed a plan, and he needed it now.

The picture of Jax and Regina intruded into his thoughts, speeding his pace—and his determination. His only hope was that Raul had taken him seriously and believed he wouldn't show without proof Regina was alive and well.

He shoved a hand through his hair. *Well* was such a nebulous term. Brooks spotted the Gideon Bible lying beside his gun and stopped short as another thought struck. Like his mother, Regina believed God controlled everything, protected those who asked. He hadn't believed that in years, but facts were facts. Due to his blundering, Regina should have died yesterday, but she hadn't. She credited him—and God—with protecting them.

Brooks rubbed the back of his neck as the truth slapped him, hard. Right now he had nowhere to turn but the God he'd abandoned long ago. "God, it's gonna take another miracle. I should have seen the truth about Jax. Don't let Reggie pay for that. She's gone through too much." Reggie's tentative smile flashed in his mind and he swallowed hard, emotion making his voice rough. "Please, keep her safe." He paced toward the door, turned back. "I know I don't deserve your help, but I'm all she's got. For her sake, will you help me get us out of this mess?"

He paced some more, forcing images of Beatrice Simms and her son away. Then he flipped through his mental Rolodex, trying to decide whom to call. He needed help, but who had the horsepower to get him what he needed in such a short time? He stopped and checked his watch as the answer occurred to him. Then he reached for his phone and dialed. "Francisco Lopez, *por favor.*"

"I'm sorry. Senhor Lopez is not in the office yet. May I take a message?" a nasally male voice inquired politely.

"This is Brooks Anderson and I need to speak with Senhor Lopez now!" He barked the last word, then lowered his voice and spoke very slowly and clearly. "You do whatever it takes to get him on the line pronto."

"I-I, um, certainly Senhor. Hold the line, please."

Brooks looked down at the bed and saw Eduardo staring up at him with wide trusting eyes. "Don't worry, kid," he murmured. "We'll keep you both safe."

"Senhor Brooks. What is it? I'm told it's urgent," Francisco said as he came on the line.

"I don't have much time, so I'll be brief. I need your help."

"Of course. Name it. Is the baby all right?"

Brooks glanced at the bed, where Eduardo sucked on his fist. "He's fine. And I intend to see that he stays that way."

"How can I be of service, Senhor?"

"Raul Carvalho has Regina and wants me to trade Eduardo for her," he stated bluntly.

The other man gasped. "Surely you won't do any such thing."

Had the other man been able to see Brooks's face at that point, he would have been chilled to the bone. "Not on your life. But that's where you come in. Here's what I need."

Several minutes later, Brooks hung up, satisfied that the other man would do exactly as he'd asked. He quickly fed Eduardo and wrestled the squirming baby into a clean diaper, then shoved all their gear into one bag. Weakness still hit him in waves, but he forced himself to march through it without slowing his pace. He didn't have time to baby himself now. He could recuperate later.

With quick efficiency, he changed his bandages, rewrapped the cloth around his middle, swallowed several pain pills, and some more antibiotics. Ten minutes later, he and Eduardo were in the back of a cab and on their way. He'd set phase one in motion. As soon as Raul called, he'd implement phase two. Please, God.

Hang on, Regina. I'm on my way.

26

In the library of his Porto Alegre home, Francisco Lopez replaced the receiver with hands that shook. He covered his face with his hands and admitted the bitter truth. He was a coward. Eduardo's life, as well as Brooks and Regina's lives, were in danger, and still he didn't give them the information that could turn the tables, that could help protect the boy.

He picked up the receiver to call Noah, then reluctantly set it back in its cradle before dialing. Noah and Carol had enough to worry about right now. He would have to handle this on his own.

Pushing the sleeve of his silk robe aside, he checked his diamond-studded watch. He had a lot to do and not much time to do it in. As he dialed a familiar number, the housekeeper came through the door, a silver breakfast tray in her hands.

He covered the receiver with one hand and said, "Thank you, Luisa. Just leave it."

By the time he'd completed the tasks Brooks had assigned him, he barely had time to gulp down the now-cold coffee and hurry upstairs to dress.

He passed his wife on the sweeping staircase. Even at this early hour, she was elegantly attired for the day, every dark curl carefully lacquered in place, her makeup artfully hiding the lines around her eyes. "Good morning, Francisco." She tilted her cheek up for his kiss, which he dutifully supplied. "Who called so early this morning?" she inquired.

Francisco forced himself to meet her assessing look straight on. "Some important business I have to attend to. It may be late tonight before I get back."

For a minute, she looked as though she might say something else, but then she simply said, "Say farewell to the girls before you leave. They miss you when you're not here." She sailed down the remaining stairs without a backward glance.

Not for the first time, Francisco wondered when he and this woman he'd once loved so desperately had become strangers who shared the same address.

Returning his thoughts to the day ahead, he hurried upstairs to his dressing room to change. As he went, he asked God to keep his family safe.

And to forgive his cowardice.

Regina woke to a world of pain. Her whole body seemed to be one mass of aching, throbbing flesh. She slowly opened her eyes, but the sunlight had her slamming her lids shut again. Instead, she tried to isolate where the pain was coming from.

She tried to swallow and realized her throat had almost swollen shut. An image of Jax with his arm around her neck flashed into her mind and she remembered. Nausea inched up the back of her throat as she wondered if, while she was unconscious, he'd finished what he started. She cautiously straightened her legs and tears of relief leaked out the corners of her eyes when she realized there was no pain. He hadn't. Though she couldn't help but wonder why not.

She tried to move and twin spasms shuddered up her arms from wrist to neck. It took her a minute to realize her hands were tightly bound behind her. Through slitted eyelashes, she took inventory of her surroundings. Water rushed nearby, so she had to be near the falls. Trees surrounded her, and off to her left she could hear children's voices above the sound of the water. Must be near one of the trails.

"So you're awake," a male voice said above her.

Regina looked up, but the sunlight behind him kept his face in shadow. He raised a hand, and Regina saw a cast on one arm and the familiar diamond ring on his left hand. Raul!

Shock loosened her tongue and the words slipped out before she thought. "Haven't we already played this scene, Raul? You hoping to do better this time?"

His backhanded slap knocked her head backward and the ring split the skin above her cheek.

Instantly, he tsked and pulled a snowy handkerchief from his pocket. He dabbed at the blood on his hand, then wiped her face. She tried to pull away, but he gripped her chin with his other hand. "Hold still. Lover boy wants you all in one piece."

She sent him a malevolent look, but he merely chuckled. "Brooks won't show up here," she declared. "I'm nothing to him. He and Eduardo are long gone. You're wasting your time."

"How touching. Both of you trying to protect the other. Too bad your efforts will be in vain. No, Regina, he'll be here. Both he and the boy. Then we'll finish what we started." He pulled her switchblade from his pocket. "And this time, I think I'll keep this with me."

Just then, Jax appeared beside Raul, holding one of her blouses. "Excellent," Raul said. "Put that one on her. We don't want Senhor Brooks to think we've in any way mistreated his little whore."

Regina kept her eyes on Raul while Jax pulled her to her feet and untied her arms. He quickly stripped her torn blouse from her and shoved her arms into the other one. As soon as he shoved the last button through its hole, he wrenched her arms behind her again and retied them. She bit back a scream as he tightened the knots until she thought he'd dislocate her shoulders.

"Ease it just a bit," Raul commanded and Jax instantly obeyed, then shoved her back on the ground. Raul carefully crouched down against a tree, one hand on his bandaged side, and sent her an amused smile. "Now, we wait."

Regina studied the man across from her, saw the malice lurking in his eyes and wondered anew that she'd been so blind. How could she not have known all along that he didn't really care about her, that his words of love were as false as his smile? "This was all part of your plan all along, wasn't it, Raul? Meeting me—courting me, as you put it—was a lie, a way to get to Noah."

"But, of course. You didn't really think a man like myself would be interested in marrying a common prostitute, did you?"

She flinched at the familiar condemnation. Would she never escape her past? But then she remembered other words, another opinion. *You deserve better,* Brooks had said. *Your sins are gone,* Christ had told her. The quiet reminders echoed in her heart and she clung to them. Not everyone saw her as Raul did.

At the thought of Brooks, panic bloomed in her heart. Was he already in the woods somewhere nearby? Maybe he just needed a bit more time to get into place. Raul looked much too relaxed, so he must be confident Brooks would appear. Worry for Eduardo raised its head, but she shoved it away. Brooks would take care of the baby. She knew that with absolute certainty. She couldn't think of a way to help except to keep this man talking, giving Brooks whatever time he needed to do whatever he planned to do. "Revenge is not the answer, you know."

"Sometimes it is necessary. My sister's blood cries out for vengeance. Even the Bible you and Noah put such stock in advocates an eye for an eye."

"It also says that vengeance belongs to God." Her throat clogged, but she forced the words out. "Irene, Eduardo, Brooks, none of them deserve this. Irene deserved to live and raise her son. Just let me go. End this now. Don't make it worse."

"As I told your friend Brooks, it's nothing personal. He knows as well as I do that one of the sad facts of war is that the innocent suffer. And die."

Regina's whole body shook as rage swept through her. "Nothing personal!" she cried. "Yo-you heartlessly blow up my best friend and then say it's nothing personal! You disgust me." She turned her head away and braced for another blow.

Raul lunged to his feet, and she cringed. Then he stopped and appeared to change his mind. She released a pent-up breath when he pulled out his cell phone instead, punching buttons quickly. "Your lover awaits, Senhor," he drawled into the phone. "Would you like to see her?"

Regina couldn't tell what Brooks said in response, but above her, Raul's face darkened. "You have the boy?" he demanded. Seconds later Raul disconnected and replaced the phone in his shirt pocket. "Get her up," he said to Jax.

Jax pulled her roughly to her feet and then propelled her out of the trees and onto the catwalk behind Raul. He set a punishing pace. As Regina hurried to keep up, she looked down once, then quickly averted her gaze.

On the Brazilian side of the falls, the walkways hugged the side of the mountain, well away from the heart of the waterfalls. Here, on the Argentine side, the catwalks were suspended a mere foot or two directly above the rushing water.

Directly under her feet, the earth fell away in an eighty-foot drop of white, churning water, crashing to the rocks below. The farther they walked, the louder the noise became. In one spot, water splashed up onto the walkway, and Regina almost lost her footing. Jax grabbed her as she fell against the guardrail and pulled her upright, shoving her ahead of him.

After that, Regina focused her gaze on the walkway, desperately ignoring the foaming water that churned beneath it. The catwalk was made of narrow slabs of concrete and as Raul stepped forward, the back end of the slab popped up under her feet. It took all her concentration to keep up with him without tripping over the bouncing slabs. The feel of them rising and falling beneath her feet, coupled with the roar of the water and the feel of Jax's hand at her back, had spots dancing before her eyes. Her breath came in shallow pants, and she knew if she didn't stop soon, she was going to be sick. Sweat poured down her back and the constant mist plastered her hair against her head.

Raul stopped suddenly, and Regina stumbled right into his back. Jax immediately yanked her backward, further disorienting her. "Put her up against the rail," Raul commanded.

Jax did, and Regina found herself leaning stomach-first over the railing, facing another section of the trail. Because Foz do Iguaçu was actually a series of waterfalls, the catwalks followed the natural contours of the converging rivers. At this particular junction, a visitor could look across to a section of the trail he'd already traversed. Regina kept her eyes forward, instead of downward. That way lay terror.

Raul again pulled out his cell phone and dialed. "Show yourself," he barked.

Across the expanse of furious water, Brooks appeared at the opposite guardrail, Eduardo cradled in his arms, wrapped securely in a blanket.

Regina tried to read his expression, but she was too far away to see anything but the grim set of his jaw and the determination in his stance. Suddenly Raul stepped up next to her and held his cell phone to her ear. She saw Brooks put his phone to his ear as well.

"Reggie? Are you okay?" Brooks had to shout to be heard above the pounding water.

"Yes. I'm fine."

"Did Jax hurt you?"

"No, he didn't." She shook her head for emphasis, needing to reassure him.

"Positive?"

"I'm okay, really. How are you and Eduardo?"

"We're both just fine. Don't worry." Then he lowered his voice, and she had to strain to hear him. "Just keep your head down. Everything's going to be okay. Trust me."

"Be careful."

Whatever else Brooks said was lost as Raul jerked the phone back. "Bring the child here."

Raul apparently wasn't pleased with whatever Brooks said, because he slammed the phone shut, cursing fluently. Then he turned to Jax. "We're meeting at the picnic area we passed earlier."

Jax frowned, arms crossed over his powerful chest. "I don't like it. It's too far out in the open."

"You don't have to like it. Just get moving."

Jax gave a mock salute and herded Regina in that direction.

Brooks hurried along the path as quickly as he could, given the bundle he carried and the hole in his side. With the ease of long practice, he relegated the pain to a distant corner of his mind. His only focus now was on his mission.

Without a sound, he darted off the path and cut through the jungle. The element of surprise would be essential here. Once he reached the picnic area, he scanned the boiling clouds overhead, grateful the sky had grown darker since he'd made the call. That was what he'd counted on. The few picnickers were hurriedly packing up their food and heading for shelter.

He set the blanket-wrapped bundle next to him and checked to be sure his gun, ammo, and both knives were ready. Anger at his long-time friend's betrayal made his movements harsh, jerky. There would be no margin for error. Raul had frustration and wounded pride on his side, fueled by his failure yesterday. He also had Jax.

On the plus side, Brooks knew exactly how the other man would react. But Jax could say the same about him, so he'd have to be careful. *I'm gonna need an edge, God.*

The patch of grass and wooden tables had emptied by the time the first drops of rain began to fall. Brooks grabbed the kid and ducked behind a stand of trees. He wouldn't make any mistakes this time. Couldn't. One corner of his mouth curved up. To his way of thinking, two against one were pretty good odds. And he had a few surprises up his sleeve, just in case. He settled in to wait.

Brooks heard them before he saw them. Interesting that they were so confident they made no effort to silence their arrival. Raul and Jax marched into the clearing, Regina between them. Each man held her with one hand and a gun in the other.

"Stop right there," Brooks called.

All three of them turned toward the sound of his voice. "Bring the boy out here," Raul demanded.

"Not until you untie Regina and back up to the tree line. When she's standing in the middle of the clearing, I'll bring Eduardo out."

"I want him out here now!" Raul shouted.

Brooks realized the other man's control was slipping fast. He had to act quickly. "Then do what I said," he returned calmly.

Raul nodded to Jax, who used a knife to slice the ropes around her wrists. Brooks's eyes narrowed as Regina rubbed her hands together to restore circulation. The swelling and bruising were easily visible, even from here. One more thing Jax would have to answer for. His expression darkened even more as Jax shoved her roughly forward. His friend's list of sins kept getting longer.

Regina walked slowly toward the middle of the clearing, looking right at him. The trust in her eyes stabbed Brooks in the heart, while the bruise on her cheek ignited his temper. She was counting on him to protect her. He planned to do much more than that. These men would pay for what they'd done to her. Brooks sent her an encouraging nod, and a smile lit her face like the sun after a storm.

"We've fulfilled our part. Now keep yours," Raul shouted.

Brooks ignored him and waited until Regina was close enough to momentarily block the two men's view of them. With his hands he signaled her to duck at his command. She nodded her understanding, and he gave her a reassuring smile. Then he lifted the baby from where it lay next to him and walked toward her, his own gun aimed at Raul.

The smile on her face faded and changed to a look of horror as she eyed the bundle he carried. *Trust me,* he mouthed, but he saw her lip begin to quiver. As he came even with her, he said the words aloud, but low enough that only she could hear them. "Trust me. Keep backing slowly toward the trees—and duck as soon as the bullets start flying."

She only stared blankly at him.

"Promise," he insisted.

He didn't start moving again until she nodded her understanding. Then he walked to the middle of the clearing and stopped.

"Set the boy down and back away."

Brooks did as he'd been told, then began backing slowly toward Regina, his eyes darting back and forth between the two men, reading their expressions. By watching their eyes, he'd know what they were planning. Behind him, he could hear Regina inching her way to safety so he slowed even further to give her time to get behind the trees. *That's my girl. Keep going; don't stop.*

Raul marched over to the baby, gun pointed at Brooks. Brooks tensed, his finger poised on the trigger and took several steps backward. Raul yanked the blanket away from the baby's face. His howl echoed in the little clearing, then he fired his gun right at the baby's middle. Bits of plastic and fluffy blue blanket flew into the air. Regina's shriek drew Raul's attention.

Even as Raul's gun came up, Brooks was in motion, diving for the other man's legs. Just before he took him down, Brooks heard the shot and Regina's muffled cry. Oh, no. It was not, by God, going to end like this.

Raul fought with everything he had, but he was no match for Brooks's rage. It didn't take Brooks long to pin the older man under him. He slammed Raul's hand against the ground until he got the gun from his grip. When he looked up, Jax was drawing a bead on Regina. Without hesitation, Brooks fired, knocking the gun away. Jax yelped and cradled his hand.

Under him, Raul bucked and tried to push him off, but Brooks simply grabbed the man's newly casted arm and shoved it against his throat, pushing down harder and harder. Looking into the other man's face, something snapped inside him.

Violence pounded through his system until his vision narrowed to the face before him. This weak and cowardly excuse for a man had killed an innocent woman, terrified a child, and mistreated the woman Brooks cared about. He wouldn't get off easy. Sliding quietly into unconsciousness was far too little punishment for what he'd done.

Fueled by adrenaline and indignation, he reached back and smashed a fist into Raul's nose. Once. Twice. "That's for Irene, you slimy lizard."

Blood spurted and Raul howled in pain. Brooks pulled his fist back and hit him again, this time in the jaw. "And that's for the way you scared Regina to death." Bone cracked with a familiar snap.

"Please," Raul begged, blood pouring out of his nose. "I'm your uncle."

It was exactly the wrong thing to say. It simply added more fuel to the inferno of Brooks's anger. He hauled off and slugged the man again, in the mouth this time. "Then that's for trying to kill my brother."

Raul moaned and turned his head to the side. He spit out two teeth. Brooks didn't care; all he saw was the man responsible for it all. He raised his fist.

Again. Again. Again.

Hands around Raul's head, Brooks prepared to snap his neck and finish him off. He hesitated as his mind registered that Raul had stopped fighting.

The haze cleared as he wiped sweat from his face with a bloody hand, then checked the other man's pulse. An odd mix of relief and disgust filled him as his fingers found it, weak and thready, but there. The scumbag didn't deserve to live.

"Might as well finish him off," Jax drawled from behind them. "You know you want to. And he certainly has it coming."

Brooks raised his head and eyed the blond man standing before him. Brooks didn't know him.

He and Jax had both killed in the line of duty, but never an enemy who was no longer an immediate threat. He'd lost control for a minute, but he'd stopped short of killing Raul. When had Jax changed? Or was he seeing his friend's true nature for the first time?

Brooks eyed the blood dripping from Jax's right hand and the gun his friend held steady in his left. Both of them had deadly skill with either hand.

Without so much as a flicker of warning, Jax calmly fired his gun, killing Raul instantly.

Brooks jumped to his feet, and Jax smiled. "Figured that would get you up. Now, you know the drill. Gun down on the ground and slide it over to me. Then both knives."

Against his will, Brooks momentarily cut his eyes toward the trees where Regina had fallen.

"Don't worry about her, friend. I'll make sure her death is quick." When he reached over to scoop up Brooks's gun, he added, "'Course I plan to enjoy that luscious bod of hers again first." Evil glinted in his smile.

Brooks fisted his hands at his sides as the trees took a slow spin. Pain hazed his vision and threatened to cut off his breath. He shook his head. He had to stay alert, because he still had a job to do. Based on what Jax just said, Regina was still alive. He focused on that. *God? Are you getting all this?*

"Why'd you do it?" Brooks asked as he pulled his knife out of his boot. The question was a stalling tactic, but he also wanted to know. How did a good guy turn bad?

Jax shrugged. "This little scene? Money. Why else?"

"Raul paid you to help him do what? Track us?"

"Among other things. Let's go. Get the other knife. I have a date."

"What other things?" Brooks asked, ignoring the implications of that last statement. He reached for his back sheath.

"Explosives. Tracking info." He waited a beat. "An ambush."

It took a moment for his words to sink in. At first, Brooks thought he'd misunderstood, then everything inside him went still.

"You were responsible for the ambush." His mind darted back and forth, trying to absorb this. Then it flashed back to the sight of those two broken bodies, mother and son, their lives draining into the dirt. Innocent victims. Behind that thought came images of all the men he'd lost, friends to both him and Jax. He squeezed his eyes shut. "That was for money, too?"

"Of course." Jax shrugged negligently, but then grimaced. "You weren't supposed to live to tell about that little incident."

Only the gun trained directly at his heart—and the knowledge that Regina was still alive—kept Brooks from ripping Jax's throat out. He had other priorities. Besides, some men weren't worth killing.

"Let's you and me take a little walk. Seems you're so distraught over your girlfriend's death, you're planning a dive off the catwalk."

Brooks snorted. "Nobody will believe that."

Jax quirked a brow. "Won't they? Given the way you've been acting lately, even your mother will buy it."

"And there won't be any bullet holes to explain."

"Exactly. Now walk." Jax pointed with his gun, and Brooks slowly set off in that direction.

As they walked, Brooks kept his ears tuned to the sound he waited for, but by the time they reached a secluded section of the catwalk, he hadn't heard anything.

"Climb up," Jax instructed. "Wait. Take your shoes off. Goes to intent."

As Brooks bent and grabbed his boot heel, Jax commented, "You and I could have made a fortune together. We're a good team—except for your unfortunate code of honor." He snorted and gestured with the gun.

"You and I are nothing alike," Brooks spat as he pulled off the boot. "Nothing." He pulled off his other boot and flung it at Jax. The boot caught his friend off guard and sent the gun flying. It sailed over the railing.

Jax recovered quickly, and in the blink of an eye they were locked in hand-to-hand combat. They'd trained together, practiced together for so many years they were evenly matched. Brooks's wounded side hampered his movements, but so did Jax's injured hand.

Brooks kicked at Jax's hand; the other man blocked it with his arm. Jax sent a powerful punch toward Brooks's injured side; Brooks spun away. Back and forth, bouncing off trees, ricocheting against the railing, neither man gave an inch and went directly for his opponent's weak spots.

After his encounter with Raul, Brooks's strength was almost gone. He had to make his move now, especially since Jax didn't appear nearly as winded.

With one mighty lunge, he grabbed Jax and forced him back against a tree. He shoved his arm across the other man's windpipe, trying to hold it there until he lost consciousness.

Jax's eyes were almost closed when he somehow found a last burst of energy. He thrust himself away from the tree with enough force to throw Brooks slightly off balance and hurl both of them back toward the railing. Just before impact, Brooks spun sideways.

After that everything seemed to move in slow motion, each movement captured like separate images in a digital slide show.

Jax's momentum carried him into the railing. He was moving so fast his legs flipped up and over his head, propelling him over the edge.

Panic widened Jax's eyes as he fell over, heading toward the eighty-foot drop, feet first. Without conscious thought, Brooks reached out a hand as the other man went by, grabbing Jax by the wrist. He braced himself against the railing, and the impact when he stopped Jax's fall almost yanked his shoulder from its socket.

Brooks looked down at Jax, dangling by one arm, then at the boiling cauldron of water below.

"Just. Let. Go." Jax spit the words.

"No." Bracing his feet more securely, Brooks reached out with his other hand, but he couldn't grasp Jax's other wrist. The one he had hold of was the injured one.

Jax hung there, kicking his legs, and Brooks' grip slipped slightly. "Hold still," he hissed.

"Let go," Jax repeated. "You know I would, in your place."

"That's how you and I are different," Brooks grunted. "I don't betray my friends."

They stayed that way for what seemed like hours, staring at each other. Brooks's arm ached, but he refused to let go. He tried to re-adjust his grip, but when he looked down again, he saw what Jax intended a split second too late.

Even as he shouted, "No!" Jax kicked his legs far out over the water and used his momentum to break Brooks's grip on his wrist. Without a sound, he disappeared into the foaming water.

Brooks leaned over the rail, searching for a glimpse of the other man, but it was as if he'd never been. He saw nothing but rushing, pulsing water shooting down toward the next level of falls.

Brooks turned away, then mustered his last reserves of strength and headed back to the picnic area. He was still several hundred yards away when he heard the welcome blades of the chopper. Bursting through the clearing, he saw Regina being loaded onto a stretcher.

"How is she?" he shouted to Francisco Lopez, running up alongside the stretcher. His heart pounded as he looked at her. She lay still, unmoving, her eyes closed, her skin a pasty white. Had he been too late? *Please, God. No.*

Francisco must have seen the look on his face, for he leaned close to be heard above the rotor blades. "They said the bullet hit her shoulder. No vital organs. She should be fine."

Francisco signaled to the men to load the stretcher into the chopper, then put a hand on Brooks's arm to detain him when he would have climbed in after her. "Where is your friend?"

"Dead." In short, curt, sentences, Brooks told the other man what had happened.

"Let's get you aboard and cleaned up," Francisco said. Then he grimaced. "I'm sure your former boss will send a crew to search for the body. He says you have some explaining to do."

Before he climbed aboard, Brooks looked around. "How's Eduardo?"

"He's just fine," Francisco assured him. "Olga is even now spoiling the boy rotten—safely in a hotel room under armed guard, of course."

Brooks gave the other man a weary smile and climbed aboard.

27

REGINA FLOATED IN A COTTONY WORLD OF MUTED BLEEPS AND MURmured voices, somewhere between sleep and wakefulness. She tried to marshal her thoughts, to figure out where she was and what had happened, but coherent words and phrases hovered just out of reach. She wanted to open her eyes, but her lids were too heavy to lift.

She thought someone hovered nearby, could sense another presence beside her. She heard a deep voice sometimes. Did it belong to whoever kept watch? She wondered briefly if she should be afraid, but she wasn't.

Tentatively, she moved one hand and immediately felt it clasped in another and held tight. Hard, warm, and calloused, that grip seemed somehow familiar and made her feel safe and secure. Protected.

She slept on.

Brooks sat beside Regina's hospital bed and watched over her as she slept. With her dark hair spread out across the pillow, surrounded by white bedding, she looked like an angel.

Maybe Noah wasn't that far wrong to name the children's home House of Angels. Regina was certainly one.

His wound had been thoroughly cleaned and examined, and the doctor had praised Regina's medical skills. A woman of many and varied talents, his Regina. Too bad most people either saw her pretty face and sordid past, or they saw her frumpy clothes and looked right through her.

He ran a careful finger over the healing bruise on her cheek, and a spurt of anger lanced through him. He hated men who used their strength to hurt women.

As she had several times during the past two days, Regina began to cry in her sleep. Twin tears slid down her face and into her ears. Those silent tears made Brooks ache with an urge to soothe her pain. He had a burning need to make things right for her—and to see that they never went wrong again.

The thought had startled him initially. But after two days, he'd stopped fighting it. This woman and her happiness mattered to him. The admission frightened him, but he finally accepted it as truth.

Brooks tenderly brushed the wetness away and leaned over to whisper the same words in her ear he'd said before. "Shh, it's okay, Reggie. Eduardo is safe. No one is going to hurt him. You're safe, too."

She still mumbled and twitched anxiously, and he wanted to add that no one would ever hurt her again, either, but he couldn't make false promises. A woman like her was strong enough not to need them. He stroked her hair and crooned softly in her ear until she settled back into restful slumber.

The nurse bustled in and sent him a dour look. "You won't be any good to her if you don't take care of yourself first, Senhor. Go back to your room and lie down."

Since she'd said the same thing at least three times today alone, Brooks merely sent her a stony look. "I'm not going anywhere. My side can heal here as well as in a hospital bed."

"You had a pretty serious concussion, too, Senhor."

It wasn't the worst one he'd ever had, but he didn't think that would reassure the militant fiftysomething woman. "I'm fine."

Actually, the dressing down he'd gotten from his former boss via telephone had given him a much worse headache than the blow to the head. The man had given him a good thrashing for not telling him what was going on—especially since he had had Jax under surveillance for quite some time. If he'd communicated instead of being his usual independent, stubborn self, his former boss had raged, some of this mess might have been avoided. He had a valid point, so Brooks didn't defend his actions.

He checked his watch and sighed. Apparently the fearsome nurse didn't know he'd checked himself out earlier. He needed to swing by House of Angels, pick up Eduardo, and head for the airport. He'd been hoping Regina would wake up before he left and give him one last glimpse of those gorgeous brown eyes, but he had run out of time.

Slowly, he leaned forward, careful of the bandage on her shoulder. She was healing well, the doctors said, and they attributed her semiconscious state to painkillers and total exhaustion. She would be fine, they insisted.

The familiar guilt gnawed at him as he studied her face. If not for him, she wouldn't be here. His erstwhile boss had termed Brooks's decidedly unauthorized mission a success, but Brooks wasn't buying it. This shouldn't have happened. And for that, he was profoundly sorry. *Let her be happy.*

"Good-bye, Reggie," he whispered. Pulling back, he gave in to temptation and brushed his lips lightly over hers. Once, and again. She tasted so sweet, so completely Regina. He cupped her uninjured cheek in one hand and gave it one more caress before slowly drawing his hand away. He took a last look and stepped back, turning toward the door.

"Stay," she croaked. "Please."

He spun around and saw that her eyes were open and looking right at him. Pleading. Just as he had before, he wished he were another kind of man. Wished he lived a different kind of life. One without so many uncertainties, so many ghosts. But he didn't. Regret weighted his steps as he moved back to the bed and enfolded her small hand in both of his. "I can't. I have to go."

"Eduardo?" Fresh tears spilled over as she said his name.

"I'll take care of him. I won't forget my promise to you."

She nodded and swallowed hard. "Thank you for saving my life."

He wanted to howl at her calm acceptance. "If not for me, you wouldn't be here."

Regina smiled through her tears and lifted her other hand to cup his cheek. "If not for you, I wouldn't be alive. God sent you as my guardian angel."

When he started to deny it, she placed a finger over his lips. "You gave me a gift, two gifts, really."

He didn't understand, and his puzzled look must have told her so.

"You kept Eduardo and me safe. You gave us both the gift of life, of safety."

When she fell silent, the question popped out before he could stop it, even though some instinct warned against what she might say. "And the second?"

"You taught me that not all men are the same. You saw the real me, and you liked me anyway."

"What's not to like?" he returned with a smile. "You're a beautiful lady, Regina da Silva. And I don't just mean under that awful sweater. You are giving and caring and someday, some man will recognize that."

She didn't say anything, but he saw the accusation there: she'd already found him, and he was leaving. He opened his mouth. Closed it. Looked away. He wanted to tell her he cared about her. That maybe someday . . . He left the thought unfinished. His life at the moment was nothing but unfinished business. The best thing he could do for both of them was to let her live in peace.

He placed a gentle kiss on her forehead. "Thank you for the gift you gave me—of knowing you."

At the door he paused with his hand on the knob and added, "I'll notify you when Eduardo is settled with his new family."

28

I *CAN'T.*

Brooks's words echoed in Regina's heart long after he'd gone, and she had no more tears left to cry. There was a wealth of regret behind the simple phrase. She knew its source, understood its origin, and still wished with all her heart that she could change his mind. Ironically though, his determination to stick to his guns, to do what he'd said without turning right or left, was one of the things she admired most about him. It was also the very thing keeping them apart.

As she lay there, wondering how she would survive the long, lonely years ahead, she heard a commotion in the hallway. Hope fluttered in her heart. He'd changed his mind and come back.

The door to her room burst open and a strange man in a suit marched in. The faint hope died a silent death, leaving only emptiness behind.

"Regina da Silva?" the man demanded.

She struggled to a sitting position, hissing in a sharp breath at the pain in her shoulder. "Who wants to know?"

"Senhor Lopez is here to see you." Suit jacket flapping open to reveal his shoulder holster, the man spun on his heel and left, banging the door shut behind him.

Within seconds it opened again, and Francisco Lopez breezed in, his handsome face wreathed in smiles. He swooped down on the bed and snatched one of her hands, placing a gallant kiss on the back of it. "How are you, my dear? I've been so worried."

"Much better, thank you," she replied politely. She didn't think he wanted to know about her heartbreak.

"Where's Eduardo?" he asked accusingly, scanning the room as though she'd hidden him behind the water pitcher.

"He's safely on his way to the United States, Senhor,"

His disappointment showed in the sudden slump of his shoulders. "I had hoped . . ." He glanced her way for a brief moment, and Regina saw such grief and regret etched in his face, her throat closed. In that instant, the truth dawned as well. This man was Eduardo's father.

"He'll be well taken care of. Carol will see to it."

"I know she will." He narrowed his gaze, then asked slowly. "You've figured it out, haven't you?"

Regina nodded.

"I never meant for it to happen, never meant to hurt Irene. Never meant to hurt my family."

"But you did."

He ran a hand through his hair. "Yes, I did."

The silence stretched as he paced her room for several minutes, then stopped abruptly. "I'm trying to make amends. I'm withdrawing from public life and will try to rebuild my family. It's the least I can do."

The implications of his simple statement were enormous, as was the price he was paying for his affair with Irene. But Regina had to admire his desire to take responsibility—even if it came much too late. "You would have made a good president for Brazil."

"My family needs me more," he said simply. Then he cleared his throat. "I came by to thank you for all you did for Eduardo. You were truly his angel." He thrust a piece of paper into her hand. "I wanted to give you this, for the House of Angels."

Regina took the check he held out and gasped at the amount. "You don't have to—" she began.

"Yes, I do. You are a remarkable young lady, Senhorita da Silva." He turned, one hand on the doorframe. "I hope your young man will soon realize that."

By the time they walked off the jetway in Orlando, Brooks wasn't sure who was more tired and cranky—him or Eduardo. There had been several delays, and neither of them had gotten any real sleep. He had a new appreciation for mothers who kept small children entertained on long flights. He felt ten years older and smelled like day-old fish. Eduardo wasn't exactly squeaky clean either.

None of that deterred his mother in the least. She latched onto both of them with the determination of an octopus, touching every part of them she could reach, wrapping her arms securely around them and refusing to let either one move more than an inch away from her.

Brooks finally unwound one arm from about his neck and broke her hold. "Ease up, Mom. You're choking the little guy."

Carol blushed and cuddled Eduardo closer still. "I was so worried," she admitted. Then her chin lifted in a gesture so like Regina a sharp jolt of pain shot through him. "It's a maternal thing, trust me on this."

"Let's get the luggage taken care of," he suggested, steering them toward baggage claim. He normally traveled only with carry-ons, but that would have been more than even he could handle, what with Eduardo and his assorted paraphernalia to deal with onboard.

Almost an hour later, they finally headed toward the airport exit with Eduardo strapped in a car seat in the back, loudly protesting this sudden confinement.

Carol reached into the back and gave him a bottle. Within moments, blessed peace reigned in the car. Brooks eased his death grip on the steering wheel and glanced at his mother. "How's Noah?"

A mixture of hope and pain showed clearly in her face. "He's holding his own. He'll be glad you asked about him."

Brooks waited for her to plead with him to go to the hospital with her, but she didn't. Instead she said, "Let's get you and Eduardo home and settled." She stroked a hand down his arm. "You both look beat. And from where I'm sitting, a bath couldn't hurt either one of you."

Her statement shocked a laugh out of him, but his thoughts immediately veered to the memory of Regina, hair plastered to her head after her bath in the river, brown eyes wide with shock after losing her fake glasses.

This had to stop. She was a lovely woman, would make some man a fantastic wife one day, but he wasn't the right man.

Stay. Please.

How long would the memory of her face as she'd asked him that torment him?

29

THE NEXT DAY, BROOKS PACED THE HALLWAY OUTSIDE NOAH'S HOSPITAL room, wondering what to do next. He'd been standing there long enough for the nurses to give him questioning looks as they walked by, but he still didn't make a move toward the door. Finally, he gripped the door handle and strode into the room, figuring he'd make it up as he went along.

When he saw his father lying in the hospital bed, he was glad for his military training. Otherwise, there was no way he could have kept from flinching. This frail-looking old man in the bed was not his father. Couldn't be. Noah was tall and broad-shouldered, larger than life. This man just looked weak and sick.

While he searched for words, the familiar gray eyes opened and instantly filled with tears at the sight of him. "You came," his now-hoarse voice croaked.

Brooks nodded, hardening himself against the way those tears affected him.

"Is Eduardo safe?" Noah asked, his gaze sharp with concern.

"He's at the house with Mom," Brooks replied.

Noah studied him for a moment and then sighed. "I'm not his father, you know."

Brooks raised a brow. "Aren't you?"

"No. I'm not."

"I saw a photo of you and Irene while she was pregnant. Looked an awful lot like another photo I remember." He tried and failed to keep the accusation out of his voice.

"That was completely innocent, I promise you. There was nothing between Irene and me." Noah shook his head slightly, as though bewildered by the accusation. "She and Regina are like daughters to me."

"The other photo wasn't innocent," Brooks said bluntly.

Noah flinched as though he'd been struck, but his gaze never wavered. Brooks had to give him points for courage. "No, it wasn't. And it's high time I apologized for that."

Weak or not, Brooks wasn't letting the old man off that easily. "Are you sorry for the photo or for the affair?" he asked bluntly.

If possible, Noah seemed to shrink before his very eyes. But then he seemed to gather his strength. The determination in his gray eyes reminded Brooks of the man he'd loved, idolized, as a child. "I was wrong to have an affair, wrong to betray your mother, wrong for not making it right years ago." When he paused, Brooks steeled himself for excuses, but none came from his father's lips. "But I'll never be sorry that I'm your father, never be sorry Carol is your mother."

"You hurt her."

"Yes," Noah admitted.

"I don't just mean back then, but for the last thirty-some-odd years." Anger rose in him, making his voice harsh. "All she wanted was for you to love her with everything you've got. It wasn't too much to ask."

The words hung in the air between them while the machines continued their rhythmic bleeps and beeps. "No, it wasn't. She deserved that and much, much more." Noah brushed at the tears streaming down his cheeks, and Brooks averted his gaze, uncomfortable as always, with his father's free displays of emotion. "I've asked your mother to forgive me and she has." When Brooks looked into Noah's eyes to test the truth of that statement, his father pierced him with a direct look. "Now I'm asking you to do the same."

Brooks twisted his hands tightly at his sides. "It isn't that simple."

"No, it isn't. But it would be a start."

"I'll think about it," Brooks said, and left the room.

"Telephone, Regina," Olga said, peering around the office door. Brooks had promised to call when he had Eduardo safely settled with his new family. A smile started forming on Regina's lips when Olga added, "It's Senhora Anderson." She poked an imperious finger in Regina's direction. "And as soon as you are finished speaking with her, you are going to bed. You just got home from the hospital. The account books can wait another day."

Regina tried to hide her disappointment and managed a wan smile. "But there may be another child who can't." She held up a hand to still Olga's protest and then picked up the receiver. "Hello, Tia Carol."

"I'm so glad you're home from the hospital. How is your shoulder?"

"Getting better, thank you."

"I wanted to let you know that Nathaniel and Eduardo are safely here."

He was officially done with her, then, Regina thought. He wouldn't even call to let her know they'd arrived safely.

As if she'd read her thoughts, Carol continued, "Nathaniel planned to call you himself, but he's at the hospital with Noah, and he didn't want you to worry."

"He went to see Tio Noah?" the question slipped out before she caught herself.

"Yes. Maybe they'll finally—" Carol's voice stopped abruptly, as though she'd said too much.

"Brooks told me a bit about the past, Tia. It's okay."

Regina could hear the tears in Carol's voice even as she laughed. "Those two are a lot alike, no matter how much they deny it. They're both stubborn as Missouri mules and dumber than bricks about some things."

"I think you're right," Regina agreed.

In the pause that followed, Regina wondered what Carol was thinking.

"He cares for you, you know."

"Pardon?"

"Nathaniel. He cares about you, but like his father, he's too stubborn to admit it."

Regina ignored the way her heart pounded in her chest. "He has no room in his life for a woman like me," she said quietly.

Carol's voice turned sharp. "That's the past talking, Regina. You are not a woman like me. You're a marvelous person with a heart of gold. You deserve to be loved, deserve a home and family of your own."

"I love him," Regina whispered. "But he doesn't want me."

"Don't be too sure of that." Then she paused and said carefully, "Nathaniel has some things in his life he needs to sort out."

"You mean with Tio Noah and what happened to make him quit the Rangers. And with God."

Carol's voice held surprise. "He told you quite a bit."

"Some," Regina allowed. She had more questions she wanted to ask, but didn't. If and when she got answers, she wanted them from Brooks.

"Give him time, Regina."

As the days stretched into weeks, Regina decided Carol's last words were nothing more than what she thought her former charge wanted to hear. Because there was no word from Brooks. No telephone call, no postcard, nothing that indicated he even remembered the time they had spent together.

Instead of lessening, the ache in Regina's heart grew, until she feared it would swallow her whole. She couldn't eat, couldn't sleep, could barely think. She missed Brooks with such longing, it emptied her of all other emotions. She missed his strength, missed his smoldering looks, his careful touches, his oh-so-rare grins. She found she even missed his stubbornness. But most of all, she missed the sense of safety he surrounded her with.

Regina moved through her days like a mechanical doll, making the appropriate responses, but her eyes were lifeless, dead. Olga took to watching her with worried eyes and hovering at her elbow, food of one sort or another always slipped into the pocket of her apron, ready to coax Regina into taking a few bites.

The nights were the worst. When the rest of the children slept, she stood by Eduardo's empty cradle and wrapped her arms around her middle, aching as she remembered the feel of his small body next to hers. She started avoiding mirrors again, too, because whenever she did, she remembered Brooks telling her she was beautiful.

One night, a month after she'd returned to House of Angels, Regina pushed the invoices back into the file folder, pushed up from her desk and began turning off the lights. It was late, and she'd put off going to bed as long as possible. She dreaded night. During the day, the children kept her going, kept her so busy she didn't have time to think about Eduardo or Brooks, to wonder what they were doing, who they were with. But at night, when all was quiet, the pain became unbearable.

And the dreams, she couldn't take the dreams anymore. All of them were of Brooks, telling her he loved her. She dreamed of herself, rounded with his child, and of Eduardo, growing into a sturdy little boy under their loving care. Impossible, wrenching dreams that left her feeling worse and worse. When would her heart learn to let go and be content with what she had, not with what could never be?

When a quiet knock sounded at the front door, she jumped, and clutched her robe more firmly about her. Maybe another orphan had found the courage to escape the *favelas*.

Or maybe the knock signified something more sinister.

Slowly, she headed down the hall, anxiety in every step. The last time someone showed up this late, it was Brooks, and shots followed soon after.

She peeked through the small peephole and saw a pair of battered cowboy boots. Her heart stopped and then started again in a thundering rhythm. She shook her head to clear it, but the image remained. Surely she had fallen asleep and was dreaming all this.

He knocked again. "Regina, open up," he commanded softly in his wonderful growl.

Dazed, she did and stood gripping the edge of the door for support. She blinked rapidly. He was really here.

"Hi," Brooks said.

She stared. "Hi."

He glanced behind him, then shifted Eduardo to his other arm. "Can we come in?"

For the first time she noticed the wrapped bundle he held, and her arms shot out. Brooks handed the baby to her and then guided them both inside to her office. This time, instead of going to the battered chair before the desk, he led them to the sagging couch and sat down beside her.

Regina glanced from one to the other, but couldn't decide which one to study first, so she started with the smallest and decided to work her way up from there. She kissed Eduardo's soft cheeks and laughed when he gurgled in response. "You've grown so much," she murmured, tickling his tummy and patting his little hands together.

Several minutes went by before she raised her head from her careful study of the baby and met Brooks's steady gaze. Myriad emotions swirled in the gray depths of his eyes, but she couldn't identify a single one. She wanted to ask what he was doing there, why he'd come back, but her heart feared the answer. Surely there was some mundane reason for his sudden appearance with Eduardo. So she asked the safest question first. "Why did you bring him back to Brazil?"

Instead of answering, he stood. "I need to get something from the car. I'll be right back."

Moments later, Regina looked up from caressing Eduardo's soft skin to see Brooks hunker down before her with a large box in his hand. "Trade you," he said softly.

Slowly, reluctantly, she handed him the baby and grasped the box. "What is it?"

He smiled, that slow melting smile that turned her knees to mush. "Why not open it and find out?"

Because she'd had so few gifts in her life, packages were something to be savored, the act of opening them stretched out as long as possible. Slowly, she peeled back the expensive wrapping paper, careful not to tear it.

She slid a finger under the tape sealing one edge of the box, then moved to open the other edge. She glanced at Brooks, but his eyes gave nothing away. They stayed on hers, alert, watchful. Inch by slow inch, she lifted the lid. Her hands began to shake as she separated layers and layers of white tissue paper until she reached the treasure below.

She gasped. Never had she seen such beautiful fabric. It was snow-white satin, covered in lace and tiny seed pearls.

"What—" she began, but Brooks interrupted.

"Take it out of the box so you can see it."

Regina stood and Brooks drew the box away so the full length of the dress cascaded to the floor. It had long sleeves and a high neck and looked like something a princess would wear.

Or a bride, she realized numbly. It was a wedding dress.

She looked at Brooks in confusion and saw him drop to one knee before her, Eduardo securely tucked against his shoulder. "Will you marry me, Regina?"

"But why?" she blurted, confused.

His expression grew tender, rueful. "Because I can't stand being without you, because I want you with me every day and night of my life." He paused and sent her a wry grin. "And because I'm adopting Eduardo, and I don't want to be the only one getting up with him in the middle of the night."

He needed her, but he hadn't said a word about love. And he still didn't know the details of her past. Old insecurities reared their head. Maybe when he knew, love wouldn't matter anyway. "You don't know about everything, about what I've done." She pushed the words out in a rush and lowered her head.

His finger gently tilted her chin up so she had to meet his eyes. "What's done is done, Reggie. It's over, in the past.

What matters is what comes next." He paused to run his finger slowly down her cheek. "I don't know all the details, but I know enough to know it doesn't matter. If you want to talk about it sometime, we can. If you don't, that's okay, too." He grasped her chin again. "But I promise you right here and now, Reggie, we'll take it slow."

He smiled that smile, and the tight knot in her belly slowly unfurled. "I can't promise not to try to get you used to my touch, but I'll never rush you. Never hurt you. Someday we'll make love, not just have sex." His expression sobered. "And if you can't have children, then we'll adopt a few, or a dozen. As many as you want."

Tears ran down her cheeks. "You'd be okay with that?"

He stroked a hand down her cheek, taking the tears with it. "I'm rather partial to adoption, myself."

Regina scrambled to take in everything he'd told her. "Wait. You're adopting Eduardo?"

"No. I mean, yes. We're adopting him, you and me."

He was so adorable when he was flustered, Regina laughed.

"But what about the other couple . . ." she couldn't bear to think there was a woman out there aching because Eduardo had been snatched from her arms.

"My mother persuaded them that a certain other child would be a much better match for their family. By the way, Mom thinks you and I would be the ideal parents for Eduardo."

Married? He wanted to marry her? She couldn't quite take it in. Questions, she had so many questions. "If we were to, um, get married, where would we live? What about your job?"

"I told Uncle Sam I wasn't coming back." His eyes twinkled, and she gaped. She'd never seen him look so at ease, almost carefree.

But she had to ask about the shadows in his past, too. He had accepted hers, but had he made peace with his own? "Have you let it go?"

His smile faded, and she saw that while the pain lingered, the self-recrimination wasn't there anymore. "Jax set up the ambush. He and Raul were working together, even then."

"Oh, Brooks, how awful. I'm so sorry." She searched for more words, but couldn't find the right ones. What could she say? No wonder he had wanted no part of her and Eduardo. They reminded him too much of a past failure.

He cupped her cheek. "You told me I wasn't God, that I couldn't control everything, and I've finally realized you're right. Think I'll let God handle that part." He took a deep breath. "I'll always hate that they died, but I'm learning to let it go."

Regina's heart filled with pride, not only that he'd accepted his failure, but that he'd been willing to tell her about it. He wasn't a man to spew his deepest thoughts for all the world to hear. "So what will you do now?" she asked.

Brooks recovered first and smiled, though the grin seemed tight around the edges. "I hear that a certain orphanage needs a codirector and a certain relief organization needs the occasional worldwide troubleshooter. I think I have a pretty good shot at getting the job."

Her eyes widened even further. "You mean you're working for Tio Noah?" As the implication of that sunk in, a fresh slew of tears filled her eyes and clogged her throat. "When did he die?" she whispered.

He stood quickly. "No, baby," he hastened to reassure. "Noah's still alive, doing better actually, and he and I got a few things straightened out."

There was a wealth of things that statement left out, but it was enough for a start.

"By the way, I discovered that Francisco is Eduardo's father."

Regina nodded her head sadly. "Yes, I know. He admitted it while I was still in the hospital. Poor Irene." She told him about Francisco's decision to leave public life.

"At least he's trying to make things right with his family." Brooks transferred Eduardo to his other shoulder and cupped her cheek. "But you still haven't answered my question. Will you marry me and put me out of my misery?"

She hesitated, the old fears and doubts whispering in her ear. "Why do you want to marry me?"

He looked stunned by the question and a scowl formed between his brows. "I love you. Why else would I want to marry you?'

"Well, you never mentioned it."

"I thought you knew."

She smiled demurely. "Women like to hear the words."

He looked her right in the eye. "I love you, Regina da Silva. Today. Tomorrow. Always."

"Mmmm." She snuggled close and kissed the side of his neck.

"Men like to hear the words, too," he whispered in her ear, wrapping his free arm around her.

"Really?" she teased, then gave a long-suffering sigh. "Oh, all right. If you insist."

"Why you little rascal," he growled, tickling her waist.

She giggled. "Careful of the baby."

"Regina," he ground out.

She flung her arms around his neck, wrapping her arms securely around both her men. "I love you, Nathaniel Brooks Anderson. Today. Tomorrow. Always."

Epilogue

Three weeks later

BROOKS STOOD AT THE FRONT OF THE OLD CATHEDRAL AND DECIDED Regina had to be the most beautiful woman he'd ever seen, certainly the most beautiful bride ever to grace a church aisle. She looked absolutely amazing in the dress he'd given her, just as he'd known she would. He searched for the right word and decided she looked like an angel. His angel.

But was she done worrying? he wondered. The night he came back, he'd had to tell her that Raul was the man who'd attacked Noah that long-ago night and killed her unborn baby, too. It wasn't news you could absorb quickly. The effects lingered.

But as Brooks studied her face as she slowly walked down the aisle on Jorge's arm, his anxiety eased. Her brown eyes sparkled, and there was a bounce in her step. Jorge walked tall and proud beside her. She looked like a woman who not only knew she looked gorgeous, but felt that way, too. And so she should. She was his bride, and as far as he was concerned, they started fresh, as of today. Whatever had gone before was gone, without the power to hurt them.

Brooks shifted his gaze to the front pew, where his mother sniffed quietly into a lace handkerchief. Beside her, Olga bounced Eduardo on her knee, her old eyes suspiciously moist. He winked.

Behind them, the pews were packed with squirming children in their Sunday best, all trying to sit still for their beloved Regina. He smiled as he heard their delighted whispers and saw their pointing fingers when she appeared. He felt like giggling and pointing himself.

Then Regina arrived at the altar and smiled at him. He smiled back, and nothing else mattered.

"Time to go, Reg," he whispered in her ear several hours later. The courtyard of House of Angels was filled to bursting with laughing children and carefree adults. If he smiled any more he knew his face was going to split right down the middle. And if he didn't get to touch his new wife soon, he'd spontaneously combust.

She looked up at him and smoothed the scowl forming between his brows. "Don't look so ferocious. They just want to wish us well."

"They've been doing it for days," he groused.

"Just a little while longer . . ." she pleaded.

He met her laughing gaze. "Five minutes. After that I'll haul you over my shoulder and drag you out of here. I'm tired of sharing." He kissed her hand and let her go.

But he didn't go far. Brooks followed his bride around the yard as they bid farewell to the guests, a guiding hand at the small of her back, easing her ever closer to the gate leading to the street.

When he got her into position, he grabbed her hand and took off at a trot, dragging her with him. "Let's go, Reg."

She squealed, hiked her dress up with one hand and ran down the street with him to the rental car he'd stashed there for just this purpose.

Brooks drove like a madman, whipping around corners, blasting through intersections with no more than an obligatory honk. He couldn't wait to get her alone. She looked at his determined expression and laughed—though she gripped the dashboard with both hands.

Several decades later, they arrived at their hotel. Another eternity crawled past before they reached the honeymoon suite. He closed the door behind them and flicked on the radio.

"May I have this dance, Mrs. Anderson?" he asked, holding out his hand.

"Of course, Nathaniel," she replied, moving into his arms.

He started to protest, but as he held her close, he decided Nathaniel wasn't such a terrible name after all.

"You looked beautiful today," he whispered.

"I felt beautiful today."

He leaned away from her then, needing to reassure. "Don't ever be afraid of me, Reg."

"I won't," she promised, "even when you growl and stomp."

He grinned at her cheekiness, delighted with this lighter, carefree side of her. "So how long do you think it will take to get you out of this lovely dress?"

"Why don't you find out?" she replied with a saucy toss of her head.

Brooks searched her eyes for a telltale flicker of anxiety, a hesitation, but there was none. Only love shone from her warm brown eyes. It humbled him and made him surer than ever that he'd treat her the way she should be treated.

With reverent hands, he undid the buttons down the back of her dress and slowly peeled it off her, her smile all the encouragement he needed. Then he stood stock still as she divested him of his tie, jacket, and shirt.

When it was his turn again, he peeled off the rest of her clothes, stopping along the way to plant tender kisses on every new inch of skin he uncovered, delighting in the taste and feel of her.

Taking her cues from him, she kept her eyes on his as she returned the favor, placing gentle kisses all over his skin.

When they finally lay down on the bed together, they were both naked, both vulnerable, and neither was afraid. With infinite care, he slowly, deliciously made her his.

His angel. Today. Tomorrow. Always.

A Note on *Angel Falls*

Dear Reader,

Welcome to Southern Brazil—an area of incredible beauty and heartbreaking contrast! My father was born and raised in Porto Alegre. Growing up, I watched my parents send clothes and supplies to orphanages there. When I visited Brazil with them several years ago, I finally understood why. Poverty abounds and walls topped with broken glass protect the wealthy from gangs of street children who steal and scavenge to survive.

What kind of person would you become if you grew up on the streets, abandoned and abused? What if someone rescued and loved you? How would that change your life? Those questions became Regina, the heroine of *Angel Falls.* A former street child, she uses her switchblade to protect the orphanage children—and keep men at a distance.

Regina needed a very special hero, so I looked to our military, people I hold in the highest esteem. But how would a confident, well-trained warrior respond to failure? That wondering became Brooks, the hero of *Angel Falls.*

Their journey takes them to Iguaçu Falls, which straddles the border between Brazil and Argentina. It's one of the world's largest waterfalls and makes Niagara Falls seem tame by comparison. As I slid along swaying, rickety catwalks, soaked to the skin, the thundering water disappearing right under my feet, I knew this had to be the site of *Angel Falls'* climactic scene.

I titled the story *Angel Falls* since the children call Regina "Miss Angel" of House of Angels orphanage, and she realizes she's *fallen* in love with Brooks at Iguaçu Falls. Because the street children of Porto Alegre are near and dear to my heart, some of the book's royalties will go to charities working there. Thank you for being an "Angel" to them.

I hope you'll visit me online at: www.BusyWomenBigDreams.com or e-mail me at: connie@conniemann.com. I'd love to hear about any of your adventures in relief work. Or just pop in to say hello.

Tchau!
Connie Mann

Discussion Questions

1. If you had grown up on the streets like Regina, how would you view your past? What kind of person would you be?
2. Regina can never have children because of someone else's cruelty. What if someone stole your most cherished dream? How would you move beyond that?
3. Some are born rich; others poor. How do you reconcile that with a gracious, loving God?
4. Brooks can't move on in life until he forgives his father. Are there people you have had a hard time forgiving? Does forgiveness mean giving them a "pass" on their actions?
5. The villain of *Angel Falls* believes in the Old Testament idea of, "an eye for an eye." Do you believe revenge is justified?
6. People died during Brooks's last mission, and he feels responsible. Is his guilt true? Or misplaced? Why or why not?
7. Carol Anderson, Noah's wife, raised another woman's son as her own—and loves him fiercely. Would you have made the choices she did?
8. The theme of forgiveness runs through *Angel Falls*. How have you applied forgiveness in your life?
9. Both Brooks and Regina act against their own best interests to keep Eduardo safe. Think about a time in your life when you have done something similar.
10. Brooks is afraid to fail again. Have you ever felt that way? How did you find the courage to try again?
11. Regina uses her switchblade to protect herself, physically and emotionally. What "weapons" do you carry to keep others at bay?
12. The Bible says Christ's forgiveness washes our sins as white as wool. Do you believe that?

Want to learn more about author
Connie Mann and check out other great fiction
from Abingdon Press?

Sign up for our fiction newsletter at
www.AbingdonPress.com/Fiction
to read interviews with your favorite authors, find tips
for starting a reading group, and stay posted on what
new titles are on the horizon. It's a place to connect
with other fiction readers or post a
comment about this book.

Be sure to visit Connie online!

www.BusyWomenBigDreams.com